A MONTH BY THE LAKE
& OTHER STORIES

H.E. BATES

A MONTH BY THE LAKE
& OTHER STORIES

INTRODUCTION BY ANTHONY BURGESS

A NEW DIRECTIONS BOOK

Editor's Note: Following the title story, "A Month by the Lake," first published in 1964, the stories proceed in chronological order, covering the years 1926–1972. Thanks are due to the author's widow and his son, Richard Bates, who have approved this selection, and to Professor Dennis Vannatta, author of a critical study on Bates (Twayne Publishers and G. K. Hall, 1983), for his advice. This too, is the place to gratefully acknowledge the help of my New Directions colleague Laurie Callahan.—G. J. O.

Manufactured in the United States of America
First published clothbound and as New Directions Paperbook 645 in 1987

New Directions books are printed on acid-free paper

Library of Congress Cataloging-in-Publication Data

Bates, H. E. (Herbert Ernest), 1905–1974.
    A month by the lake and other stories.

    (New Directions paperbook ; 645)
    I. Title.

PR6003.A965A6
1987   823'.912   87-5680
ISBN 0-8112-1035-9
ISBN 0-8112-1036-7 (pbk.)

New Directions Books are published for James Laughlin
by New Directions Publishing Corporation
80 Eigth Avenue, New York 10011

SECOND PRINTING

CONTENTS

H.E. BATES—AN INTRODUCTION

The sixties were not a bad time for the British. The prime minister Harold Macmillan told them on television, with an Edwardian snarl, that they had never had it so good. It was the era of the Beatles, the miniskirt, the sexual scandal which dislodged the politician Profumo, the first James Bond films, and a general air of sybaritism and self-satisfaction (it was soon blown away). Even writers, who do not usually do well, were doing well. But the atmosphere of monied ease which some writers showed was partly due to subventions from the Arts Council. One lady novelist who received a sum of money from that body said that she needed it desperately: "I have to go to Lord's to watch cricket in the afternoons, and, not writing, I have to have a subsidy." There were some of us who growled at this. It seemed that these governmental hand-outs went to the idle who should continue that gentlemanly tradition of not producing very much—best exemplified by E.M. Forster and T.S. Eliot and (ladylike) Virginia Woolf. Writers who wrote for a living and, of necessity, wrote much, who never debased themselves by begging for money from the State and lived on earnings from the open literary market seemed to be looked down upon. Herbert Ernest Bates was one of these, and I was another.

I wrote a long letter to the *Times Literary Supplement* denouncing idle writers confirmed in their idleness by State subsidies, and Bates wrote another. He alleged that much of this money went straight into the pockets of the brewers and distillers. He was denounced for his denunciation. But, as he said to me, he had worked hard at writing all his life and seen little reward for it. He recognised a spiritual kinship with the great Edwardians—H.G. Wells, Chesterton, Belloc, Arnold Bennett—who were proud of their industry and scorned to ask favours. He never received any literary prizes. When, with his sequence about the Larkin family, beginning with

The Darling Buds of May, he found a popular audience, the reviewers tried to belittle him. This, however, was difficult. He wrote too well, even at a popular level. He attained mastery of the novel, novella and short story forms early, and he never lost his touch. He died too young, at sixty-nine, and he still had much to do.

Bates was born in 1905 and thus belongs to the generation which produced Evelyn Waugh, Graham Greene and Anthony Powell. He was perhaps luckier than they in gaining encouragement early, for it was Edward Garnett (of whom Bates wrote a study in 1950) who promoted the publication of his first novel *The Two Sisters* when Bates was only twenty-one. Garnett was publisher's reader for several successive firms and, though his taste was not always sure— he failed dismally to appreciate the genius of James Joyce—he pushed the work of Conrad, D.H. Lawrence, Forster, Dorothy Richardson and W.H. Hudson. His patronage of the young Bates enabled an author born to prolificity to start being prolific early.

Some fiction writers are naturally novelists, others naturally short-story writers. V.S. Pritchett, perhaps England's greatest contemporary master of the short story, has never really succeeded with the novel, and the same may be said of William Sansom. The distinction of Bates is that he has been equally masterful with both forms. The short-story volumes—*The Woman Who Had Imagination* (1934), *The Flying Goat* (1939) and *The Beauty of the Dead* (1940)—match the novels *The Fallow Land* (1932) and *Love for Lydia* (1952) for skill in psychological penetration and spare style that has a greater resonance than appears on the surface. When Graham Greene called Bates an English Chekhov he was paying a tribute that is made to too many short-story writers. It meant that he was good, serious, accomplished. It is to the credit of a government department that it was willing to harness this artistic skill to the national effort in World War II.

There have always been war artists and war chroniclers, but never before had there been a war short-story writer. Bates, as Flying Officer X, brought his sharp eye and his sharper compassion to the activities of the Royal Air Force, showing what was going on in the minds of the flyers, their doubts, fears, sufferings, successes. And not only the flyers but their sweethearts and families. It was not patriotic writing of the kind that the Great Patriotic War produced in Soviet Russia; it was low-keyed as to sentiment, far from flag-waving, essentially human and quietly compassionate. "It's Just the Way It Is," in this volume, is a good example. Narrative style is pared to nothing; everything is left to dialogue; it may well be too subfusc a piece of writing to please Americans brought up in a more ebullient tradition, but it represents what a lot of British writing of the period was like. Paradoxically, it owes something to Hemingway. I remember seeing a brief film made from it when I was a soldier during the war—one of the short movies put out by the Ministry of Information to precede the main feature. I was deeply moved, and I'm moved again when I re-read the story.

What ought to strike the newcomer to Bates's short stories is the variety of tone, the manner in which the vocabulary expands or contracts to fit the subject, and the faultless ear for human speech. In that nothing much seems to happen—only a nuance of change in relationships, a minimal modification of attitude—Bates is seen clearly to be in the tradition of Chekhov, to whom one ought to add the Joyce of *Dubliners*. The O. Henry tradition of the twist in the tail is not here; rather what we have is what Joyce called the epiphany—the showing forth of some small human truth in rather drab and ordinary human circumstances. "She stood staring at all this for some time longer. She had forgotten her shoes and now she dared not go back for them. Her eyes were big and colourless. One of her small stony lips was held tight right above the other and it might have been that she wished, after all, that she too was dead." That is the end of "Death and the Cherry Tree." Just a wish, not even that—just the possibility of a wish, a velleity. It's enough.

As a British writer of fiction myself, though totally unskilled in the short story and all the readier to admire those who succeed in a flimsy but difficult form, I am naturally pleased to be presiding over the introduction to the American public of a fellow-Briton in danger of neglect. It may be that writers who do not attain thorough mastery of literary forms are the most suitable subjects for critical reappraisal or academic promotion—writers who are ambiguous, or whose imperfections may really be cunning symbol-ism. Writers who succeed in what they are doing but do not suggest any new technical or psychological paths tend to be ignored in the colleges. The good read is not enough for some readers. I would never suggest that Bates opened up new territory, but he achieved such sovereignty of what literary land he inherited that he deserves the homage of our uncomplicated enjoyment. I hope that this small selection (for which I thank America) will lead readers to his larger works—such novels as *Fair Stood the Wind for France*, and such novellas as those which honour a simple English family. Bates's affection for ordinary people is one of his shining virtues. But he himself, as I knew, and as this compilation should make clear, was, is, far from ordinary.

1987   Anthony Burgess

A MONTH BY THE LAKE
& OTHER STORIES

A MONTH BY THE LAKE

Over the lake the weather had settled into such tranquil late magnificence that Miss Bentley had decided to stay another month: the entire month of October.

Already in the distances the morning mountains sometimes revealed the thinnest night-caps of pure fresh snow; but below them, by noon, every fissure in the bare perpendicular falls of rock was distinctly carved, clear dark purple in the sun. Even farther below them the masses of pine and chestnut and beech and walnut caught the smouldering light of afternoon like clusters of solid coral, pale amber, bronze or bright rusty from the harsh heat of summer. Still farther below them the vines on their narrow terraces were hung with palest ripe green grapes, misted with olive bloom. Farthest below of all, below the umbrella pines, the erect black plumes of cypresses and the shining flowerless thickets of camellia, tender torches of oleanders still bloomed along the lakeside: pure white, pale yellow, pink and vermilion, flowering in front of houses that melted into the honied impermanence of soft distances until they were nothing but stumps of burned-down candles melting in pearly air.

One by one Miss Bentley had watched the guests of the white *albergo* depart until now, at last, only herself and Major Wilshaw remained. By noon, now, Major Wilshaw too would be gone: a ghost departed with the family of machine-tool manufacturers from Milan, charmers all, the husband a joker in cool sky-blue suits, the wife a splendid cushion of dark fat velvet, the two little girls like sallow angels for whom Major Wilshaw was fond of doing tricks with handkerchiefs, English pennies and bits of string.

With them had gone the two American ladies, school-teachers from Ohio, who had become ill, as Miss Bentley had firmly predicted they would, from living too much on ice-water, green salad and uncooked pears. And with them all the rest whose time or money or interest was not unlimited: the Swiss honeymooners from Schaffhausen, the German chemist and his wife from Frankfurt, the two couples from Yorkshire whom Miss Bentley had christened the gawpy-talkies, the car dealer and his alleged wife, really mistress, from Brussels—mistress, Miss Bentley was sure, because she always passed him the sugar at breakfast, although he clearly never took sugar in his coffee—and finally the sock-knitting English governess with the silent, fallow-timid boy from Turin, a little wooden human carving snatched from the shadows of some impossible Catholic altar.

Now, when Major Wilshaw had gone, there would be no one left but herself; Maria, who cleaned the bedrooms; Enrico, who waited at table; the two cooks and Signora Fascioli, who owned the hotel.

Alone, she would watch the lamps of summer burn quickly out; she would eat another ton of spaghetti—Bolognese or Milanese on alternate days, except Sundays, when it was tagliatelli—peel with meticulous care the last of the pears and purple figs, manicure her nails every Wednesday and Saturday, wash her hair every Friday, swim when she felt like it and take at least one more excursion by funicular to the Monte and look down for the last time on the lake below—its great pattern of inlets and curves, she always thought, so like some great blue glass lioness, sprawled and glittering between the mountains and the plain.

From her favourite place on the patio, a viewpoint from which she could watch the lake-steamers glide like long white water-birds from the gap between the two islands opposite the hotel, Miss Bentley watched Major Wilshaw come down the hotel steps, folding up, with care, the bill he had just paid.

"Ah! there you are. Thought I should find you here."

The most remarkable feature of Major Wilshaw was not, in Miss Bentley's eyes, the singularly fine straight nose; or the way the greyish hair crinkled bushily into his neck, or the sharp pale blue eyes; or the fact that he had, with his loose brown trousers, bright bluc shirt and chrome yellow tie, a rather gay, gamey appearance, an air of wishing to be something rather dashing.

To Miss Bentley the most remarkable feature about Major Wilshaw was his small flat pink ears. They were not only exceptionally small for a man who was thickish, upright and rather tall. They were very delicately, very intricately fashioned. Nothing in the entire human body, Miss Bentley would tell herself, had quite the same fascinating quality as ears. All the attraction of mood and response and character and emotion lay, of course, in the mouth and eyes: everyone knew that. But ears were, Miss Bentley thought, far more wonderful. Ears were unchanging and undying. They remained, in some strange way, uncoarsened, undepraved, unwrinkled and unaged by time. In the ears of the aged you could see the flesh of youth; in a sense they were immortal and never grew old.

Perhaps it was for this reason that Miss Bentley always greeted Major Wilshaw with oblique, off-the-target glances, never looking him straight in the eyes.

"Well: I'm afraid it's good-bye."

"Oh! come, surely not good-bye," Miss Bentley said. "Say *arrivedérci*."

She smiled, putting her book on the little white wooden table at her side. At forty-seven she could give Major Wilshaw a few years, she thought, though perhaps not very many. His hair was already grey; her own was still a rich honey brown, without a touch of age.

"What time does your train go?" she said. "I forget."

The train, she knew quite well, went at half past twelve. She saw it regularly every day, creeping up from Milan along the lakeside.

"Half past twelve."

"Really! I thought it was earlier."

"No: half past," the major said. "Twelve thirty-one to be exact."

Something, she suddenly thought, seemed to be troubling him. He took from his pocket his newly paid hotel bill and began to examine it covertly.

"So you're really going," she said.

"I'm really going."

"Which way are you going?" she said. "You did tell me. I forget."

She had not forgotten. She knew very well that he was going by way of Domodossola, the Simplon, Brig, Montreux, Lausanne and the spaces of France beyond.

"Via Domodossola, the Simplon, Brig, Montreux and that way," he began to say and then broke off, looking perplexed. "I don't think my bill's quite right," he said, "it doesn't somehow—"

A little fussily the major began to examine the bill, turning his head sideways towards her, so that once again she could see the fine, small ears. Miss Bentley thought there were many ears, even male ones, that were like sea-shells; but the fascination of Major Wilshaw's ears was much more like that of certain flowers. Perhaps that was ridiculous and which particular flower they most resembled was something that, so far, had persisted in eluding her; but she was perfectly sure that, one day, she would discover which one it was.

"No: it isn't right," he said. "They've charged me far too much—"

Folding and re-folding the bill, he looked up at her, helpless and troubled.

"May I look?" she said. "Perhaps—"

"Please," he said. "Please. I always say it pays to check these things—"

Miss Bentley took the bill, read through it once and gave it back to him.

"It adds up all right to me," she said. "I think you're adding the one as a one instead of as a seven. See?—it has the little stroke across its middle."

"Of course, of course, how stupid," the major said.

Below, across the lake, the peep of a steamer whistle broke the tranquil morning air, echoed across the flat honey-blue water and re-echoed in the scarcely visible mountains.

"That's the twelve o'clock steamer," Miss Bentley said.

"Already?" the major said. "I'm afraid I must go if it is. I'm afraid it's good-bye."

"Are you always nervous when you travel?" Miss Bentley said.

"Well, not exactly nervous. But you know—"

"Just in a state of this and that. I know," she said. "You feel you're neither here nor there."

That, he had noticed, was a favourite phrase of hers: a state of this and that. She was rather given to such odd, half-slangy quips that hit off moments, people and moods with dry and sometimes satirical exactitude.

"That's it, that's it," he said. "A state of this and that. Wondering if you've got everything. If there's anything you've forgotten."

"And have you got everything?"

"I think so, I fancy so." Uncertainly he fumbled at the pocket of his jacket. "I checked—"

"Ticket?"

"Yes, yes. Ticket."

"Passport? You told me you once forgot your passport."

"In my suitcase."

"Never keep it in your suitcase," she said. "You're done if someone snitches it. Suitcase and passport gone in one. Always keep it on you."

"Of course, of course," he said. "I'll do it. I'll see to that."

"Well then," she said, "if you've got everything."

She got up and the major extended his hand.

"Well, good-bye, Miss Bentley. It's been absolutely—"

"Oh! not here," she said. "I'm coming down the steps."

"How nice of you, how kind," he said. "There's absolutely no need—"

Miss Bentley was suddenly aware, as she descended the white steps of the terrace slightly behind him, of two eventful things. The first was the unexpected elucidation of the private mystery that had troubled her ever since the first evening she had seen the major doing tricks for the amusement of the two sallow little angels from Milan.

It was the sudden revelation that the major's left ear was, more than anything, like a small pink rose. The particular rose she had in mind was flattish, inclined to be oval in shape, and mysteriously crinkling to a soft inner heart.

"So it is," she said and the major, turning to say "Pardon?" saw on her face a look of extraordinary revelation.

"Did you say something?"

"No," she said. "No. Nothing at all."

A moment later she was aware of the second event. Voices were suddenly laughing gaily in Italian by the front door of the hotel. Signor Fascioli was rushing down the steps, laughing too. And there, by the door of a cream familiar Fiat, were the two sallow little angels from Milan, dancing up and down, yellow dresses flouncing. The splendid dark fat cushion of a wife was there and Signor Bompiani, gay and immaculate in light blue linen, was waving both hands above his head in the direction of Miss Bentley and Major Wilshaw, giving greeting in the manner of a boxer:

"Major! Miss Bentley! We are here! Back again! Time for a nice cup of tea!"

This was his favourite, much-repeated joke about the English.

"Not to *stay*?"

"To stay. Of course. The weather is so beautiful—*bella, bella bella*—To stay, of course!"

"*Molto bella*," Miss Bentley said. "Oh! so beautiful. How nice to see you."

"Shake hands, Major, shake hands."

"The major is going," Miss Bentley said. "You're just in time to say good-bye."

"The major is going? No? Where? Why? Away? Not—"

"Away," the Major said. "England."

"We arrive. You depart. That's very sad. That's not very well arranged, Major—"

The two sallow little angels began dancing about Major Wilshaw, pleading in Italian, pulling his sleeves and hands.

"They wish a trick!"

"Oh! no. I'm sorry. I must get the train—"

"They wish one trick before you go!"

"It's getting awfully late—"

"In the car they speak of nothing but tricks. Tricks from the major. They wish all the time tricks from the major!"

"Just one then. One quickly—"

The major, stooping down, began to do his little trick with English pennies. It consisted, in essentials, of losing the pennies one by one in the hair of—but suddenly, in surprise, Miss Bentley was not watching.

In the excitement she had not noticed, by the door of the car, a girl with smooth fair hair, wearing a plain black skirt, rather full, and a plain white blouse. Nor had the major seen her either; but now, suddenly, the trick completed, he straightened up, turned and caught sight of her standing there.

Miss Bentley had never seen in the eyes of a girl a look of such open unequivocal indifference, so cool in contemplation, and suddenly Signor Bompiani was saying:

"Ah! badly arranged again, forgive me, badly arranged. I am so sorry—this is Miss Beaumont. She is with us for three months to learn Italian and also to teach the kids a little English, I hope. Miss Beaumont, please to allow me to introduce Miss Bentley and Major Wilshaw."

"How do you do," Miss Beaumont said.

On the major's face a stunned, excruciating look of pure shyness developed into one of actual embarrassment. Opening his mouth to speak he succeeded only in giving a brief gape of astonishment. At the same time he averted his face, as if unable suddenly to look at the girl.

"The taxi has been waiting ten minutes, Major Wilshaw," Signora Fascioli said. "You will miss the train—"

"Oh! must you go, Major?" Signor Bompiani said. "No more tricks?"

"I must go, I must really get on. I'll say good-bye—"

"Good-bye then, Major. Good-bye," Signor Bompiani said.

"You will miss the train, Major!"

"Good-bye! Good-bye!" the angles shouted.

"Not good-bye," Miss Bentley said. "*Arrivedérci!*"

"*Arrivedérci!*" everyone shouted. "*Arrivedérci!*"

"*Arrivedérci!*" the major said. "Good-bye."

Framed against the exquisite background of the lake, the major lifted his hand and took off his small green homburg hat in farewell. Behind him the mountains, half-dissolved in dreamy amber haze, threw into sharp relief the yellow tie, the glazed blue eyes and above all the small pink ears for which Miss Bentley felt she had found, at last, the perfect, happy comparison.

She, too, raised her hand, waving it in farewell; and then realized, a moment later, that the eyes of the major were not looking back at her. Nor were they looking at Signora Fascioli, the Bompianis, Maria and Enrico, or the little angles who, no longer dancing, were simply crooking slow, sad fingers.

They were not even looking at Miss Beaumont. With melancholy transparence they appeared to be held in a trance by which it seemed almost certain for a second or two that the major had forgotten who and where he was. He stood for a moment longer in this lost enchantment, eyes blank and almost white in the sun, and then suddenly turned and groped into the taxi.

"Come back next year!" Miss Bentley called and down on the

lake the short rude peep of the departing steamer mocked the flawless distances in answer.

Three quarters of an hour later, sitting alone at her table under the arbour of Virginia creeper at the end of the patio, Miss Bentley was raising a glass of *valpolicella* to her lips in readiness to wash down the last mouthful of *spaghetti bolognese*. The glass never reached her lips and as she set it slowly down on the table, with a surprise far greater than she had seen on the face of Major Wilshaw when he had first become aware of the cool detached Miss Beaumont, her mouth too fell open, as the major's had done, with a gape of astonishment.

The major himself was just driving up to the hotel in an open taxi, holding his green homburg hat on his knees.

Her first impulse, as the taxi drew up, was to call out to him. Then she checked it. A great air of preoccupation shrouded the major, who was staring down at his feet.

She turned quickly to glance at the Bompianis and Miss Beaumont, lunching at their long table at the farther end of the arbour. The two children were drinking red wine in water and Miss Beaumont, with white meticulous fingers, was washing, peeling and eating a bunch of pale green grapes. Miss Beaumont, she realized for the first time, was, in her thin, measured way, a very pretty creature.

When she looked back at the road through the screen of Virginia creeper leaves she saw Maria was helping to unload the major's suitcases but that the major had already disappeared. Instinctively she looked up towards the window of the room he occupied on the second floor of the hotel and then realized how stupid it was to expect to see him there so quickly or even to see him there at all. At the same time she found herself suffering from the temporary illusion that the major had, after all, not appeared on the road from the lake so suddenly.

"It was probably," she thought, "that I just wanted him to appear."

Three or four minutes later Enrico, the thin hollow-eyed waiter, came out of the hotel carrying tablecloth, napkins, cutlery, pepper and salt pots and a small white plate. She watched him lay the table that the major always occupied and then, when he had finished, called him over.

"Is there another visitor?"

"The table," he said, "is for Major Wilshaw."

"The major left this morning for Domodossola."

"The major is back."

"Did he miss the train?"

"I think so, madam. I don't know."

"Bring my fruit," she said, "will you please?"

For the next three quarters of an hour she sat washing and peeling the grapes and dark blue figs of which she never tired. She washed the fruit slowly and thoughtfully, watching with fascination the pearls of air gather delicately on the grapeskins under the water, her eyes at the same time ready to lift themselves towards the door of the hotel.

After twenty minutes the Bompianis got up from their table. Mrs. Bompiani, who did not speak English, smiled in Miss Bentley's direction as she rose. Mr. Bompiani, red-flushed beneath the eyes from wine, smiled at Miss Bentley too and said simply, with satisfied brevity: "Shut-eye." The two children waved spidery fingers and Miss Beaumont, who had changed her white blouse for a scarlet sleeveless one, seemed to begin to smile and then decided not to.

After the voices of the children had died away the afternoon became quite silent, wrapped in thin hot haze. The lake took on a golden glassy skin, without a stir of air. Once Enrico appeared at the door of the hotel, looked in Miss Bentley's direction, saw that she was still peeling grapes and then went away.

It was nearly an hour before she saw the major, who had changed now into a light shantung suit slightly creased from packing, with a brown silk shirt and pale green tie, walking towards her under the screen of Virginia creeper.

"I suppose you're surprised?"

"Not a bit," she said. "I felt all along you'd mistaken the time of the train."

"I didn't miss the train."

He glanced round as if, she thought, looking for the Bompianis, and then said:

"May I join you? I'm not eating."

"No lunch?"

"They're bringing me some coffee."

She sat for some moments contemplating in silence the small pink ears. She thought there seemed something covert, complicated and sad about Major Wilshaw, more especially about the eyes, which were downcast as he played with a spoon, not often looking up at her.

"So you came back."

"I came back."

She decided suddenly, for no reason, not to ask why.

"You should have something to eat," she said. "You look tired."

"Do I? I don't feel it," he said. "I'll be all right with just the coffee."

Flawlessly the lake lay shining in the afternoon sun, the oleanders alight along the shore. She found herself not only extraordinarily glad that he was back but even happier not to be alone. Then when Enrico brought the coffee she found herself instinctively passing the sugar, saying:

"Sugar? You take a lot, I know."

Thoughtfully unwrapping the sugar cubes, Major Wilshaw stared with light blue eyes at the hazed quiet skin of the lake.

"What do you do when you suddenly have damn funny impulses?" he said.

She found herself laughing.

"Oh! I suppose you don't have such things," he said.

"Why not? I have wild, unconquerable desires too," Miss Bentley said, "if it comes to that."

She was sorry, a moment later, that she had mocked him. That was rather her way sometimes, she thought, to mock, to be a little trite. It was not really herself who spoke on such occasions. It was really—puzzled, she shied away from a complexity too difficult to explain.

"I'm talking about an impulse that stops you," the major said.

"Not the other kind."

"Not the urging, to-hell-with-it-kind?"

"No. The sort with a voice," he said.

This is too ridiculous, she thought. Men simply don't talk like this. Nor women either.

"No, seriously, seriously," he said.

"You're going to tell me you were walking across the station, ready to get on the train, when a voice said, 'Don't go. Don't do it. Go back to the *Albergo Bianco* and stay a few more days.' "

"Something like that."

"That was simply commonsense speaking. You needn't have gone in the first place. You know that. In this marvellous, wonderful weather."

"I know it sounds silly—"

"Not a bit. Not silly at all. Commonsense. The sanest, most sensible thing to do. Who'd leave all this if they didn't have to? Look at it!" With rapturous hands she pointed down to the lake laced in its tender honey-skin of autumn light. "Not me, that's certain. I'm not sure I shan't stay all winter."

He started to speak, then stopped and poured himself more coffee. She pushed the sugar-bowl across to him a second time and then watched him unwrap two of the papered cubes and drop them in the cup.

"You're walking along a street to go somewhere. You know perfectly well where you're going—what time and so on and all that. And suddenly you don't go. You're turned back by something and the whole day, perhaps a great bit of life, is different. You've done that surely?"

Of course she had done that, she told him. Everybody had done that.

"Do you feel life has a pattern?" he said. "A predetermined one, I mean?"

"Oh! Heaven help us," she said. "Don't go into that. If I'd felt my life had had a predetermined pattern I'd probably have cut my throat at the age of six."

She laughed again, but she noticed he did not laugh in reply.

"How long are you going to stay?" she said, "now you're back?"

He simply shrugged his shoulders slightly, an almost imperceptible muscular quiver, and again lifted his coffee cup.

"Stay a whole month," she said. "Stay until another impulse strikes you."

He gave the faintest of smiles and then started biting his lip.

"Well, here we all are again," she said, "anyway. You, the

Bompianis, those two little angels and me. I think it's absolutely
wonderful."

"Yes."

"Do you remember that picnic we had in the mountains?" she
said. "Do you suppose we could manage another picnic like that?
I'd cheerfully arrange it if the Bompianis would offer the car like
they did last time. I'm sure they would, except that this time, of
course, there's Miss Beaumont—"

"Oh?" He spoke very abruptly, almost sharply. "Is that her
name?"

"I think that's what they said—"

"I didn't catch it, I didn't catch it," he said.

"I shall always remember that picnic. That cold spring water the
children washed their feet in and the wild raspberries and the little
wild cyclamen they were selling along the roadside, at the village
down the valley. I'd never seen wild cyclamen before. I didn't even
know there were wild cyclamen—"

She broke off and saw, from the far-away look on his face, that
the major was not listening. Nor was he looking at her. And then
she remembered, suddenly, when she had seen that same look of
lost enchantment on his face before.

And getting up from the table, pushing away her glass and picking
up her book, she remembered Miss Beaumont. It was Miss
Beaumont who had inspired it all.

About four o'clock Major Wilshaw walked down to the town,
called at the post office and sent a telegram to the Wilshaw Light
Metal Construction Co. Ltd, of which he was managing director,
saying "Delayed for further week possibly more address me as
previously case urgency." Then he bought himself a day-old English
newspaper from the kiosk at the steamer landing stage, glanced at
the headlines and walked back to the hotel.

He had already changed his clothes a second time. Now he was
wearing a soft blue suit in mohair with a deep cream shirt and a pale
blue silk tie. His shoes were of light brown turned calf and he was
without a hat. His grey hair was well and scrupulously brushed,
giving him a certain military appearance, though in fact he was not
a military man. During the war he had joined up in his age-group as

his turn came and had risen to the rank of major in the Royal Engineers purely because he was an engineer by profession and because establishment happened to call for another major at a certain time. He never stopped to ask why, after the war, he continued to use his rank. A great many majors and quite a few captains did and he never stopped to ask why the did so either. During a war so many people got into the habit of using ranks and after the war it was natural and easy to go on with it as before.

At fifty-one he was unmarried, successful, prodigiously competent, and, as he liked to think, very young in mind. His impression of Miss Bentley was that she was, in spite of her ungreyed brown hair, her liveliness of speech and generally pleasant air, well settled in middle age. He thought that he could give her quite a few years. One of the things that success in business enabled him to do was to expend a good deal of time, care and money on his choice of clothes. He thought a man ought not only to dress well but, rather like an animal adopting protective colouring, to dress according to his immediate surroundings. That was why he wore simple plain blue suits at the office, sober clerical greys when he did business in London and now, on the lake, a variety of light, sunny blues, yellows, browns and greens that matched the burning autumn mountains, the honey expanses of water, the oleanders, the Italian-ate villas and skies. That, he thought, was the kind of thing that kept him young.

During the three weeks he had been on the lake he had become quite friendly, in an unadventurous detached sort of way, with Miss Bentley. She was what he called a decent old stick. She was not at all bad-looking, he thought, and she dressed herself rather as his secretary in the office did, neatly and freshly, with what he called a slightly starched-and-ironed effect. She used just enough make-up to keep herself from dullness. Her hands and hair were always scrupulous. He was unaware that she found the shape of his ears both baffling and attractive or that she had searched for a long time for a fitting description of their delicacy. She had a certain mustardy sense of humour, a little dry and hot on the tongue as it were, and when she trotted out phrases like "Oh! I have wild and unconquerable desires if it comes to that" he knew she was merely being funny and that she didn't mean it at all. Or perhaps, he thought, it was a sort of protection against something, though what it was he didn't know.

What Miss Bentley called his rather gay and gamey air rose largely from his choice of clothes; but it sprang also from a conviction that he was attractive to girls. He rather fancied himself in that way. At home, in the town where the Wilshaw Light Metal Construction Company occupied several pleasant acres of ground, he ran about in an open cream sports car, played tennis, belonged to a country club and knew of one or two hotels in the country where the food was good. From time to time he struck up acquaintances with girls who also ran about with him in the sports car, played tennis, belonged to the country club, went to eat with him in country hotels and then, for some reason he could never define, suddenly left him to marry men who toiled in printing works, ran unsuccessful market gardens or were just plain ten-pound-a-week clerks in offices. He could never understand these things; it puzzled him always to wonder why.

At fifty-one his figure was still good, if a little solid, the stomach muscles still hard and taut, and one of the things he did rather well was to play tennis. On holidays he always took a couple of rackets with him, together with a supply of good correct clothes. But people generally, he thought, didn't play tennis quite so much as before and he found it always rather hard to get a partner.

Once he asked Miss Bentley if she played and all he had got was one of her mustardy answers:

"Oh! Love and all that. No. I'm afraid it never attracted me. Oh! except one thing—that business of love meaning nothing. Why does it? Of course one knows it does anyway, but did some cynic start the game?"

As he walked back along the road to the hotel he remembered his tennis. He remembered too his explanation of why he had suddenly changed his mind about the train to Domodossola. It wasn't a specially good explanation. It was true, in a sense, that he had been brought to a sudden standstill by a voice. But the voice was neither that of a mystic warning him to go back nor of a guardian angel seeking to change the course of his destiny. He hadn't on the whole been very explicit about it, but it was the best he could do. The voice was really the voice of Miss Beaumont—not so much her speaking voice, in reality, as the voice communicating itself to him through the cool calm blue eyes—suddenly binding him in a compelling, instantaneous attraction.

When he reached the hotel he saw with considerable pleasure that Miss Beaumont was sitting on the terrace with the Bompiani children. The girl, who had been drinking coffee, looked splendidly fair, cool and bored as she stared at the lake below. The two little girls, who had been drinking orange juice, now greeted him with lips stained with bright yellow moustaches, shouting:

"Tricks! Tricks! Tricks! *Prego, prego*! Tricks!"

"Good afternoon." He smiled with charm and friendliness at Miss Beaumont, who herself stared in answer. "May I sit down?"

"Tricks! Tricks!"

"I suppose you wonder why I'm back. Absolutely impossible to resist the lake in this weather, that's all—I just couldn't resist it." Miss Beaumont neither smiled nor made a comment. "Don't you think it's beautiful?"

"I like Garda better."

He started to do his tricks. He was, he thought, rather good with the tricks. Children always liked them. He had first taken up tricks and conjuring generally as a boy, and by now he had forgotten the best of them. But at home he still had the first box he had bought with his pocket money, still neatly packed away in his bedroom, after forty years. Among the tricks was a very good one by which you turned water into wine. There was also another in which you invited several people to write whatever they liked on a paper, seal it in an envelope and hand it to you. Then, one by one, you held the envelopes up to the light, concentrated for a few moments and then, before opening the envelope, told the audience exactly what they had written. It was always a tremendous, baffling success but of course you needed a collaborator.

On the table were a few wrapped cubes of sugar left over from Miss Beaumont's coffee. He palmed them, made a few mysterious dabs at the air and then produced them from the ears of the Bompiani little girls.

Shrieking with laughter, they broke into brief wild English:

"More! Again! More, more!"

"Ah! and now where? Now?"

Opening his hands, he revealed them both quite empty.

"Gone, you see, gone. Gone!—where?"

Baffled, as they always were, the little Bompiani children searched his inner sleeves. Deftly, in triumph, he produced the sugar from the side of Miss Beaumont's hair.

It was clear, in a moment, that Miss Beaumont did not think the trick either very successful or very amusing, but the little Bompiani angels danced with delight, half-hysterically.

"Freda! Freda! Freda!" they said.

"Ah! yes, that time it was Freda," he said. "Sugar in Freda's hair. But not now—not this time. This time in—!"

"Rosali! Rosali!"

To shrieking laughter he opened his hands and again they were empty.

"I'm afraid I've done this trick so many times it's getting stale," he said.

"Yes," Miss Beaumont said. "I suppose it must be."

"I'll have to think up new ones. I know several. It just needs thinking."

"Yes."

"Do you play tennis?" he suddenly said.

"Occasionally."

"Oh! really! oh! fine. They have very good courts at the Splendide that you can hire. I wonder—"

"I haven't a racket."

"I always bring two," the major said. "It would be awfully nice if you'd care to—perhaps tomorrow?"

"Tomorrow we go to Orta."

"Well, there's plenty of time. How long are you here?"

She shrugged her shoulders.

"Three weeks. A month. I wouldn't know."

"Then there's bags of time," the major said. "By the way the swimming is pretty good in the lake. The water's still warm. Do you—"

"Tricks! Tricks!" the children shrieked. "Tricks!"

The insistent voices pierced the afternoon air wildly, maddening as discharging pop-guns.

"Tricks! Sugar in Freda's hair! Tricks!"

"Oh! my God, these kids," the girl said. "Three weeks of this will drive me batty."

"Let's have a drink this evening somewhere," the major said. "We could nip down into the town—"

Before Miss Beaumont could answer, and as if by a process of telepathy, Miss Bentley appeared at the door of the hotel, calling the major by name, waving a handful of letters.

"Anything to post, Major Wilshaw?"

"No, I don't think so. Many thanks."

"I'm walking to the town before dinner—I just wondered—nothing you want?"

He called no, nothing, thanking her all the same, and Miss Bentley called back:

"Are the children restless? Would they care to come?"

"May they really?" Miss Beaumont said. "Isn't it an awful trouble?"

"Absolutely not."

Miss Bentley, calling the little angels, held out both hands. Major Wilshaw called back something about his tricks being exhausted and how he would have to think up new ones and then remembered something else and said:

"Oh! there is just one thing you could do for me, Miss Bentley. That's if it's no trouble. If you haven't too much to do yourself—"

"I'm picking up a couple of dresses, that's all," Miss Bentley said. "I must have something new if I'm to stay here another month."

"Excuse me a moment," the major said to Miss Beaumont. "Don't run away."

Walking across to Miss Bentley he stopped half-way, took from his pocket a fountain pen and notebook and wrote something down, afterwards tearing out the page.

"Just a telegram if you wouldn't mind. I think it'll be five hundred lire. Something like that—"

"Oh! not to worry now," Miss Bentley said. "I'll tell you at dinner—"

"Awfully kind of you, Miss Bentley. More than kind."

"Not a bit," she said. "Come along, angels. No, no, no! Take care! Don't run into the road!"

Back at the table, sitting facing Miss Beaumont, looking into the

cool prepossessing eyes, wonderfully blue and bored, the major felt
run through him the first of a series of exciting, scurrying emotions
and tried suddenly to disguise them by an appearance of casualness:

"She's an awfully decent old stick, really. Terribly kind. Quite
witty too. Sits hours staring at the lake, dreaming. Quite happy, I
suppose, wondering what she might have had—"

"And what might she have had?"

The major, unable to put into words what Miss Bentley might
have had, suddenly felt obliged to change the subject and looked up
at the hills.

"You can walk quite a way through the vineyards," he said.
"There's an old back road goes up behind the hotel and you come
out above the terraces. It's a magnificent view. Would you care to
walk up?"

"Oh! it's awfully hot—"

"Still two hours before dinner," the major said. "There's a little
trattoria up the top where we could get a glass of wine."

"I don't like wine," the girl said. "By golly, the time drags here. I
thought it was later."

By the time the major and Miss Beaumont had reached the upper
terraces of vines, from which the view over the descending trellises
of misty olive fruit was, as the major had said, so magnificent, Miss
Bentley had reached the post office down in the town.

There, for the first time, she looked at the major's telegram.

"Please post soonest box conjuring tricks bottom left hand corner
wardrobe dressing-room," it read, "regards Wilshaw."

As the days went past Miss Bentley continued to sit on the
terrace, watching the sky, the mountains, the lake and the steamers
crossing the lake; watching too the oleanders still opening fresh
sprays of white, pink, vermilion and yellow flower.

After a week or so the gathering of grapes began on the
terraces above the hotel and all day she could hear the voices of
workers calling, chattering and laughing across the vineyards. In
mornings of exquisite light she watched the mountains emerge
from shrouds of mist, mostly a pure ochreous bloom, occasionally pale rose and more rarely still a tender egg-shell green
below which distant houses looked more than ever like squat
white candles gently melting; sometimes making in the mellow

air the only visible division between land and water, just as the thin snow caps made the only perceptible division between land and sky.

She also watched Major Wilshaw. For the first few mornings he appeared on the terrace with his customary fresh briskness, immaculate. She saw him look with eagerness from table to table, searching for Miss Beaumont, who was never there. At the fourth morning he inquired for her.

"Miss Beaumont not down?"

"She never eats breakfast."

"No?" He appeared startled, even shocked. "Not eat breakfast? How—"

"She told me so."

After that Major Wilshaw did not appear for breakfast either.

He would appear instead about eleven o'clock, carrying a towel, ready for his swim.

"Miss Beaumont not about?"

"Haven't seen her."

"She was coming for a swim at eleven o'clock." He glanced hurriedly at his watch, fretting. "It's a quarter past already."

"She hates getting up," Miss Bentley said. "There are people who do, you know."

The major fretted until a quarter to twelve and then said:

"Damn. I hate missing my swim. I hate swimming by myself too."

Miss Bentley did not answer but found herself looking obliquely, instead, at the small fresh pink ears. This glance seemed to startle the major into new thoughts and he said:

"I suppose you wouldn't care to come? No, I don't suppose—"

She smiled in her quizzical, rather ironic way.

"Are you asking me?"

"Oh yes—I'm sorry, Miss Bentley. Of course I am, of course."

"Thank you. If you'll wait for me I'll get my costume."

Ten minutes later they were walking down the steps of the terrace when Miss Beaumont appeared at the foot of them.

"Where on earth have you been?"

"Waiting," the major said. "Here on the terrace. Waiting. Have you only just—?"

"I was here all the time," Miss Beaumont said. She spoke frigidly. "In the garden. In the garden was where you said."

Humbled and confused, the major made groping attempts at apology, almost stuttering. Miss Beaumont, cooler than ever, more aloof and more distant, gazed into air. Miss Bentley said nothing but:

"Well, if we're going, shall we go?"

The figure of Miss Beaumont was virginal, slender and wiry, with small, sharp, up-pointed breasts. As she walked she held her shoulders well back, self-consciously, swinging her hands elaborately. The major, as the three of them walked down the hillside towards the lake, seemed stunned and mesmerized by this, keeping his eyes fixed on her in a stupor of admiration, not once glancing at Miss Bentley.

In the hot brilliant noon unexpected numbers of people were swimming in the lake or lying on concrete, below lines of bathing huts, sunning themselves.

As he saw them the major hurried forward, murmuring something about grabbing a cubicle before it was too late, and then came back, three or four minutes later, dismayed.

"Rather as I suspected," he said. "Only two huts left. Do you mind?—you will have to share I'm afraid. I'm awfully sorry—"

"Oh! that's all right," Miss Beaumont said and stared away, glassily.

Only five minutes later the major saw a white-costumed Miss Bentley emerge first from the cubicle, smiling strangely. Sitting on warm concrete, he was dangling his legs above the lake and turned in time to see the smile break into open laughter.

"What are you laughing at?"

"Oh, nothing."

"It seems to tickle you tremendously all the same."

Once again Miss Bentley's strange smile broke into open laughter.

"Not going to share the joke?"

"Oh, it was nothing," Miss Bentley said. "It was just that I don't think Miss Beaumont liked sharing the cubicle, that's all. She's rather shy."

Before the major could make up his mind what to say about this Miss Bentley was lying full length on the concrete. With sensations of surprise and disbelief he found himself staring at her figure, relaxed and brown in its white two-piece suit in the sun. It was a remarkably taut, clean, smooth figure for a woman to whom, as he thought, he could give a few years. The legs were firm, hairless and shapely. The flesh on the rather long sloping shoulders was wonderfully clean and golden and the bust held itself upright, like that of a girl, self-supported.

Miss Bentley, who had closed her eyes for a moment or two against the brilliance of the sun, now opened them suddenly and found the major staring at her body. With warm, unsurprised, unequivocal eyes she looked straight back at him and said:

"By the way, I meant to have asked you. Have your tricks come?"

"No. I can't understand it. It's been nearly two weeks now. It's rather tiresome. The children keep pestering and I promise them every day."

"Could they be held by the Customs?"

"Good gracious." The thought had on Major Wilshaw the effect of revelation. "I never thought of that."

"I think you'll probably find that that's what happened," Miss Bentley said.

He was about to say something about what a genius she had for putting her finger on the solution to a problem when he turned and saw that Miss Beaumont had left the cubicle and was walking across to where he and Miss Bentley sat by the lakeside.

Seeing her, he was unaccountably depressed by an effect of flatness about the dark red costume. The legs were extraordinarily thin, like a boy's, and too hollow at the thighs. He experienced the impression that Miss Beaumont, who looked so arrestingly pretty in cool silk frocks, now looked meagre, a mere slice of a girl, skimpy. He was so uneasy that he could not think what had happened to her.

He stood up. At the same moment Miss Bentley stood up too, erect and full, her brown hair remarkably thick and bright against the golden sloping shoulders. Miss Beaumont was tying a red bathing hat on her head and this, as it enclosed her hair, made her look more than ever like a boy. Immature and white, her shoulders were awkwardly twisted, showing salt-cellars.

"Ah! there you are at last," the major said. "Ready?"

"There's no great hurry, is there?" she said.

With studied rapture Miss Bentley turned and stared into the tranquil heart of the lake, disturbed here and there only by the faintest silver ruffles, little islands of coat-of-mail that drifted, sparkled, took to air and floated away.

"Heavens, this lake looks as deep as the end of time this morning," she said. "Don't you think so? I've noticed it before on these hot, still days."

She turned to Miss Beaumont, whose toe-nails were painted red, giving her a still more unreal, doll-like appearance.

"I'll give you one guess how deep it is," Miss Bentley said.

Miss Beaumont too gazed at the lake, silent, evidently not wanting to guess at its depth and giving once more, as a consequence, an impression of compressed virginal aloofness.

"Fourteen hundred feet they tell me," Miss Bentley said.

A moment later she dived. As she did so Major Wilshaw realized that he had never seen her swim before. He had no idea whether she swam well or badly.

A second later he realized that she had totally disappeared. The great depth of the lake had swallowed her. In a stupefying moment of astonishment, followed by shock, he was pained by an unpleasant sensation. He was unaware of giving a gasp of alarm or of walking several paces towards the edge of the water and, at last, of letting out a half-choked breath, part in relief, part in sheer admiration, as Miss Bentley surfaced thirty yards away, turned belly-wise like a clean white fish and floated in the sun.

As his alarm drained away he turned to see Miss Beaumont sitting down.

"What was all the fuss about?"

"Fuss? Oh, nothing. I just wondered when—Aren't you coming in?"

"Not yet," the girl said. "I'm rather chilly. I'll lie in the sun."

He turned from the flat figure to face a sun that, even at the angle of October, sliced at his eyes with clear hot brightness. A moment later he dived and swam slowly and unhurriedly out to where Miss Bentley floated, face upwards, perfectly still.

To his fresh surprise she again had on her face the strange smile that had mystified him a few minutes before.

"No idea you swam so well."

She did not answer. Instead, for the second or third time, the smile broke into actual laughter.

"Oh! look, aren't you going to share this joke with me?"

"Some jokes make you laugh more when you don't share them," Miss Bentley said. "They sort of evaporate when you start telling."

"I've got an idea it's about me," he said.

"Oh! good lord no."

"About Miss Beaumont then?"

Again she did not answer and he knew now that the joke, whatever it was, was about Miss Beaumont.

He paddled water. Small brilliant pearls of water lay in the hollow above Miss Bentley's breasts. She kept her hands flicking, fin-like, at full length and the smile on her face did not fade.

"Might just as well tell me."

"I don't think it would be fair on Miss Beaumont."

It suddenly amused her to tease the major and with lazy strokes she started swimming on her back, towards a diving raft that lay fifteen yards away. He followed at a slow crawl, keeping some distance behind.

On the raft two muscular, good-looking Italians, about twenty or so, sleek, with black hair, walnut bodies and brief blue swimming trunks, watched her come in, heave herself to the raft and sit dripping in the sun. She lifted herself aboard the raft in one easy swinging movement and the Italians smiled across at each other as the major followed, heaving himself up with difficulty, in several puffing movements, his own weight too much for him, so that in the end Miss Bentley stretched out and gave him a hand.

"Funny how I've never seen you down at the Lido before," the major said. "How did you get so brown?"

"You always come in the mornings," Miss Bentley said. "I always come in the afternoons, when you're napping. I have lunch earlier than you."

She turned and lay on her back, wet hair spread outwards, and the two Italians stared at her full, prostrate body as it glittered in the sun.

The major lay down too and after five minutes or so turned his head, saw that her eyes were closed and said:

"Going to swim any more?"

"I think so, yes. And you?"

"I don't think so. I think I'll lie in the sun."

A moment or two later she dived, came up only a few yards away and started to swim with an easy crawl along the path of the sun. Almost immediately she had dived the taller, older of the two young Italians dived too and swam with long strokes after her.

Miss Bentley, turning some moments later to float on her back, found him smiling brilliantly alongside her.

"Hullo."

"Hullo," she said.

"Hot today." His smile was very white. A crucifix glittered gold on the wet black hairs of his chest. "Are you thirsty?"

"Not very. Why?"

"I thought if you thirsty you have drink with me?"

Miss Bentley smiled, lapping water with outstretched fingers.

"That sounds nice. Did the other one dare you?"

"Did what? *Prego?*"

"Oh! it doesn't matter. Where do you drink anyway?"

He pointed shorewards with a very brown, very well-manicured hand.

"At the little *caffè* at the end of the Lido. Just there. You take coffee, vermouth what you like. Oh! him?" he said, pointing back to the raft. "He's my brother."

Miss Bentley, not answering at once, turned to see where the major was. She discovered him to be sitting upright on the raft, watching her. The sight of him sitting there gave her so much satisfaction that she smiled again and then turned, still smiling, to the Italian boy.

"I don't think my friend would like it."

"No? You have to ask him?"

"No, but—"

She gave him the kind of glance that Major Wilshaw often found quizzical, sometimes ironical, but not really coquettish, and the boy seemed to find it so attractive that he swam closer.

"Then will you come?"

"I don't think so. I think my friend would be very jealous. I think he wouldn't like it."

"Jealous?" the boy said. "It's very good to be jealous. That's good."

She felt his hand brush itself quickly across her back.

"He's watching. Another thing—You're much too close to me."

"Of course," he said. "If I didn't want to be close to you I would be sitting on the raft. Like your friend."

Slowly and boldly his eyes travelled the full length, from hair to toes, of her floating body.

"Will you come now?" he said. "They have very good *orvieto* at the *caffè*. After the swim it very good—"

"Supposing I preferred coffee?"

"Very well, then. Good. Coffee!—"

He smiled handsomely, brilliantly again, with vanity, pleased with himself. "I suppose he does it every day," she told herself and smiled too.

As they swam shorewards together he kept very close to her and once or twice he touched her arm, but she did not protest or move away. Nor did she once look back to where a stunned Major Wilshaw, squatting on the raft with his arms huddled across his knees, was staring at her across the tranquil surface of the lake, solemnly, with disbelieving eyes.

It was after five o'clock when she was sitting on the patio, drinking tea with slices of lemon in it, and Major Wilshaw appeared. It was the first time she had seen him since midday and now he was carrying a parcel in his hands.

"You were quite right about the tricks," he said. "There was a mess-up about a customs form. Cost me another five hundred lire but anyway I've got them now."

"The children will be thrilled."

The major continued to stand by her table, a little coolly, as if purposely intending not to sit down.

"Won't you have some tea?" Miss Bentley said. "We could easily ask for another cup."

"I had a cup in the town."

He shifted uneasily from one foot to another, at the same time changing the parcel from hand to hand.

"You disappeared rather quickly all of a sudden this morning," he said.

"Oh! did I?"

"I thought it was rather swift."

She played with a slice of lemon in her cup, submerging it and poking at it thoughtfully with a spoon.

"I didn't want to play gooseberry," she said, "that's all."

"I don't know about gooseberry."

She did not answer; she drank tea instead and the major went on:

"After all, the three of us went down together and I naturally thought—You didn't come back to lunch, either, did you?"

"No," she said. "I had lunch at the *caffè*."

"Oh?" he said. "With the two Italian boys?"

"With one of them."

She looked up as she said this and she thought the face of the major flushed.

"He's rather nice," she said. "And I think rather well off too. His father makes motor tires."

The major, lifting his head suddenly, made a quick short noise of expiration, somewhere between a snort and a sigh.

"What was all that in aid of?" Miss Bentley said.

"Nothing. Only I didn't think you were a pick-up."

"Of course it was a pick-up." She said this with deliberate emphasis and it amused her to see his face as she teased him.

"Well!" he said. "Well!"

"What's wrong with a pick-up?" she said. "After all, thousands of women all over the world are simply longing for a pick-up. It's all they dream about. Every night. Every day."

"Yes, but really I must say it's rather surprising in *you*, isn't it?" the major said. "And with—with this boy."

"Why with me? And why not with a boy? After all," she said, "you have your Miss Beaumont."

"That's rather different."

"Is it?" she said. "I don't see how. Miss Beaumont and the Italian boy are about the same age as each other. So are you and I."

"Yes, but I mean. With an older woman and a young—"

He broke off suddenly, unable to complete the sentence in which he was clearly going to say that he thought that when women of her age chose to consort with young men of twenty it was something rather cheap, unladylike and distasteful. After this he stood stiffly, almost to attention, with an air of offence, not speaking.

"I'm sorry if I made you angry."

"Oh! you didn't make me angry." She looked up to see a flush of anger on his face and felt extraordinarily pleased that it was there. "Not a bit."

Pleasantly, coolly and without haste, aware of the major's discomfort, she poured herself another cup of tea, put sugar and lemon into it and stirred it delicately with her spoon.

"What about the tricks?" she said. "Will you do them tonight?"

"That's really what I wanted to see you about," the major said. He relaxed a little. He even allowed himself the beginnings of a short stiff smile. "You see it's slightly awkward—"

"In what way?"

"Well, in at least one of the tricks, probably two, I need a collaborator and I rather thought—"

"Wouldn't Miss Beaumont do?"

"Oh! no, no, no, no. I don't think so. You see—"

"When is all this going to be?" Miss Bentley said and again she turned on him her slightly quizzical, slightly ironical smile. "This trickery and collaboration?"

"I thought if we rehearsed a bit we could do it by tomorrow night."

She drank the remainder of her tea. And then, wiping her lips and the tips of her fingers with a paper serviette, which she afterwards crumpled up in her hands, she came to a sudden decision which astounded herself.

"I'm afraid I can't tomorrow," she said. "I'm driving into Pallanza to have dinner with this young man."

She looked up suddenly to see the effect of her words on the major and found his face unexpectedly blank and the colour of greyish cardboard.

"I see," he said and then turned suddenly and walked away across the terrace and into the hotel, leaving her staring at the lake, across the pink-blue surface of which a steamer was cutting, like a white knife, a path against the sun.

Suddenly, as he disappeared, she was aware of feeling uneasy, no longer so confident in herself. The tea and the lemon abruptly started to repeat themselves and she knew that if she were not very careful they would bring on an uncomfortable attack of heartburn.

The following evening, shortly before seven o'clock, she started to walk into the town. As she went down the steps of the hotel Major Wilshaw appeared suddenly from the garden, almost as if he had been waiting in hiding, hoping to catch her.

"I thought you were driving to Pallanza."

"So I am. But something happened to the boy's car and he said would I walk to meet him."

The major stood awkwardly, first on one foot, then the other. She thought he combined an appearance of great smartness with considerable uneasiness as he fingered the lapel of his suit of navy blue mohair. A little cream handkerchief showed triangular-wise from the breast pocket. He fingered that too and said:

"Actually Miss Beaumont and I are dining out too. It's nice to have a change sometimes."

"Oh! Where?"

"At the Splendide. We can dance there."

She moved to go away.

"Oh! about the tricks," he said.

"Yes?"

"I've got it all fixed for tomorrow. I want to do it properly. Signora Fascioli says I can use the writing-room. Of course I shall invite her."

"Naturally."

He suddenly made such a mess of fingering the handkerchief that he pulled it out in entirety, together with a small silver pencil, which fell on the steps.

"That wasn't very clever," he said, without laughing. "I'll have to do better than that."

She began to feel highly uneasy herself as he stooped to pick up the pencil.

"Well, I'll have to fly now," she said. "I'll be late otherwise."

Fumbling hopelessly with pencil and handkerchief he said: "What I wanted to say was would you?—you know, just help a bit?— tomorrow?"

"If you think I'd be any good."

"Of course, of course. Thank you. Well, I mustn't keep you—"

She hurried away, not looking back. She kept up a quick pace for a hundred yards or so and then fell into a slow, dawdling walk. Across the lake, where the sun had already set, an orange-green glow, touched with purple, lay softly on the more distant water. The mountains above it were also purple, except at the tips. There they were pink-amber in the afterglow, and along the shore and in the valleys the lights of towns were coming on.

In the town she bought an English newspaper. Then she went into a small side-street restaurant and ordered an omelette and made it last as long as she could. In the paper she read, as she sipped at a glass of *valpolicella*, that the weather in London was unusually cold for mid-October. Snow had already fallen in the Cairngorm mountains of Scotland. An actress she had once seen in a play had died from an overdose of sleeping tablets. Some shares she held in rubber had fallen six points or so.

After the omelette she ordered cheese and fruit. Then, because there were many grapes on the dish, both green and black ones, she made the cheese and fruit last almost twice as long as the omelette had done. By that time she had read most of the things in the paper.

Afterwards she ordered coffee and sat for some time trying to work out how long it would take anyone to drive to Pallanza, have dinner at leisure and drive back again. She supposed that she ought to add to this another half an hour, or even more, for saying good-night to a young, handsome and easy-spoken Italian with plenty of energy, money and time to spare and she decided it would be at least eleven o'clock before she dare be seen walking up the steps of the hotel, where on hot nights guests often sat until midnight, talking.

By this time it was only nine o'clock and she ordered a brandy with fresh coffee and started to do the crossword in the newspaper. The words of the crossword did not come to her very easily. She found herself thinking of Major Wilshaw and Miss Beaumont and what dinner might be like at the Splendide and if the band was good for dancing. She smiled once into space as she remembered the incident in the bathing cubicle when she and Miss Beaumont were undressing together but the waiter misinterpreted the smile as a gesture that she wanted him and came over, bowing, and said:

"Yes, signora? Is something you wanted?"

"Just the bill," she said and wondered miserably what had made her say so.

As she walked slowly back along the promenade by the lakeside the night was extraordinarily warm and still and she could sometimes catch the faint vanilla-like scent of oleanders blooming under the street-lights, about the path.

Then a hundred yards away from the entrance to the Splendide she saw the unmistakable figure of Major Wilshaw, with Miss Beaumont, leave the hotel, cross the street and come straight towards her.

In panic she turned completely round, walked back several yards and hid behind a clump of oleanders, from which she pretended to be gazing, with her face in her hands, at the lights of Pallanza, several miles away. As the major and Miss Beaumont passed her she heard the major say, without drawing any answer from Miss Beaumont:

"I should like to have had little invitation cards printed. Fun for the children, I thought. But then of course, there isn't time and I'll have to write them."

As they passed out of hearing Miss Bentley suddenly hated herself for the stupid evening she had spent and then hated Miss Beaumont even more for not responding with a single word to the major's charming thought.

The major walked on with Miss Beaumont until they came to a *caffè* where, between small candle-lit tables, a two-piece orchestra consisting of piano and piano accordion were playing. Dinner at the Splendide had been taken in a large, echoing, chandeliered room in which the seven waiters had outnumbered the guests by two and there had been, because of the lateness of the season, no dancing.

One of the things the major had discovered he disliked most in life was dancing on a floor, between very small tables, measuring perhaps six feet by four, and he began to think with envy of Miss Bentley, dining quietly at Pallanza, perhaps under one of those charming arbours of vines so common to Italy, or under a canopy of trained chestnut branches.

"Oh! this is fun," Miss Beaumont said. "I feel like sticking a candle in your hair."

"Oh, please don't."

"Oh, come on," she said. "Take your back hair down. Have fun. Somebody told me this is the place where they dance on the tables."

The two-piece band poured music down his throat from a distance of two yards like a blast from a furnace door. The hard thin body of Miss Beaumont flung him from side to side. Her breasts pressed against him with the hardness of two shapely little Easter eggs and now and then she chanted into his ear, in an abrasive voice, the brittle, chirpy words of songs she knew.

"And relax, relax," she said. "Let your feet go. Your bones are set. Let your feet go."

Some time later they were served with a luke-warm soup that looked like porridge and that the major discovered, with violent distaste, was made entirely of garlic, finely shredded. With difficulty and wretchedness he ate several spoonfuls, washing it down with sharp red wine, and wondered miserably how long his breath would smell.

"Glorious fun," Miss Beaumont said. "Come on, you old candlestick, dance with me."

Later, towards eleven o'clock, a young Italian girl danced on a table, to be joined presently by one of the waiters. Miss Beaumont climbed on a table and started dancing too, kicking her thin legs, shouting to the major to join her. The table was not large enough for two and he succeeded in getting up on another, but some moments later the table suddenly collapsed and the major fell heavily, bruising his shin against a chair. When he tried to dance again the garlic, quarrelling already with the wine, started repeating violently, making him belch, and he felt strong waves of hot nausea begin to rise.

When Miss Beaumont came down from the table and danced with him on the floor again she said:

"What on earth are you hobbling for?"

"I barked my shin. It's rather painful."

"Oh! rub it with brandy!" she said. "You won't die."

After that they drank more red wine, followed by a sweet liqueur tasting strangely of perfumed oranges. It too quarrelled with the garlic and soon a painful area of burning, deep and formidable, settled about the major's chest.

As he drove Miss Beaumont home in a taxi, soon after one
o'clock, he could not decide if she were tipsy, happy or merely
excited, but suddenly he decided to interpret her mood as one in
which, at all costs, she longed for him to kiss her.

To his surprise, as his hands touched her body, she pushed him
away.

"If you're going to kiss me, kiss me," she said. "Don't creep all
over me."

The major, who had no intention of creeping all over her and
who also flattered himself that he was capable of reasonable behaviour, did not know what to say. The attempt to kiss her,
when he made it at last, was not successful, partly because, perhaps for the twentieth or thirtieth time, the garlic again began
to rise.

Up in his room the major discovered, after an hour, that he
could not sleep at all. The garlic, the sharp red wine, the
strange orange liqueur and a repetitive taste of a portion of
scampi he had eaten at dinner quarrelled with continual violence just above his heart.

He got up at last, switched on the light and unpacked the box
of tricks that had given him so much pleasure as a boy. He
decided to put in some practice on the tricks but after some
moments he discovered that he had, over the years, forgotten
most of them, particularly the one where he needed the collaboration of Miss Bentley.

Depressed and worn out, he went to the window and stared at
the diminishing number of lights on the shores of the lake below. As he stood there a car drew up outside, its door banged,
and he looked down to see a woman alighting.

Though the woman was in fact Signora Fascioli coming home
late from visiting her eldest sister in Arona he was sure, in the
darkness, that it was Miss Bentley, at last returning from Pallanza.

The thought depressed him more than ever. He experienced a
pitiful moment of jealousy and then decided he hated himself as
much as Miss Bentley. The garlic began to rise again and he drank
several glasses of water, together with three aspirins, before going
back to bed, to lie there miserably wondering how many coffee

beans he would have to chew in the morning before he was again a
civilized, presentable man.

The following evening, after dinner, the major put on his little
performance of tricks in the writing-room. He had gone to the
trouble of writing out little cards of invitation, which the Bompiani
children clutched with delight and on which he described himself as
Major Paulo: the Magic Wanderer. He had remembered in time that
he had called himself *the Magic Wanderer* as a boy. It was still rather
good, he thought. The *Major Paulo* was an afterthought and
because of it Miss Bentley grasped, for the first time, that his name
was Paul.

The Bompiani family, with Miss Bentley, Miss Beaumont,
Signora Fascioli, Maria, Enrico and the two cooks sat in rows
of chairs. The major had the tricks set out on a table covered
with a red cloth he had borrowed from Signora Fascioli. He
had rehearsed the tricks very hard during the late morning and
afternoon and he had let Miss Bentley into the necessary secrets
of collaboration. She seemed in some way subdued, her enthusiasm restricted, he thought, but he hoped things would go very
well all the same.

When he appeared, bowed and took up his magic wand the
Bompiani family led the applause and the children stood up,
clapping and dancing.

"Thank you, thank you," he said. "Thank you. Now, ladies and
gentlemen, *signori e signore*, if you will let me have your kind
attention, a few examples of the magic art—"

Miss Beaumont stared with stony eyes. Miss Bentley felt unaccountably nervous, still despising herself. The Bompiani children
shrieked far too much, she thought, and the whisperings of Maria
and one of the cooks, in local Italian, got on her nerves.

The major first did a trick where he turned water into wine. That
always went well. He was pleased that there were many "Bravos!"
mostly led by Signor Bompiani and taken up by the two little angels
in a chanting chorus. After this he did a trick in which he made a
fool's cap of thick white paper, poured a glass of milk into it and
then abruptly screwed up the empty fool's cap and threw it away.
That went very well too and again there was much applause, many

"Bravos!" and much admiring laughter. Before, during and after each trick he waved his magic wand.

After several other tricks, including one in which he cut a thick silk rope in half and joined it together again, and then a piece of baffling illusion with a black box, the time came for him to collaborate with Miss Bentley.

"For this trick I also need the collaboration of the audience," he said, "Signor Bompiani—perhaps you would be good enough to translate please?"

Signor Bompiani, who had a melodious, easy voice, translated at some length, so that by the time he had finished Miss Bentley felt more unsure of herself than ever. She found herself wanting the trick to succeed even more than the major did and she began to be afraid that the two cooks, who looked dopey as they listened, did not understand.

"It is all very simple," the major said. "You will each write whatever you like on a piece of paper, put the paper into an envelope and then seal it down. Please remember what you have written, because I shall then take each envelope *and, without opening it*, tell you what it is."

"We write in Italian or English?" Signora Fascioli said.

"Whichever you like," the major said. "But in Italian only the simple words!"

Miss Beaumont, who looked more distant than ever, was seen to dash off a single word. Signor Bompiani wrote three pieces, one each for the little angels. The cooks and Enrico sucked their pencils. Someone was heard distinctively to say *O! Sole Mio* and behind Miss Bentley there were sudden reproving cat-like hissings.

The major collected the envelopes. As he collected them he chattered a good deal, in traditional conjuring fashion, distracting attention and at the same time creating an air of expectancy.

"Now!" he said. "I am ready to read your minds. Envelope Number One!"

He stared with intensity, for twenty seconds or so, at the first envelope, holding it up to the light of the central chandelier.

"I think," he said at last, "yes, I think I penetrate the veil of the first mind. I think I know what words this envelope contains. Yes!" He spoke slowly, passing his hands in mystical, groping fashion in

front of his eyes. "I think—yes, I am sure." With drama, flourishing the envelope, he proclaimed: "I think the words this envelope
contains are *The spring in the mountains*." He paused. "Did anyone
write that?"

The major had arranged with Miss Bentley that at this point
there should be a dramatic pause: almost as if the trick, in its first
moment, had failed. Miss Bentley, as she heard her own words read
out, felt her throat become harsh and dry. She was unable to frame
her words. She felt as if years went by before she was able to say,
quietly:

"Yes. I wrote *The spring in the mountains*."

The major made a gesture of modest triumph. There was again
much applause. "Bravo! Bravo!" everyone said and Signor Bompiani exclaimed in round, melodious English: "Jolly good, major.
Jolly good."

While this was going on the major swiftly tore open the envelope,
memorized its contents and picked up the next one. Holding it up
to the light he suddenly said:

"Ah! I know what you are saying. You are saying that when I
hold the envelope up to the light the envelope becomes transparent.
That is not so. Signor Bompiani—would you oblige? Take the
envelope please and hold it up to the light. Is the envelope
transparent or not?"

Signor Bompiani took the envelope and held it up to the light.

"Thick as London fog," he said. "Can't see a blooming thing."

"Thank you, sir," the major said. There was some laughter. One
of the cooks giggled. The two Bompiani angels started giggling too.
"Yes, this one I think is easy. Did someone write *God Save the
Queen*?"

"Guilty," Signor Bompiani said. "I wrote it for this one," and
picked up the younger of the two children and put her on his knee.

"Bravo!" everyone said, with applause. "Bravo!"

The trick, Miss Bentley thought, was going quite well after all.
The worst, she felt, was over. She sucked her lips in relief, feeling
saliva flow warmly down to her throat, melting the dry harshness
there. She had now no more to do except listen and during the next
few moments she heard Signora Fascioli confess to have written, in
English, *There'll always be an England*, and Signor Bompiani, also in

English, to *A nice cup of tea*. It was Enrico who had written *O Sole Mio* after all.

Suddenly it seemed to Miss Bentley that the major grew uneasy. After Enrico's *O Sole Mio* he seemed all at once to lose buoyancy. She thought he looked irritated, flushed and a little under pressure.

"This envelope contains only a single word," he said in a slow voice, at last. "*Candlestick*. Did someone write that? *Candlestick?*"

"I did," Miss Beaumont said.

"Thank you," the major said. His voice carried a thin, restrained note of sarcasm. "Thank you."

From that moment the trick began to go wrong. Miss Bentley sat watching the major's small pink ears flush to a dark, bruised red. After the neat envelope he paused, looked very confused, said something about "it's very hard to concentrate on this one. I have to confess this one is very difficult," and then looked into the audience and said:

"Was there someone who didn't write *anything?*"

No one answered.

"Signor Bompiani."

Signor Bompiani translated. One of the cooks raised her hand and said something. The Italians laughed and Signor Bompiani translated what the cook had said.

"She wrote nothing, she says. She says she hadn't time to think. She requires a lot of time for thinking."

The major made a regretful gesture of resignation and said the spell was broken. The children, who had not understood the trick in the first place, looked more than ever mystified, and the major consoled them into fresh delight and giggling by producing round, bright pink sweets from their hair.

"Shame!" Signor Bompiani said. "Won't you go on? It was marvellous."

"It is too difficult now," the major said. "The spell is broken."

"Still, it was marvellous," Signor Bompiani said. Starting to applaud, he looked for approval towards his wife, who smiled also. "Marvellous!" she said with her handsome, fat, velvety lips and applauded too.

"I can't think how you do it, Major," Signor Bompiani said and then everyone said, "Marvellous!" or "Bravo!" and clapped their hands.

Only Miss Beaumont, Miss Bentley noticed, did not clap her hands. Instead she took out her lipstick and touched up her lips and while the major did a final trick of pulling unending streams of coloured paper from his mouth, Miss Bentley, watching her, wondered what *Candlestick* meant and why it had offended the major into sarcasm. She supposed Miss Beaumont in turn wondered what *The spring in the mountains* meant and she hardly knew herself what had made her choose the words. They had come to her suddenly, in a moment of mysterious enlightenment, in the odd way that things sometimes do, without thought or premeditation.

She discovered suddenly that she had been lost in a little daydream in which her eyes had been fixed once again on Major Wilshaw's ears. Hastily she re-focused her eyes to find that Signor Bompiani was making a little speech, partly of thanks and partly, as it turned out, of invitation.

"On behalf of you all I thank the major most profoundly for a wonderful treat—is that the word?—treat? Yes? A great treat, Major, thank you." The audience, led by Signor Bompiani, applauded once again. "And now, something else. The Bompianis, I am sad to say, must go back to Milano the day after tomorrow."

"Oh, no. No, no," the major said. "That's too bad."

"Work. One must work," Signor Bompiani said. "Still, what about a picnic? A farewell, final picnic? Tomorrow?"

While Signor Bompiani was saying this Signora Fascioli slipped out of the room, beckoning Enrico, Maria and the two cooks to go with her.

"What do you say? Where shall we go? Where we went before?—to the place in the mountains?"

"Splendid," the major said. "Couldn't be better."

"Good," Signor Bompiani said. "The only trouble is that we are one more this time. That makes it more difficult for the car."

"It's easy to hire another car," Miss Bentley said. "The major and I would stand for that."

Miss Beaumont suddenly spoke for only the second time.

"Or you could ask your Italian boy-friend along," she said. "That would even up the party. He has a car."

Before Miss Bentley could recover from annoyance and astonishment Signor Bompiani was saying:

"Oh! Oh! Boy-friend? Miss Bentley?— an *Italian* boy-friend?"

"We simply had a swim together."

"Oh?" Miss Beaumont said. "I'm sorry. I thought it was lunch. And dinner too."

Miss Bentley suddenly found herself in a hideous trap, not knowing what to answer. She was saved by Signor Bompiani, who laughed melodiously and said with generosity:

"Well, of course, invite him. The car would be most useful. It would be fun. What is his name? Perhaps we know him? Do you know his name?"

"I think his name is Balzari," Miss Bentley said. "His father manufactures motor-car tires. But we—"

"Of course we know him! Very well. Of course, Balzari. They have a villa here. Which boy is this?—the elder or the younger? There are two brothers."

"I think his name is Vittorio—"

"Vittorio—the elder one. The other one is named Carlo, of course," Signor Bompiani said. "Nice boys, I shall telephone him myself."

He began to take charge of the party, talking generously of drinks, occasionally saying, "Let's all have a nice cup of tea," his favourite joke about the English, shepherding everyone forward to the patio, where little green and crimson lights were hung about the arbours of trellis work. Miss Bentley took the opportunity of hurrying ahead, murmuring about the need for her wrap and how she would get it from upstairs. The Bompiani angels clung to the major, one at each hand, with their mother just behind, leaving Signor Bompiani and Miss Beaumont to come from the writing-room last, together.

"Well, Freda, that was nice, eh?" He patted Miss Beaumont in a friendly way on the shoulder. "Didn't you enjoy that? Didn't you think the trick with the envelopes was a good one? I can't think how the major does it at all."

"I know how it's done," Miss Beaumont said. "It's as old as the hills."

Upstairs, in her room, where the lights of the lake shining

through the slats of the Venetian blinds made cage-like bars on the white ceiling, Miss Bentley sat looking at her quivering, foolish hands.

For the picnic lunch there were large piles of cold pork and salami, pink stacks of ham, two dishes of pâté, a whole *Bel Paese*, large nests of hard-boiled eggs, much bread and two baskets of fruit, mostly green and black grapes, with a few last blue figs and big butter-coloured pears. There were four flasks of *valpolicelli* to drink, with white vermouth for those who preferred it, and mineral water for the angels. Miss Bentley and Signora Bompiani separated the slices of meat and laid them thickly on rounds of buttered bread. Miss Beaumont tied bibs on the children while Signor Bompiani and Vittorio, the Italian boy, who to Miss Bentley's relief had driven up with the major in his car, opened and poured out the wine. All across the mountains a still sharp light lay wonderfully distilled above the distances, with pure noon transparence, and the lake, more than ever like a pale blue glass lioness, was clearly visible below.

"Shall we drink to our meeting next summer?" Signor Bompiani said. Gaily he raised his glass to everybody; the wine glowed with a brilliant heart of fire in the sun. "Let's drink to that, shall we?"

"Cheers," the major said. "*Salut. Santé*. And everything else besides. To next year."

Everyone drank wine as they sat about on short grass burned to bleached matting by the long summer. From somewhere higher up the slope, among the rocks, the sound of a spring breaking and beginning to run down the mountainside was the only sound in the fresh bright air except the sound of voices.

"Will you come back next year, Major?"

"My goodness I hope so."

"And what about you, Miss Bentley?"

Miss Bentley, caught unawares by the question, did not know what to say.

"I may do," she said. "I shall see—"

"Or perhaps you prefer Pallanza?" Miss Beaumont said.

Looking up suddenly at this remark, Major Wilshaw saw on Miss Bentley's face something he had never seen there before. She had

totally lost her look of assurance. Her expression was one of
indecisive, rather helpless pain and suddenly it hurt him to see it
there.

"Well, Pallanza is very nice," Signor Bompiani said. "But not so
nice as this. What do you say, Vittorio? You like Pallanza?"

"No. Pallanza's noisy," the boy said.

In panic Miss Bentley wondered how long the conversation
would go on but the major said quickly, changing the subject almost
desperately, that he thought the nicest place he had seen in all Italy
was a little town in one of the steep river valleys between Bolzano
and Venice. Tobacco grew all along the sides of the valley and he
thought it was very lovely there.

"Stupid of me, though," he said. "I can't even remember the
name of it now."

"Ah, Venice," Signor Bompiani said. "Venice." He turned to the
boy. "Vittorio really comes from Venice, don't you?"

"My family has a house there."

Part of a slice of ham hung down from the astonished lips of Miss
Beaumont as she heard this. Her eyes fixed themselves on Vittorio
Balzari with unbelief, fascination and with less coolness than she
reserved for Miss Bentley and Major Wilshaw. Then she became
aware of the pink trembling piece of ham dangling from her lips and
pushed it hastily in and said:

"You have three houses? One in Milan, one in Venice, and one
here?"

"Four, really," he said. "My mother has a flat in Rome too."

Miss Beaumont swallowed her ham and tried to look as if, every
day of her life, she heard of people who had houses in each of four
illustrious and beautiful towns in Italy.

"How nice," she said. "Don't you find it hard to get servants for
all these places?"

"No," he said. "In Italy we have plenty."

"How many do you need for four houses?" Miss Beaumont said.

"I think we have twenty-seven—no, twenty-eight—waiters," he
said.

Everyone laughed at this, especially the three English, who were
delighted at the misuse of the word waiters. Even Miss Bentley
laughed. The major was quick to notice on her face a little break in

the veil of pained, indecisive tension. He was glad he had been skilful in changing the subject of Pallanza.

Through the rest of the lunch he found himself looking more and more at her face, which from his lower position on the slope appeared to him framed completely against the sky, clear sharp blue above the mountains. And presently he found that he was looking at her, though he did not realize it at first, with tenderness. He felt he suddenly wanted to leave the pleasant arena of the laughing picnic and walk with Miss Bentley somewhere farther up the slopes, among the rocks, in complete solitude, where the spring rose.

Then he remembered the sentence she had written for the trick, *The spring in the mountains*, and he wondered what could have made her write the words. She had been very quiet, almost without a word, throughout the entire picnic. Now a puff of breeze had blown a few strands of her brown hair down across her forehead and eyes and in preoccupation she had not pushed it back again. He watched this brown curl of hair with new fascination and thought it gave her a certain lightness, a prettiness, he had never seen there before.

Then he was aware of Vittorio filling up his glass again and Signor Bompiani, who loved any excuse for drinking and even more for proposing a toast, raised his glass to everyone again and said:

"We have already drunk to next year. Now let's drink to this year. It's been wonderful."

Everyone drank and agreed it had been wonderful.

"And to our English friends."

"Thank you. And to our Italian friends."

"Thank you, Major. Most kind."

"And to the children. Our little angels," the major said. "If only we could all grow up so beautiful."

Everyone laughed at the ambiguity of this remark, which Signor Bompiani translated for his wife, and Miss Beaumont said, "Thank you," with the faintest, most distant touch of sarcasm.

Then the two children suddenly raised their glasses of mineral water and drank too, to the amusement of everybody, and there were fresh shrieks of laughter.

"Any more ham?" Signor Bompiani said. "No more ham? No

more salami? No more cheese? No, no, not for me." He laughed
loudly. "If I eat more I must take too much shut-eye!"

As the major watched Miss Bentley quietly peeling a ripe fig and
then sucking the light pink flesh from the broken purple balloon of
skin he made up his mind that he would, somehow, get her to walk
with him, after lunch, farther up the mountainside. His only fear
was that Vittorio would ask her first and again he felt a stab of
jealousy about the boy and the journey to Pallanza, which had
ended with the miserable fiasco of Miss Beaumont, the garlic and
the incident of the candlestick, that blistering, sarcastic, crushing
word.

Then he saw, after a time, that Signor Bompiani and his wife were
already asleep among the rocks. The children were resting too,
stretched out in the sun. Miss Bentley and Miss Beaumont were
packing up the picnic things, disdaining help from men, though
Vittorio was hovering near them: waiting, the major hoped, for
Miss Beaumont to be free.

For five minutes he wandered away among the rocks, hoping that
when he got back again Miss Bentley would be alone. When he did
get back she was alone but, like the Bompianis, already lying down
among the rocks, in the sun, with eyes closed.

He lay down too, the sun hot on his face, the air powdery dry
with a smell of thin autumnal earth long burned by summer. There
was not a sound in the air except the sharp falling water of the
spring rising invisibly, some distance up the gorge, from the rocks.
Vittorio and Miss Beaumont had wandered away too and even the
children did not stir.

He found he could not close his eyes at all. For a long time, lying
face sideways, he watched Miss Bentley. The strand of hair had
fallen down, for a second time, across her face. He wondered again
what had happened at Pallanza to make her so unhappy and why
she had written the words about the spring.

Suddenly she opened her eyes and lay there looking at him. He
stared back at her without a flicker. Her eyes had no movement
either. Her stare was profound, enraptured and mute and for a long
time the two of them lay there in a trance, looking at each other,
never moving, in air so quiet that the major could separate each
sound of falling water from the other as clearly as notes on a flute.

It was a spell he never wanted to be broken but the children, leaping up suddenly, broke it with laughter. Hearing them, the Bompianis woke too and Signor Bompiani said:

"Well, did you sleep, Major? I dreamed I was the owner of a banana plantation on some island somewhere. How do you account for that? Too much salami and cheese I suppose."

A few minutes later Vittorio and Miss Beaumont came back: Miss Beaumont, the major thought, looked thinly haughty; Vittorio rather baffled. Seeing them, Signor Bompiani said he was glad they were back. The air was far up and so late in the year got cold very quickly. For the children's sake they ought to go.

Two minutes later, although it was only three o'clock, the sun dipped behind a bastion of westerly mountainside, leaving a sheet of cold purple shadow through which the sound of spring water seemed suddenly to fall with iciness.

"Time for a nice cup of tea!" Signor Bompiani said: his favourite joke about England.

He led the way down the mountainside, carrying the younger child. The major carried the other angel and the rest followed, single file, with the picnic baskets.

At the foot of the path, just before they reached the cars, Signor Bompiani turned and called back:

"By the way, Major, when do you leave?"

"Not sure. I've stayed over three weeks longer than I meant already."

Signor Bompiani turned again and called back.

"What about you, Miss Bentley?"

Miss Bentley seemed to hesitate uncomfortably before answering. With a curiously constricted feeling about his heart the major stared ahead across the lake, waiting for what she had to say.

"Two days after you," Miss Bentley said. "Sunday."

"Well, make the most of them," Signor Bompiani called.

The major felt himself sharply catch his breath, but whether in relief or astonishment or from the sudden chill of the air he never knew. Half an hour later the two cars, descending rapidly, were down in the warmth, among the still-blooming oleanders, of the lakeside.

Two mornings later Miss Bentley sat on the terrace, staring at a

boiled egg. She could not think what had caused her to order a
boiled egg for breakfast and she was just thinking that, after all, she
did not want it very much when the major appeared.

"Do you mind if I join you?" he said. "Is that a boiled egg you've
got?"

"I thought I'd order one."

"I think I might order one myself."

The major rang a bell on one of the trellis posts along the terrace
and, when Enrico came, ordered a boiled egg.

"Four minutes," he said.

It was, it seemed to him, the longest four minutes of his life. Like
Miss Bentley he did not know what prompted him to order the
boiled egg and he knew, some time before it came, that he did not
want it very much either. A recollection of Pallanza, Miss Beaumont's sarcasm about his tricks, the strange moments when he had
stared at Miss Bentley at the picnic and above all the fact that Miss
Bentley was going away next morning made him something more
than tongue-tied and uneasy. He felt a little sick too.

"Do start," he said. "Don't wait. Mine is sure to be some time."

Miss Bentley picked up a knife and prepared to slice the top off
her egg. The morning sun drew from the knife blade a flick of silver
light as, almost at once, she laid it down again.

The major, not daring to ask her what her plans were for her last
day by the lake, raised his face to the sun and said:

"The sun's really quite warm when you think it's nearly November."

"Yes, it's quite warm."

"It's really been quite exceptionally warm all the month."

"Exceptionally warm," she said. "Even the Italians say it's been
exceptionally warm."

Presently the egg arrived and the major found himself staring at
it, unable to attack it, exactly as Miss Bentley had done.

"It seems awfully quiet without the Bompianis," he said.

She looked away at the lake. "Yes," she said.

"They were so gay."

"I suppose they were. The children got on your nerves sometimes."

"Oh! did they? I never noticed that."

Miss Bentley looked from the lake to her egg and then back to the lake again. As she did so the major remembered the morning, almost a month before, when she had said good-bye to him, checked his hotel bill for him and had talked to him, with such efficient assurance, about the necessity of not packing his passport and ticket with his luggage. Then she had kept her eyes fixed on the side of his face and it was he who was nervous. Now she simply stared at the egg and the lake and could not look at him.

He tapped at the top of his egg with a spoon.

"I thought—"

"What are—"

The major stopped tapping the egg.

"I'm sorry. Please—"

"It's nothing," Miss Bentley said, "I was only going to say—I mean you're up rather early. Are you having a swim today?"

"No. As a matter of fact," the major said, "I was thinking of going up to the mountains."

"By funicular?"

"No. You can get a bus to that village—the one where the level crossing is—and then walk from there."

"It's quicker by funicular."

A sudden impression that the egg might not be very fresh caused him to feel a wave of nausea. It caught in his throat. He swallowed, pushed the egg away and found himself saying:

"I suppose you wouldn't care to come? We could probably get a bite at the village and a glass of wine."

"I really ought to do my packing."

"It really won't take all that long," the major said. "I plan to be back by three."

She made another meaningless gesture with the knife, picking it up as if to attack the egg and then putting it down again.

"I simply must do my packing," she said.

Another pointless gesture with the knife irritated him.

"You've got hours," he said. "What time does your train go tomorrow?"

"That's another thing," she said. "I've got to get my sleeper ticket fixed. I've only an open one at the moment. I ought to have done it before—"

"Perhaps you'd rather say good-bye to Pallanza?" he said. "I'll go to Locarno for the day."

The jolt of pain across her face was quick and shocked, but it followed him down the hill. Walking quickly towards the lake, angry, almost marching, he suddenly hoped he would never see Miss Bentley again. His embittered remark about Pallanza was a fitting end to something that, even before the pantomime of the eggs, had begun to swell with prickly irritations. That was the way with women. You offered, you cajoled, you were reasonable, you were generous and suddenly for no reason they took flight and hid themselves away.

He decided suddenly he was in time to catch the ten o'clock steamer, make the trip up the lake, spend the day in Locarno and come back late by train. By that time Miss Bentley would have gone to bed. In the morning he would order his breakfast upstairs, read for a couple of hours and not come down till lunch time. By twelve-thirty Miss Bentley would be gone. He would have seen the last of her.

Then suddenly he was thinking "Why the devil should I? Why, when I don't want to? Why go to Locarno when what you really want to do is to go to the mountains? Why be bludgeoned by Miss Bentley?"

He turned away from the lake and was just in time to catch a bus, in which he got a back window-seat, at the *piazza*. It took him, with many stops, up the long valley where groups of workers, some of them women still in big rice-straw sun-hats, were still gathering grapes among the vines. Over everything hung a light dust-coloured haze. The sun was hot on the windows of the bus and at one of the stops he looked out to see a hatless young Italian girl, arrogant, strong and brown as mahogany, taking off her woollen sweater among the vines. As she crossed her hands and seized the tips of the jumper and pulled it over her head she revealed underneath it the high line of her breasts, updrawn, in a white sleeveless blouse.

She laughed openly as she saw him looking at her. Then she hung the jumper over the vines and, still looking at him and still laughing, made as if to pull off the blouse too. He smiled back at her as the bus drove away and she suddenly plucked a bunch of grapes and pretended to throw it after him, following him with roving, arrogant eyes.

As the bus travelled away from the vineyards he half-wished he had got out, stopped and spent the day there. That would have been a great way to spend a day. He had always wanted to help with the vines. That would have been quite a Bacchanalian revel there, he thought, in the hot sun, in the alley-ways of vines, among the piled skips of grapes, with the brown arrogant girls.

By the time he got off the bus it was twelve o'clock. He was quite hungry and he had forgotten the look, on Miss Bentley's face, of arid, fleeting pain.

At the foot of the narrow road to the mountains stood a *caffè* where, on his first visit with the Bompianis and Miss Bentley, children had arrived, selling flowers. He sat at a table outside and waited. Beyond an open door screened by a curtain of coloured beads he could hear the family having lunch. He listened for some time to the murmur of voices and the sharp sounds of knives and forks and then pressed a bell in the wall.

A girl in a white sleeveless dress came, wiping food from her mouth with the corner of her apron.

"You speak English?"

"Little, little," she said.

She smiled as she spoke. He noticed her very slim, long fingers, almost as straight as wheat stalks and the same yellowish-tawny colour. Dark hair grew thick in her neck and under her arms and her feet were bare.

"Bring me a half bottle of *orvieto*," he said. "And some cheese."

"Bread with the cheese?"   .

She smiled again as she spoke. It was a very pleasant smile, he thought, not so bold, ripe and ready as the smile of the girl in the vineyard, but still a wonderfully pleasant, easy smile.

He responded by smiling too. She was eighteen or nineteen, he thought, though you could never tell in the south. Perhaps she was younger. "Yes , bread, please," he said and he watched the swing of her bare legs as she moved away.

When she came with the wine she smiled again, staying at the same time to talk a little and not only to uncork the wine but to pour it out for him; and once again he could not help thinking that the smile, like the smile of the girl in the vineyard, was specially, exclusively and solely for him. Wonderful, he thought, to drowse

away the whole afternoon there, repeating the wine and the smiles
until the bus came back.

"Very beautiful here," he said. "*Molto bella*. In the mountains."

"In the town is better."

"You think it's better in the town? Not in the mountains? Why?"

She shrugged her shoulders slightly and with one long finger drew
indeterminate patterns with a drop or two of spilled wine across the
table-top.

"In the town more fun."

"Oh! you know the word fun, do you?" he said.

"Yes, I know it," she said. The corners of her mouth sprang up,
quick and pretty. "You think I shouldn't know?"

They responded quickly, he thought. Bathed in a glow of
pleasure, the wine cold and fresh in his mouth, he sat for an hour
alone, gazing at the mountains. Nobody else was eating or drinking
and in the house the noises of the family gradually quietened down.

When he finally rang for the bill and the girl came he delayed her
by searching in the wrong pocket for his money and then by
producing a note for five thousand lire, hoping she had no change.
But she had change and he sat in fascination as she counted the
notes out for him on the table, his veins racing with pleasure and
satisfaction as he followed the line of her bare arms to the
shoulders, until finally he ran his fingers down her arm and pressed
a note in her hand.

"*Basta! Basta!*" she said. She swung round in a flare of fury,
pointing to the mountains. "*Basta!*" He thought she would either
strike him or spit at him before she found her English again. "We
sell wine and food here! Not *me!*"

She actually did spit as, a moment later, she turned and swung
into the house again. He picked up his change and started away up
the road, but a rattle of curtain beads made him turn suddenly and
he saw the girl appear again, this time with another, older girl,
perhaps her sister, and from the beads they mocked him.

"*Papa!*" the elder one shouted. She stuck out her tongue.
"*Papa!*"

He walked frigidly up the mountainside, among the rocks. He
suddenly felt completely stripped. He felt he would hear for the rest
of his life the jeers of the two girls from behind the curtains.

He climbed up to where the spring broke from the rocks. It was farther up than he thought and the spring itself, bursting from a wall of rock, came out faster than he remembered. Instinctively he held his hand under the descending water and the shock of it, pure ice, fell like a lock on his pulse, making him gasp for breath.

For a long time he sat listening to the water. There was nothing in it now that soothed him. It cut down into the tendons of his pride as harshly as the water itself had locked its ice on his wrist. It seemed to expose skin after skin of folly: his incredible folly about Miss Beaumont, his utter folly about the stupid, pompous tricks.

He remembered Miss Bentley. He had been, above all, an impertinent, impossible fool about Miss Bentley. With ruthlessness he had thrown at her his trite and embittered taunt about Pallanza and had fled the instant she stared at him with pain.

He started to walk back down the slope. It had been more than an hour since he had first walked up. The sun was moving rapidly westward. Already, across the fields of rock, there were big purple flanks of shadow.

Where the picnics had taken place, on a circular ledge of exposed burnt grass, the sun still shone.

He stopped suddenly at the edge of this grass and stared. In the centre of it, more or less exactly where she had lain at the picnic, Miss Bentley lay in the sun, arms outstretched, eyes closed.

He sat down. With compressed astonishment Miss Bentley opened her eyes and looked at him.

"You said you were going to Locarno."

He searched for something to say in answer. A recollection of the blistering taunt from behind the curtain of the little *caffè* shot through him and kept him silent instead. Then he remembered his own impossible taunt about Pallanza and suddenly, for the first time, he felt he began to understand her pain.

"What made you come up here?" he said.

"I came to listen to the spring."

A further recollection of the stupid evening of his tricks made him realize, for the first time too, why she had written her words about the spring. Then he was sure, suddenly, and also for the first time, that the complications about her, about himself, about everything, were slipping away.

"I'm glad you came up," he said.

He thought he saw on her face a look of inexpressible gratitude for this remark and suddenly he bent down and kissed her.

When it was over she lay, with the faintest of smiles, looking up at him.

"That was a nice impulse," she said. "Even better than the one you had when you missed the train."

"You told me to stay until a new one struck me," he said. "Do you remember?"

Miss Bentley found herself looking, as she had so often done, at the major's ears, that were so like small tight pink roses. She actually lifted her hand and touched one of them with the tips of her fingers. A moment later she felt an impulse of her own: an impulse to tell the major not only what his ears looked like but to confess that she too had been a fool and had never been to Pallanza.

Instead she checked herself. She was quiet and she stared at the sky. There were many ways of pursuing happiness and perhaps half of them were stupid. Most of the time you were a fool and the rest of it in pain.

The major, she decided, need never know about Pallanza. She merely smiled up at him and said:

"Such a nice impulse that I hope you'll be struck by it again."

"I might," he said. "On condition."

The major laughed for the first time, looking down into Miss Bentley's clear brown eyes.

"Tell me the joke about Miss Beaumont," he said. "That day at the cubicle. You remember."

Miss Bentley began laughing too.

"It wouldn't be fair on Miss Beaumont."

"Miss Beaumont has gone," the major said. "Damn Miss Beaumont."

Miss Bentley laughed again, gaily this time, with growing excitement, and then calmed herself.

"All right," she said. "Come nearer. How can I possibly tell you if you sit up there?"

Laughing again, she pulled the face of the major down to her, putting her mouth against one of his small pink ears.

"Good God," he said. "No."

"You see how unobservant men really are."

He drew slightly away from her, looking down at her body, seeing it not only as it lay there in the sunlight of afternoon but also as he had seen it, floating, unexpectedly splendid, in the lake below.

"Much depends," he said, "on what there is to observe."

She laughed again. With rising excitement he felt his hands slip to her breasts. Her thoughts were suddenly a racing jumble of bright impressions that included the sky, the mountains, the oleanders by the lakeside and the lake itself, stretched like a blue glass lioness in the autumn sun.

Suddenly she stopped laughing and was quiet again, holding his hands against her.

"Listen to the water," she said. "To the spring. Can you hear it?"

Over the mountainside there was no sound except the sound of falling water. Listening, the major heard it, as he always did, like cold music, with all its sharp and separate flutings descending rapidly and brilliantly, exhilarating in the clear still air.

Miss Bentley listened too. She supposed she had wanted all her life to listen to that sound, but now she did not hear it as the major did.

"It's like eternity, that sound," she said. With an amazement of joy she heard it pouring through herself. "The sound of a spring rising in the mountains."

(1960)*

---

*The date given at the end of each story is the date when the story was first collected.

THE FLAME

 "Two ham and tongue, two teas, please, Miss!"
"Yessir."

The waitress retreated, noticing as she did so that the clock stood at six. "Two ham and tongue, two teas," she called down the speaking-tube. The order was repeated. She put down the tube, seemed satisfied, even bored, and patted the white frilled cap that kept her black hair in place. Then she stood still, hand on hip, pensively watching the door. The door opened and shut.

She thought: "Them two again!"

Wriggling herself upright she went across and stood by the middle-aged men. One smiled and the other said: "Usual."

Down the tube went her monotonous message: "One ham, one tongue, two teas."

Her hand went to her hip again, and she gazed at the clock. Five past!—time was hanging, she thought. Her face grew pensive again. The first order came on the lift, and the voice up the tube: "Two 'am an' tongue, two teas!"

"Right." She took the tray and deposited it with a man and woman at a corner-table. On returning she was idle again, her eye still on the door. Her ear detected the sound of a bronchial wheeze on the floor above, the angry voice of a customer in the next section, and the rumble of the lift coming up. But she watched the door until the last possible second. The tray slid into her hand almost without her knowing it and the nasal voice into her ears: "One 'am, one tongue, two teas!"

"Right."

The middle-aged customers smiled; one nudged the other when she failed to acknowledge that salute, and chirped: "Bright today, ain't you!"

She turned her back on him.

"Been brighter," she said, without smiling.

She was tired. When she leant against the head of the lift she shut her eyes, then remembered and opened them again to resume her watch on the door and clock. The man in the corner smacked his lips, drank with his mouth full and nearly choked. A girl in another corner laughed, not at the choking man but at her companion looking cross-eyed. The cash-register "tinked" sharply. Someone went out: nothing but fog came in, making every one shiver at once. The man in the corner whistled three or four notes to show his discomfort, remembered himself, and began to eat ham.

The girl noticed these things mechanically, not troubling to show her disgust. Her eye remained on the door. A customer came in, an uninteresting working girl who stared, hesitated, then went and sat out of the dark girl's section. The dark girl noticed it mechanically.

The manageress came: tall, darkly dressed, with long sleeves, like a manageress.

"Have you had your tea, Miss Palmer," she asked.

"No."

"Would you like it?"

"No, thank you."

"No? Why not?"

"It's my night off. I'm due out at half-past."

She walked away, took an order, answered a call for "Bill!" and found that the order got mixed with the bill, and that the figures wouldn't add. It seemed years before the "tink" of the register put an end to confusion. The customer went out: fog blew in: people shivered. The couple in the corner sipped their tea, making little storms in their tea-cups.

She put her head against the lift. The clock showed a quarter past: another quarter of an hour! She was hungry. As if in consequence her brain seemed doubly sharp and she kept thinking: "My night out. Wednesday. Wednesday. He said Wednesday! He said—"

"Bill! Bill!"

She went about mechanically, listened mechanically, executed mechanically. A difficult bill nearly sent her mad, but she wrote mechanically, cleaned away dirty platter, brushed off crumbs—

all mechanically. Now and then she watched the clock. Five minutes more! Would he come? Would he? Had he said Wednesday?

The waitress from the next section, a fair girl, came and said: "Swap me your night, Lil? Got a flame comin' in. I couldn't get across to tell you before. A real flame—strite he is—nice, quiet, 'andsome. Be a dear? You don't care?"

The dark girl stared. What was this! She couldn't! Not she! The clock showed three minutes to go. She couldn't!

"Nothing doing," she said and walked away.

Every one was eating contentedly. In the shadow near the lift she pulled out his note and read: "I will come for you, Wednesday evening, 6."

Six! Then, he was late! Six! Why should she think half-past? She shut her eyes. Then he wasn't coming!

A clock outside struck the half-hour. She waited five minutes before passing down the room, more mechanically than ever. Why hadn't he come? Why hadn't he come?

The fair girl met her. "Be a dear?" she pleaded. "Swap me your night. He's a real flame—'struth he is, nice, quiet!"

Thirty-five minutes late! The dark girl watched the door. No sign! It was all over.

"Right-o," she said.

She sent another order down. The door opened often now, the fog was thicker, she moved busily. She thought of him when a man ordered a brandy and spilt it over her hand because his own shivered with cold. He wasn't like that, she thought, as she sucked her fingers dry.

For the first time in five minutes she looked at the door. She felt her heart leap.

He had come at last. Yes, there he was. He was talking to the fair girl. The little doll was close to him. Yes, there he was, nice, quiet handsome. Their voices crept across to her.

"Two seats? two seats?" she heard.

"Yes."

"Oh! I say! And supper?"

"Of course. And supper."

The dark girl could not move as they went out.

The door shut hard. "Two seats?" "And supper?" "Nice quiet, 'andsome." The dark girl dreamed on.

"Miss! Miss!"

She obeyed. She was sad, hungry, tired.

"Yessir?" They were middle-aged men again!

"Two teas, two tongues," said one.

"Two seats and supper?" she whispered.

"Whaaat? Two teas! two tongues! Can't you hear?"

"Yessir. Two teas, two tongues. Thank you, sir."

She moved slowly away.

"You can never make these blooming gals understand," said one man to the other.

(1928)

TIME

Sitting on an iron seat fixed about the body of a great chestnut tree breaking into pink-flushed blossom, two old men gazed dumbly at the sunlit emptiness of a town square.

The morning sun burned in a sky of marvellous blue serenity, making the drooping leaves of the tree most brilliant and the pale blossoms expand to fullest beauty. The eyes of the old men were also blue, but the brilliance of the summer sky made a mockery of the dim and somnolent light in them. Their thin white hair and drooping skin, their faltering lips and rusted clothes, the huddled bones of their bodies had come to winter. Their hands tottered, their lips were wet and dribbling, and they stared with a kind of earnest vacancy, seeing the world as a stillness of amber mist. They were perpetually silent. The deafness of one made speech a ghastly effort of shouting and mis-interpretation. With their worn sticks between their knees and their worn hands knotted over their sticks they sat as though time had ceased to exist for them.

Nevertheless every movement across the square was an event. Their eyes missed nothing that came within sight. It was as if the passing of every vehicle held for them the possibility of catastrophe; the appearance of a strange face was a revolution; the apparitions of young ladies in light summer dresses gliding on legs of shell-pink silk had on them something of the effect of goddesses on the minds of young heroes. There were, sometimes, subtle changes of light in their eyes.

Across the square they observed an approaching figure. They watched it with a new intensity, exchanging also, for the first time, a glance with one another. For the first time also they spoke.

"Who is it?" said one.

"Duke, ain't it?"

"Looks like Duke," the other said. "But I can't see that far."

Leaning forward on their sticks, they watched the approach of this figure with intent expectancy. He, too, was old. Beside him, indeed, it was as if they were adolescent. He was patriarchal. He resembled a biblical prophet, bearded and white and immemorial. He was timeless.

But though he looked like a patriarch he came across the square with the haste of a man in a walking race. He moved with a nimbleness and airiness that were miraculous. Seeing the old men on the seat he waved his stick with an amazing gaiety at them. It was like the brandishing of a youthful sword. Ten yards away he bellowed their names lustily in greeting.

"Well Rueben boy! Well Shepherd!"

They mumbled sombrely in reply. He shouted stentoriously about the weather, wagging his white beard strongly. They shifted along the seat and he sat down. A look of secret relief came over their dim faces, for he had towered above them like a statue in silver and bronze.

"Thought maybe you warn't coming," mumbled Rueben.

"Ah! been for a sharp walk!" he half-shouted. "A sharp walk!"

They had not the courage to ask where he had walked but in his clear brisk voice he told them, and deducing that he could not have travelled less than six or seven miles they sat in gloomy silence, as though shamed. With relief they saw him fumble in his pockets and bring out a bag of peppermints, black-and-white balls sticky and strong from the heat of his strenuous body, and having one by one popped peppermints into their mouths they sucked for a long time with toothless and dumb solemnity, contemplating the sunshine.

As they sucked, the two old men waited for Duke to speak, and they waited like men awaiting an oracle, since he was, in their eyes, a masterpiece of a man. Long ago, when they had been napkinned and at the breast, he had been a man with a beard, and before they had reached their youth he had passed into a lusty maturity. All their lives they had felt infantile beside him.

Now, in old age, he persisted in shaming them by the lustiness of his achievements and his vitality. He had the secret of a devilish perpetual youth. To them the world across the square was veiled in sunny mistiness, but Duke could detect the swiftness of a rabbit on a hillside a mile away. They heard the sounds of the world as though through a stone wall, but he could hear the crisp bark of a fox in another parish. They were condemned to an existence of memory because they could not read, but Duke devoured the papers. He had an infinite knowledge of the world and the freshest affairs of men. He brought them, every morning, news of earthquakes in Peru, of wars in China, of assassinations in Spain, of scandals among the clergy. He understood the obscurest movements of politicians and explained to them the newest laws of the land. They listened to him with the devoutness of worshippers listening to a preacher, regarding him with awe and believing in him with humble astonishment. There were times when he lied to them blatantly. They never suspected.

As they sat there, blissfully sucking, the shadow of the chestnut-tree began to shorten, its westward edge creeping up, like a tide, towards their feet. Beyond, the sun continued to blaze with unbroken brilliance on the white square. Swallowing the last smooth grain of peppermint Reuben wondered aloud what time it could be.

"Time?" said Duke. He spoke ominously. "Time?" he repeated.

They watched his hand solemnly uplift itself and vanish into his breast. They had no watches. Duke alone could tell them the passage of time while appearing to mock at it himself. Very slowly he drew out an immense watch, held it out at length on its silver chain, and regarded it steadfastly.

They regarded it also, at first with humble solemnity and then with quiet astonishment. They leaned forward to stare at it. Their eyes were filled with a great light of unbelief. The watch had stopped.

The three old men continued to stare at the watch in silence. The stopping of this watch was like the stopping of some perfect automaton. It resembled almost the stopping of time itself. Duke shook the watch urgently. The hand moved onward for a second or two from half-past three and then was dead again. He lifted the watch to his ear and listened. It was silent.

For a moment or two longer the old man sat in lugubrious

contemplation. The watch, like Duke, was a masterpiece, incredibly ancient, older even than Duke himself. They did not know how often he had boasted to them of its age and efficiency, its beauty and pricelessness. They remembered that it had once belonged to his father, that he had been offered incredible sums for it, that it had never stopped since the battle of Waterloo.

Finally Duke spoke. He spoke with the mysterious air of a man about to unravel a mystery. "Know what 'tis?"

They could only shake their heads and stare with the blankness of ignorance and curiosity. They could not know.

Duke made an ominous gesture, almost a flourish, with the hand that held the watch. "It's the lectric."

They stared at him with dim-eyed amazement.

"It's the lectric," he repeated. "The lectric in me body."

Shepherd was deaf. "Eh?" he said.

"The lectric," said Duke significantly, in a louder voice.

"Lectric?" They did not understand and they waited.

The oracle spoke at last, repeating with one hand the ominous gesture that was like a flourish.

"It stopped yesterday. Stopped in the middle of me dinner," he said. He was briefly silent. "Never stopped as long as I can remember. Never. And then stopped like that, all of a sudden, just at pudden-time. Couldn't understand it. Couldn't understand it for the life of me."

"Take it to the watch maker's?" Reuben said.

"I did," he said. "I did. This watch is older'n me, I said, and it's never stopped as long as I can remember. So he squinted at it and poked it and that's what he said."

"What?"

"It's the lectric, he says, that's what it is. It's the lectric—the lectric in your body. That's what he said. The lectric."

"Lectric light?"

"That's what he said. Lectric. You're full o' lectric, he says. You go home and leave your watch on the shelf and it'll go again. So I did."

The eyes of the old men seemed to signal intense questions. There was an ominous silence. Finally, with the watch still in his hand, Duke made an immense flourish, a gesture of serene triumph.

"And it went," he said. "It went!"

The old men murmured in wonder.

"It went all right. Right as a cricket! Beautiful!"

The eyes of the old men flickered with fresh amazement. The fickleness of the watch was beyond the weakness of their ancient comprehension. They groped for understanding as they might have searched with their dim eyes for a balloon far up in the sky. Staring and murmuring they could only pretend to understand.

"Solid truth," said Duke. "Goes on the shelf but it won't go on me. It's the lectric."

"That's what licks me," said Reuben, "the lectric."

"It's me body," urged Duke. "It's full of it."

"Lectric light?"

"Full of it. Alive with it."

He spoke like a man who had won a prize. Bursting with glory, he feigned humility. His white beard wagged lustily with pride, but the hand still bearing the watch seemed to droop with modesty.

"It's the lectric," he boasted softly.

They accepted the words in silence. It was as though they began to understand at last the lustiness of Duke's life, the nimbleness of his mind, the amazing youthfulness of his patriarchal limbs.

The shadow of the chestnut-tree had dwindled to a small dark circle about their seat. The rays of the sun were brilliantly perpendicular. On the chestnut-tree itself the countless candelabra of blossoms were a pure blaze of white and rose. A clock began to chime for noon.

Duke, at that moment, looked at his watch, still lying in his hand.

He started with instant guilt. The hands had moved miraculously to four o'clock and in the stillness of the summer air he could hear the tick of wheels.

With a hasty gesture of resignation he dropped the watch into his pocket again. He looked quickly at the old men, but they were sunk in sombre meditation. They had not seen or heard.

Abruptly he rose. "That's what it is," he said. "The lectric." He made a last gesture as though to indicate that he was the victim of some divine manifestation. "The lectric," he said.

He retreated nimbly across the square in the hot sunshine and the old men sat staring after him with the innocence of solemn wonder.

His limbs moved with the haste of a clockwork doll and he vanished with incredible swiftness from sight.

The sun had crept beyond the zenith and the feet of the old men were bathed in sunshine.

(1934)

SERGEANT CARMICHAEL

[I]

For some time he had had a feeling that none of them knew where they were going. They had flown over France without seeing the land. Now they were flying in heavy rain without a glimpse of the sea. He was very young, just twenty, and suddenly he had an uneasy idea that they would never see either the land or the sea again.

"Transmitter pretty u.s., sir," he said.

For a moment there was no answer. Then Davidson, the captain, answered automatically, "Keep trying, Johnny," and he answered "O.K.," quite well knowing there was nothing more he could do. He sat staring straight before him. Momentarily he was no longer part of the aircraft. He was borne away from it on sound-waves of motors and wind and rain, and for a few minutes he was back in England, recalling and reliving odd moments of life there. He recalled for a second or two his first day on the station; it was August and he remembered that some straw had blown in from the fields across the runways and that the wind of the take-offs whirled it madly upward, yellow and shining in the sun. He recalled his father eating redcurrants in the garden that same summer and how the crimson juice had spurted on to his moustache, so that he looked rather ferocious every time he said, "That, if you want it, is my opinion." And then he remembered, most curiously of all, a girl in a biscuit-yellow hat sitting in a deck-chair on the seafront, eating a biscuit-yellow ice-cream, and how he had been fascinated because hat and ice were miraculously identical in colour and how he had wanted to ask her, with nervous bravado because he was very young, if she bought her hats to match her ice-cream or her ice-cream to match her hats, but how he never did. He did not know why he recalled these moments, clear as glass, except perhaps that they were moments of a life he was never going to see again.

He was suddenly ejected out of this past world, fully alert and aware that they were not flying straight. They had not been flying straight for some time. They were stooging round and round, bumping heavily, and losing height. He sat very tense, and became gradually aware that this tension was part of the plane. It existed in each one of them from Davidson and Porter in the nose, down through Johnson and Hargreaves and himself to Carmichael, in the tail.

He heard Davidson's voice. "How long since we had contact with base?"

He looked at his watch; it was almost midnight. "A little under an hour and three-quarters," he said.

Again there was silence; and again he felt the tension running through the plane. He was aware of their chances and almost aware, now, of what Davidson was going to say.

"One more try, boys. Sing out if you see anything. If not it's down in the drink."

He sat very still. They were losing a little height. His stomach felt sour and he remembered that he could not swim.

For some reason he never thought of it again. His thoughts were scattered by Davidson's voice.

"Does anyone see what I see? Isn't that a light? About two points to starboard."

He looked out; there was nothing he could see.

"I'm going down to have a look-see," Davidson said. "It *is* a light."

As they were going down he looked out again, but again he could see nothing. Then he heard Davidson speaking to Carmichael.

"Hack the fuselage door off, Joe. This looks like a lightship. If it is we're as good as home. Tell me when you're ready and I'll put her down."

He sat very still, hearing the sound of hatchet blows as Carmichael struck at the fuselage. He felt suddenly colder, and then knew that it must be because Carmichael had finished and that there was a gap where the door had been. He heard again the deep slow Canadian accent of Carmichael's voice, saying, "O.K., skipper, all set," and then the remote flat English voice of Davidson in reply:

"All right, get the dinghy ready. All three of you. Get ready and heave it out when I put her down."

Helping Joe and Hargreaves and Johnson with the dinghy he was no longer aware of fear. He was slung sideways across the aircraft. There was not much room. The dinghy seemed very large and he wondered how they would get it out. This troubled him until he felt the plane roaring down in the darkness, and it continued to trouble him for a second after the plane had hit the water with a great crash that knocked him back against the fuselage. He did not remember getting up. Something was wrong with his left wrist, and he thought of his watch. It was a good watch, a navigational watch, given him by his father on a birthday. The next moment he knew that the dinghy had gone and he knew that he had helped, somehow, to push it out. Carmichael had also gone. The sea was rocking the aircraft violently to and fro, breaking water against his knees and feet. A second later he stretched out his hands and felt nothing before him but the open space in the fuselage where the door had been.

He knew then that it must be his turn to go. He heard Carmichael's voice calling from what seemed a great distance out of the darkness and the rain. He did not know what he was calling. It was all confused, he did not answer, but a second later he stretched out his hands blindly and went down on his belly in the sea.

[II]

When he came up again it was to find himself thinking of the girl in the biscuit-coloured hat and how much, that day, he had liked the sea, opaque and green and smooth as the pieces of sea-washed glass he had picked up on the shore. It flashed through his mind that this was part of the final imagery that comes with drowning, and he struggled wildly to keep his face above water. He could hear again the voice of Carmichael, shouting, but the shock of sea-water struck like ice on his breast and throat, so that he could not shout in answer. The sea was very rough. It heaved him upwards and then down again with sweeps of slow and violent motion. It tossed him about in this way until he realized at last that these slow, barbaric waves were really keeping him up, that the Mae West was working and that he was sinking away no longer.

From the constancy of Carmichael's shouts he felt that Carmichael must have seized, and was probably on, the dinghy. But he was not prepared for the shout: "She's upside down!" and then a moment or two later two voices, yelling his name.

"Johnny! Can year hear us? Can you hear us now?"

He let out a great yell in answer but sea-water broke down his throat, for a moment suffocated him, bearing him down and under the trough of a wave. He came up sick and struggling, spitting water, frightened. His boots were very heavy now under the water and it seemed as if he were being sucked continually down. He tried to wave his arms above his head but one arm had no response. It filled him suddenly with violent pain.

"O.K., Johnny, O.K., O.K.," Carmichael said.

He could not speak. He knew that his arm was broken. He felt Carmichael's hands painfully clutching his one free hand. He remembered for no reason at all that Carmichael had been a pitcher for a baseball team in Montreal, and he felt the hands move down until they clutched his wrist, holding him so strongly that it was almost a pain.

"Can you bear up?" Carmichael said. "Johnny, try bearing up. It's O.K., Johnny. We're here, on the dinghy. Hargreaves is here. Johnson's here. We're all here except the skipper. It's O.K., Johnny. Can you heave? Where's your other arm?"

"I think it's bust," he said.

He tried heaving himself upward. He tried again, helped by Carmichael's hands, but something each time drew the dinghy away. He tried again and then again. Each time the same thing happened, and once or twice the sea, breaking on the dinghy, hit him in the face, blinding him.

He knew suddenly what was wrong. It was not only his arm but his belt. Each time he heaved upward the belt caught under the dinghy and pushed it away. In spite of knowing it he heaved again and all at once felt very tired, feeling that only Carmichael's hands were between this tiredness and instant surrender. This painful heaving and sudden tiredness were repeated. They went on for some time. He heard Carmichael's voice continually and once or twice the sea hit him again, blinding him, and once, blinded badly, he wanted to wipe his face with his hands.

Suddenly Carmichael was talking again. "Can you hang on? If I can get my knee on something I'll get leverage. I'll pull you up. Can you hang on?"

Before he could answer the sea hit him again. The waves seemed to split his contact with Carmichael. It momentarily cut away his hands. For an instant it was as if he were in a bad and terrifying dream, falling through space.

Then Carmichael was holding him again. "I got you now, Johnny. I'm kneeling on Dicky. Your belt ought to clear now. If you try hard it ought to clear first time."

The sea swung him away. As he came back the belt did not hit the dinghy so violently. He was kept almost clear. Then the sea swung him away again. On this sudden wave of buoyancy he realized that it was now, or perhaps never, that he must pull himself back. He clenched his hand violently; and then suddenly before he was ready, and very lightly as if he were a child, the force of the new wave and the strength of Carmichael's hands threw him on the dinghy, face down.

He wanted to lie there for a long time. He lay for only a second, and then got up. He felt the water heaving in his boots and the salt sickness of it in his stomach. He did not feel at all calm but was terrified for an instant by the shock of being safe.

"There was a light," he said. "That's why he came down here. That's why he came down. There was a light."

He looked around at the sea as he spoke. Sea and darkness were one, unbroken except where waves struck the edge of the dinghy with spits of faintly phosphorescent foam. It had ceased raining now but the wind was very strong and cold, and up above lay the old unbroken ten-tenths cloud. There was not even a star that could have been mistaken for a light. He knew that perhaps there never had been.

He went into a slight stupor brought on by pain and the icy sea-water. He came out of it to find himself furiously baling water from the dinghy with one hand. He noticed that the rest were baling with their caps. He had lost his cap. His one hand made a nerveless cup that might have been stone for all the feeling that was in it now.

The sea had a rhythmical and awful surge that threw the dinghy too lightly up the glassy arcs of oncoming waves and then too steeply over the crest into the trough beyond. Each time they came down into a trough the dinghy shipped a lot of water. Each time they baled frenziedly, sometimes throwing the water over each other. His good hand remained dead. He still did not feel the water with it but he felt it on his face, sharp as if the spray were splintered and frozen glass. Then whenever they came to the crest of a wave there was a split second when they could look for a light. "Hell, there should be a light," he thought. "He saw one. He shouted it out. That's why he came down," but each time the sea beyond the crest of the new wave remained utterly dark as before.

"What the hell," he said. "There should be a light! There *was* a light."

"All right, kid," Carmichael said. "There'll be one."

He knew then that he was excited. He tried not to be excited. For a long time he didn't speak, but his mind remained excited. He felt drunk with the motion of pain and the water and sick with the saltness of the water. There were moments when he ceased baling and held his one hand strengthlessly at his side, tired out, wanting to give up. He did not know how he kept going after a time or how they kept the water from swamping the dinghy.

Coming out of periods of stupor, he would hear Carmichael talking. The deep Canadian voice was slow and steady. It attracted him. He found himself listening simply to the sound and the steadiness of it, regardless of words. It had the quality of Carmichael's hands; it was calm and steadfast.

It occurred to him soon that the voice had another quality. It was like the baling of the water; it never stopped. He heard Carmichael talking of ball games in Montreal; the way the crowd ragged you and how you took no notice and how it was all part of the game; and then how he was injured in the game one summer and for two months couldn't play and how he went up into Quebec province for the fishing. It was hot weather and he would fish mostly in the late evenings, often by moonlight. The lake trout were big and strong and sometimes a fish took you an hour to get in. Sometimes at week-ends he went back to Quebec and he would eat steaks as thick, he said, as a volume of Dickens and rich with onions and butter. They were lovely with cold light beer, and the whole thing set you back about two dollars and a half.

"Good eh, Johnny?" he would say. "You ought to come over there some day."

All the time they baled furiously. There was no break in the clouds and the wind was so strong that it sometimes swivelled the dinghy round like a toy.

How long this went on he did not know. But a long time later Carmichael suddenly stopped talking and then as suddenly began again.

"Hey, Johnny boy, there's your light!"

He was startled and he looked up wildly, not seeing anything.

"Not that way, boy. Back of you. Over there."

He turned his head stiffly. There behind him he could see the dim cream edge of daylight above the line of the sea.

"That's the light we want," Carmichael said. "It don't go out in a hurry either."

The colour of daylight was deeper, like pale butter, when he looked over his shoulder again. He remembered then that it was late summer. He thought that now, perhaps, it would be three o'clock.

As the daylight grew stronger, changing from cream and yellow to a cool grey bronze, he saw for the first time the barbaric quality of the sea. He saw the faces of Carmichael and Hargreaves and Johnson. They were grey-yellow with weariness and touched at the lips and ears and under the eyes with blue.

He was very thirsty. He could feel a thin caking of salt on his lips. He tried to lick his lips with his tongue but it was very painful. There was no moisture on his tongue and only the taste of salt, very harsh and bitter, in his mouth. His arm was swollen and he was sick with pain.

"Take it easy a minute, kid," Carmichael said. "We'll bale in turns. You watch out for a ship or a kite or anything you can see. I'll tell you when it's your turn."

He sat on the edge of the dinghy and stared at the horizon and the sky. Both were empty. He rubbed the salt out of his eyes and then closed them for a moment, worn out.

"Watch out," Carmichael said. "We're in the Channel. We know that. There should be ships and there should be aircraft. Keep watching."

He kept watching. His eyes were painful with salt and only half-open. Now and then the sea hit the dinghy and broke right over it, but he did not care. For some reason he did not think of listening, but suddenly he shut his eyes and after a moment or two he heard a sound. It was rather like the sound of the sea beating gently on sand, and he remembered again the day when he had seen the girl in the biscuit-coloured hat and how it was summer and how much he had liked the sea. That day the sea had beaten on the shore with the same low sound.

As the sound increased he suddenly opened his eyes. He felt for a moment that he was crazy, and then he began shouting.

"It's a plane! It's a bloody plane! It's a plane, I tell you, it's a plane!"

"Sit down," Carmichael said.

The dinghy was rocking violently. The faces of all four men were upturned, grey-yellow in the stronger light.

"There she is!" he shouted. "There she is!"

The plane was coming over from the north-east, at about five thousand. He began to wave his hands. She seemed to be coming straight above them. Hargreaves and Johnson and then Carmichael also began to wave. They all waved frantically and Hargreaves shouted, "It's a Hudson, boys. Wave like raving Hallelujah! It's a Hudson."

The plane came over quite fast and very steady, flying straight. It looked the colour of iron except for the bright rings of the markings in the dull sea-light of the early morning. It flew on quite straight and they were still waving frantically with their hands and caps long after it had ceased looking like a far-off gull in the sky.

He came out of the shock of this disappointment to realize that Carmichael was holding him in the dinghy with one arm.

"I'm all right," he said.

"I know," Carmichael said.

He knew then that he was not all right. He felt dizzy. A slow river of cold sweat seemed to be pouring from his hair down his backbone.

"What happened?" he said.

"You're all right," Carmichael said. "Don't try to stand up again, that's all. How's your arm? I wish there was something I could do."

"It's O.K.," he said.

He remembered the plane. The sky was now quite light, barred with warm strips of orange low above the water in the east. He remembered also that it was summer. The wind was still strong and cold but soon, he thought, there will be sun. He looked overhead at the grey-blue and the yellow-orange bars of cloud. They were breaking a little more overhead and he knew now that it would be a fair day for flying.

"Does the sun rise in the east or a little to the north-east?" Carmichael said.

They held a little discussion, and Johnny and Hargreaves agreed that in summer it rose a little to the north-east.

"In that case we seem to be drifting almost due north. If the wind helps us we might drift into the coast. It's still strong."

"It's about forty," Hargreaves said. "It must have been about eighty last night."

"It was a point or two west of south then," Johnny said.

"I think it's still there," Carmichael said.

They all spoke rather slowly. His own lips felt huge and dry with blisters. It was painful for him to speak. He was not hungry, but the back of his throat was scorched and raw with salt. His tongue was thick and hot and he wanted to roll it out of his mouth, so that it would get sweet and cool in the wind.

"Keep your mouth shut, Johnny," Carmichael said. "Keep it shut."

He discovered that Carmichael was still holding him by the arm. In the hour or two that went by between the disappearance of the Hudson and the time when the sun was well up and he could feel the warmth of it on his face he continually wanted to protest; to tell Carmichael that he was all right. Yet he never did and all the time Carmichael held him and he was glad.

All the time they watched the sea and the sky and most of the time Carmichael talked to them. He talked to them again of Canada, the lakes in the summertime, the fishing, the places where you could eat in Montreal. The sea was less violent now, but the waves, long and low and metallically glittering in the sun, swung the dinghy ceaselessly up and down troughs that bristled with destructive edges of foam. Towards the middle of the morning Hargreaves was very sick. He leaned his head forward on his knees and sat very quiet for a long time, too weak to lift his head. The sickness itself became covered and churned and finally washed away by incoming water. After this only Johnson and Carmichael troubled to watch the horizon, and they took turns at baling the water, Carmichael using one hand.

For some time none of them spoke. Finally when Johnny looked up again it was to see that Johnson too had closed his eyes against the glitter of sunlight and that only Carmichael was watching the sea. He was watching in a curious attitude. As he held Johnny with one hand he would lean forward and with his hat bale a little water out of the dinghy. Then he would transfer the hat from one hand to the other and with the free hand press the fabric of the dinghy as you press the inner tube of a tyre. As he pressed it seemed flabby. Then he would look up and gaze for a few moments at the horizon, northwards, where at intervals the sea seemed to crystallize into long lips of misty grey. For a long time Johnny sat watching him, following the movements of his hands and the arrested progress of his eyes.

Very slowly he realized what was happening. He did not move. He wanted to speak but the back of his throat was raw and his tongue was thick and inflexible. When he suddenly opened his mouth his lips split and there was blood in the cracks that was bitterly salt as he licked it with his tongue.

He did not know which struck him first: the realization that the thin lips of grey on the horizon were land or that the dinghy was losing air. For a second or two his emotions were cancelled out. The dinghy was upside down; the bellows were gone. He felt slightly light-headed. Above the horizon the clouds were white-edged now, and suddenly the sun broke down through them and shone on the line of land, turning the lips of grey to brown. He knew then that it was land. There could be no mistake. But looking down suddenly into the dinghy he knew that there was and could be no mistake there either.

He began to shout. He did not know what he shouted. His mouth was very painful. He rocked his body forward and began to bale excitedly with his free hand. In a moment the rest were shouting too.

"Steady," Carmichael said, "steady."

"How far is it away?" Hargreaves said. "Five miles? Five or six?"

"Nearer ten."

"I'll take a bet."

"You'd better take one on the air in the dinghy."

It was clear that Hargreaves did not know about the air in the dinghy. He ceased baling and sat very tense. His tongue was thick and grey-pink and hanging out of his mouth.

It seemed to Johnny that the dinghy, slowly losing resilience, was like something dying underneath them.

"Now don't anybody go and get excited," Carmichael said. "We must be drifting in fast, and if we drift in far enough and she gives out we can swim. You all better bale now while you can. All right, Johnny? Can you bale?"

Baling frantically with his one hand, looking up at intervals at the horizon, now like a thin strip of cream-brown paint squeezed along the edge of the sea, he tried not to think of the fact that he could not swim.

All the time he felt the dinghy losing air. He felt its flabbiness grow in proportion to his own weight. It moved very heavily and sluggishly in the troughs of water, and waves broke over it more often now. Sometimes the water rose almost to the knees of the men. He could not feel his feet and several times it seemed as if the bottom of the dinghy had fallen out and that beneath him there was nothing but the bottom of the sea.

It went on like this for a long time, the dinghy losing air, the land coming a little nearer, deeper-coloured now, with veins of green.

"God, we'll never make it," Hargreaves said. "We'll never make it."

Carmichael did not speak. The edge of the dinghy was low against the water, almost level. The sea lapped over it constantly and it was more now than they could bale.

Johnny looked at the land. The sun was shining down on smooth uplands of green and calm brown squares of upturned earth. Below lay long chalk cliffs, changing from sea-grey to white in the sun. He felt suddenly exhausted and desperate. He felt that he hated the sea.

He was frightened of it and suddenly lost his head and began to bale
with one arm, throwing the water madly everywhere.

"We'll never do it!" he shouted. "We'll never do it. Why the hell
didn't that Hudson see us! What the hell do they do in those fancy
kites!"

"Shut up," Carmichael said.

He felt suddenly quiet and frightened.

"Shut up. She's too heavy, that's all. Take your boots off."

Hargreaves and Johnson stopped baling and took off their boots.
He tried to take off his own boots but they seemed part of his feet
and with only one arm he was too weak to pull them off. Then
Carmichael took off his own boots. He took off his socks too, and
Johnny could see that Carmichael's feet were blue and dead.

For a minute he could not quite believe what he saw next. He saw
Carmichael roll over the side of the dinghy into the sea. He went
under and came up again at once, shaking the water from his hair.
"O.K.," he shouted, "O.K. Keep baling. I'm pushing her in. She'll
be lighter now."

Carmichael put his hands on the end of the dinghy and swam
with his feet.

"I'm coming over too," Hargreaves said.

"No. Keep baling. Keep her light. There'll be time to come over."

They went on like this for some time. The situation in the dinghy
was bad, but he did not think of it. His knees were sometimes
wholly submerged and the dinghy was flabby and without life. All
the time he hated the sea and kept his eyes in desperation on the
shore. Then Carmichael gave Hargreaves the order to go over and
Hargreaves rolled over the side as Carmichael had done and came
up soon and began swimming in the same way.

They were then about five hundred yards from the shore and he
could see sheep in the fields above the cliffs, but no houses. The
land looked washed and bright and for some reason abandoned, as
if no one had ever set foot there. The sea was calm now, but it still
washed over the dinghy too fast for him to bale and he still hated it.
Then suddenly Johnson went over the side without waiting for a
word from Carmichael, and he was alone in the dinghy, being
pushed along by the three men. But he knew soon that it could not
last. The dinghy was almost flat, and between the force of the three

men pushing and the resistance of water it crumpled and submerged and would not move.

As if there were something funny about this Johnson began laughing. He himself felt foolish and scared and waited with clenched teeth for the dinghy to go down.

It went down before he was ready, throwing him backwards. He felt a wave hit him and then he went under, his boots dragging him down. He struggled violently and quite suddenly saw the sky. His arm was very painful and he felt lop-sided. He was lying on his back and he knew that he was moving, not of his own volition but easily and strongly, looking at the lakes of summer sky between the white and indigo hills of cloud. He was uneasy and glad at the same time. The sea still swamped over his face, scorching his broken lips, but he was glad because he knew that Carmichael was holding him again and taking him in to shore.

What seemed a long time later he knew that they were very near the shore. He heard the loud warm sound of breaking waves. He was borne forward in long surges of the tide. At last he could no longer feel Carmichael's arms, but tired and kept up by his Mae West, he drifted in of his own accord. The sun was strong on his face and he thought suddenly of the things he had thought about in the plane: the straw on the runways, his father eating the currants, the girl in the biscuit-coloured hat. He felt suddenly that they were the things for which he had struggled. They were his life. The waves took him gradually farther and farther up the shore, until his knees beat on the sand. He saw Carmichael and Johnson and Hargreaves waiting on the shore. At last new waves took him far up the shore until he lay still on the wet slope of sand and his arms were outstretched to the sky.

As he lay there the sea ran down over his body and receded away. It was warm and gentle on his hands and he was afraid of it no longer.

(1943)

IT'S JUST THE WAY IT IS

November rain falls harshly on the clean tarmac, and the wind, turning suddenly, lifts sprays of yellow elm leaves over the black hangars.

The man and woman, escorted by a sergeant, look very small as they walk by the huge cavernous openings where the bombers are.

The man, who is perhaps fifty and wears a black overcoat and bowler hat, holds an umbrella slantwise over the woman, who is about the same age, but very grey and slow on her feet, so that she is always a pace or two behind the umbrella and must bend her face against the rain.

On the open track beyond the hangars they are caught up by the wind, and are partially blown along, huddled together. Now and then the man looks up at the Stirlings, which protrude over the track, but he looks quickly away again and the woman does not look at all.

"Here we are, sir," the sergeant says at last. The man says "Thank you," but the woman does not speak.

They have come to a long one-stored building, painted grey, with "Squadron Headquarters" in white letters on the door. The sergeant opens the door for them and they go in, the man flapping and shaking the umbrella as he closes it down.

The office of the Wing Commander is at the end of a passage; the sergeant taps on the door, opens it and salutes. As the man and woman follow him, the man first, taking off his hat, the woman hangs a little behind, her face passive.

"Mr. and Mrs. Shepherd, sir," the sergeant says.

"Oh, yes, good afternoon." The sergeant, saluting, closes the door and goes.

"Good afternoon, sir," the man says.

The woman does not speak.

"Won't you please sit down, madam?" the Wing Commander says. "And you too, sir. Please sit down."

He pushes forward two chairs, and slowly the man and the woman sit down, the man leaning his weight on the umbrella.

The office is small and there are no more chairs. The Wing Commander remains standing, his back resting against a table, beyond which, on the wall, the flight formations are ticketed up.

He is quite young, but his eyes, which are glassy and grey, seem old and focused distantly so that he seems to see far beyond the man and the woman and even far beyond the grey-green Stirlings lined up on the dark tarmac in the rain. He folds his arms across his chest and is glad at last when the man looks up at him and speaks.

"We had your letter, sir. But we felt we should like to come and see you, too."

"I am glad you came."

"I know you are busy, but we felt we must come. We felt you wouldn't mind."

"Not at all. People often come."

"There are just some things we would like to ask you."

"I understand."

The man moves his lips, ready to speak again, but the words do not come. For a moment his lips move like those of someone who stutters, soundlessly, quite helplessly. His hands grip hard on the handle of the umbrella, but still the words do not come and at last it is the Wing Commander who speaks.

"You want to know if everything possible was done to eliminate an accident?"

The man looked surprised that someone should know this, and can only nod his head.

"Everything possible was done."

"Thank you, sir."

"But there are things you can never foresee. The weather forecast may say, for example, no cloud over Germany, for perhaps sixteen hours, but you go over and you find a thick layer of cloud all the way, and you never see your target—and perhaps there is severe icing as you come home."

"Was it like this when—"

"Something like it. You never know. You can't be certain."

Suddenly, before anyone can speak again, the engines of a Stirling close by are revved up to a roar that seems to shake the walls of the room; and the woman looks up, startled, as if terrified that the plane will race forward and crash against the windows. The roar of airscrews rises furiously and then falls again, and the sudden rise and fall of sound seems to frighten her into speech.

"Why aren't you certain? Why can't you be certain? He should never have gone out! You must know that! You must know it! You must know that he should never have gone!"

"Please," the man says.

"Day after day you are sending out young boys like this. Young boys who haven't begun to live. Young boys who don't know what life is. Day after day you send them out and they don't come back and you don't care! You don't care!"

She is crying bitterly now and the man puts his arm on her shoulder. She is wearing a fur and he draws it a fraction closer about her neck.

"You don't care, do you! You don't care! It doesn't matter to you. You don't care!"

"Mother," the man says.

Arms folded, the Wing Commander looks at the floor, silently waiting for her to stop. She goes on for a minute or more longer, shouting and crying her words, violent and helpless, until at last she is exhausted and stops. Her fur slips off her shoulder and falls to the ground, and the man picks it up and holds it in his hands, helpless, too.

The Wing Commander walks over to the window and looks out. The airscrews of the Stirling are turning smoothly, shining like steel pin-wheels in the rain, and now, with the woman no longer shouting, the room seems very silent, and finally the Wing Commander walks back across the room and stands in front of the man and woman again.

"You came to ask me something," he says.

"Take no notice, sir. Please. She is upset."

"You want to know what happened? Isn't that it?"

"Yes, sir. It would help us a little, sir."

The Wing Commander says very quietly: "Perhaps I can tell you a little. He was always coming to me and asking to go out on

operations. Most of them do that. But he used to come and beg to
be allowed to go more than most. So more often than not it was a
question of stopping him from going rather than making him go. It
was a question of holding him back. You see?"

"Yes, sir."

"And whenever I gave him a trip he was very happy. And the
crew were happy. They liked going with him. They liked being
together, with him, because they liked him so much and they
trusted him. There were seven of them and they were altogether."

The woman is listening, slightly lifting her head.

"It isn't easy to tell you what happened on that trip. But we
know that conditions got suddenly very bad and that there was bad
cloud for a long way. And we know that they had navigational
difficulties and that they got a long way off their course.

"Even that might not have mattered, but as they were coming
back the outer port engine went. Then the radio transmitter went
and the receiver. Everything went wrong. The wireless operator
somehow got the transmitter and the receiver going again, but then
they ran short of petrol. You see, everything was against him."

"Yes, sir."

"They came back the last hundred miles at about a thousand feet.
But they trusted him completely, and he must have known they
trusted him. A crew gets like that—flying together gives them this
tremendous faith in each other."

"Yes, sir."

"They trusted him to get them home, and he got them home.
Everything was against him. He feathered the outer starboard
engine and then, in spite of everything, got them down on two
engines. It was a very good show. A very wonderful show."

The man is silent, but the woman lifts her head. She looks at the
Wing Commander for a moment or two, immobile, very steady,
and then says, quite distinctly, "Please tell us the rest."

"There is not much," he says. "It was a very wonderful flight, but
they were out of luck. They were up against all the bad luck in the
world. When they came to land they couldn't see the flarepath very
well, but he got them down. And then, as if they hadn't had
enough, they came down slightly off the runway and hit an
obstruction. Even then they didn't crash badly. But it must have

thrown him and he must have hit his head somewhere with great force, and that was the end."

"Yes, sir. And the others?" the man says.

"They were all right. Even the second pilot. I wish you could have talked to them. It would have helped if you could have talked to them. They know that he brought them home. They know that they owe everything to him."

"Yes, sir."

The Wing Commander does not speak, and the man very slowly puts the fur over the woman's shoulders. It is like a signal for her to get up, and as she gets to her feet the man stands up too, straightening himself, no longer leaning on the umbrella.

"I haven't been able to tell you much," the Wing Commander says. "It's just the way it is."

"It's everything," the man says.

For a moment the woman still does not speak, but now she stands quite erect. Her eyes are quite clear, and her lips, when she does speak at last, are quite calm and firm.

"I know now that we all owe something to him," she says. "Good-bye."

"Good-bye, madam."

"Good-bye, sir," the man says.

"You are all right for transport?"

"Yes, sir. We have a taxi."

"Good. The sergeant will take you back."

"Good-bye, sir. Thank you."

"Good-bye," the woman says.

"Good-bye."

They go out of the office. The sergeant meets them at the outer door, and the man puts up the umbrella against the rain. They walk away along the wet perimeter, dwarfed once again by the grey-green noses of the Stirlings. They walk steadfastly, almost proudly, and the man holds the umbrella a little higher than before, and the woman, keeping up with him now, lifts her head.

And the Wing Commander, watching them from the window, momentarily holds his face in his hands.

(1943)

The Flag

"We are surrounded by the most ghastly people," the Captain said. All across miles of unbroken pasture there was not another house.

Up through the south avenue of elms, where dead trees lifted scraggy bone against spring sky, bluebells grew like thick blue corn, spreading into the edges of surrounding grass. The wind came softly, in a series of light circles from the west. Here and there an elm had died and on either side of it young green leaves from living trees were laced about smoke-brown brittle branches. In a quadrangle of wall and grass the great house lay below.

"You never really see the beauty of the house until you get up here," the Captain said. Though still young, not more than forty-five or so, he was becoming much too fat. His ears were like thickly-veined purple cabbage leaves unfurling on either side of flabby swollen cheeks. His mouth, pink and flaccid, trembled sometimes like the underlip of a cow.

"They have killed the elms," he said. "Finished them. They used to be absolutely magnificent."

He stopped for a moment and I saw that he wanted to draw breath, and we looked back down the hill. Down beyond soldierly lines of trees, the tender lucent green broken here and there by the black of dead branches, I could see a flag waving in such intermittent and strengthless puffs of air that it, too, seemed dead. It was quartered in green and scarlet and flew from a small round tower that was like a grey pepper-box stuck in the western arm of the cross-shaped house.

Now I could see, too, that there were four avenues of elms, repeating in immense pattern the cross of the house below. As we stood there, the Captain making gargling noises in his throat, a cuckoo began calling on notes that were so full and hollow that it

was like a bell tolling from the elms above us. Presently it seemed to
be thrown on a gust of air from the tip of a tree, to float down-wind
like a bird of grey paper.

"There she goes," I said.

"Tank emplacements mostly," the Captain said. His face shone
lividly in the sun, his lip trembling. "The place was occupied right,
left and centre. We used to have deer too, but the last battalion
wiped them out."

The breath of bluebells was overpoweringly sweet on the warm
wind.

"When we get a little higher you will see the whole pattern of the
thing," the Captain said.

Turning to renew the ascent, he puffed in preparation, his veins
standing out like purple worms on his face and neck and forehead.

"Tired?" he said. "Not too much for you? You don't mind being
dragged up here?"

"Not at all."

"One really has to see it from up here. One doesn't grasp it
otherwise. That's the point."

"Of course."

"We shall have a drink when we get back," he said. He laughed
and the eyes, very blue but transparent in their wateriness, were sad
and friendly. "In fact, we shall have several drinks."

It was only another fifty yards to the crown of the hill and we
climbed it in silence except for the hissing of the Captain's breath
against his teeth. All the loveliness of spring came down the hill and
past us in a stream of heavy fragrance, and at the top, when I
turned, I could feel it blowing past me, the wind silky on the palms
of my hands, to shine all down the hill on the bent sweet grasses.

"Now," the Captain said. It was some moments before he could
get breath to say another word. Moisture had gathered in confusing
drops on the pink lids of his eyes. He wiped it away. "Now you can
see it all."

All below us, across the wide green hollow in which there was not
another house, I could see, as he said, the pattern of the thing.
Creamy grey in the sun, the house made its central cross of stone,
the four avenues of elms like pennants of pale green flying from the
arms of it across the field.

"Wonderful," I said.

"Wonderful, but not unique," he said. "Not unique."

Not angrily at first but wearily, rather sadly, he pointed about him with both arms. "It's simply one of six or seven examples here alone."

Then anger flitted suddenly through the obese watery-eyed face with such heat that the whole expression seemed to rise to a bursting fester, and I thought he was about to rush, in destructive attack at something, down the hill.

"It was all done by great chaps," he said, "creative chaps. It's only we of this generation who are such absolute destructive clots."

"Oh! I don't know."

"Won't even argue about it," he said. His face, turned to the sun, disclosed now an appearance of rosy calm, almost boy-like, and he had recovered his breath. "Once we were surrounded by the most frightfully nice people. I don't mean to say intellectual people and that kind of thing, but really awfully nice. You know, you could talk to them. They were on your level."

"Yes."

"And now you see what I mean, they've gone. God knows where but they're finished. I tell you everything is a shambles."

Across from another avenue the cuckoo called down-wind again and over the house I saw the flag lifted in a green and scarlet flash on the same burst of breeze. I wanted to ask him about the flag, but he said:

"It's perfectly ghastly. They've been hounded out. None of them left. All of them gone—"

Abruptly he seemed to give it up. He made gestures of apology, dropping his hands:

"So sorry. Awfully boring for you, I feel. Are you thirsty? Shall we go down?"

"When you're ready. I'd like to see the house—"

"Oh! please, of course. I'd like a drink, anyway."

He took a last wide look at the great pattern of elm and stone, breathing the deep, almost too sweet scent of the hill.

"That's another thing. These perishers don't know the elements of decent drinking. One gets invited to the dreariest cocktail parties. The drinks are mixed in a jug and the sherry comes from

God knows where." Anger was again reddening his face to the appearance of a swollen fester. "One gets so depressed that one goes home and starts beating it up. You know?"

I said yes, I knew, and we began to walk slowly down the hill, breathing sun-warm air deeply, pausing fairly frequently for another glance at the scene below.

"How is it with you?" he said. "In your part of the world? Are you surrounded by hordes of virgin spinsters?"

"They are always with us," I said.

He laughed, and in that more cheerful moment I asked him about the flag.

"Oh! it's nothing much." He seemed inclined to belittle it, I thought. "It gives a touch of colour."

"I must look at it."

"Of course. We can go up to the tower. There's a simply splendid view from there. You can see everything. But we shall have a drink first. Yes?"

"Thank you."

"My wife will be there now. She will want to meet you."

Slowly we went down to the house. About its deep surrounding walls there were no flowers and the grass had not been mown since some time in the previous summer, but old crucified peaches, and here and there an apricot, had set their flowers for fruiting and it was hot in the hollow between the walls. At the long flight of stone steps, before the front door, the Captain said something in a desultory way about the beauty of the high widows but evidently he did not expect a reply. He leapt up the last four or five steps with the rather desperate agility of a man who has won a race at last, and a moment later we were in the house.

In the large high-windowed room with its prospect of unmown grass the Captain poured drinks and then walked nervously about with a glass in his hand. I do not know how many drinks he had before his wife appeared, but they were large and he drank them quickly.

"Forty-six rooms and this is all we can keep warm," he said.

When his wife came in at last she was carrying bunches of stiff robin-orange lilies. She was very dark and her hands, folded about the lily stalks, were not unlike long blanched stalks of uprooted flowers themselves. She had a hard pallor about her face, very beautiful but in a way detached and not real, that made the Captain's festering rosiness seem more florid than ever.

I liked the lilies, and when I asked about them she said:

"We must ask Williams about them. I'm frightful at names. He'll know."

"Williams knows everything," the Captain said.

He poured a drink without asking her what she wanted and she seemed to suck at the edge of the glass, drawing in her lips so that they made a tight scarlet bud.

"Are you keen on flowers?" she said.

I said "Yes," and she looked at me in a direct clear way that could not have been more formal. Her eyes had slits of green, like cracks, slashed across the black.

"That's nice," she said.

"Has Williams done the cabbages?" the Captain said.

"What cabbages? Where?"

"He knew damn well he had cabbages to do," the Captain said. "I told him so."

"How should I know what he has to do and what he hasn't to do?" she said.

"How should you know," he said. He drank with trembling hands, trying to steady himself a little. He went to the window and stared out. The room was so large that his wife and I seemed to be contained, after his walking away, in a separate and private world bordered by the big fireless hearth and the vase where she was arranging flowers. She smiled and I looked at her hands.

"Williams will tell you the name of the flowers if you like to come along to the conservatory before you go." She did not raise her voice; there was no sound except the plop of lily stalks falling softly into the water in the vase. "He would like it. He likes people who are interested."

She dropped in the last of the lilies and then took off her coat and laid it on a chair. It was black and underneath she was wearing a yellow sweater of perpendicular ribbed pattern over a black skirt. It went very well with her black hair, her white long face and her green-shot eyes.

I heard the Captain pouring himself another drink, and he said:

"What about the tower? You still want to go up?"

"I really ought to go."

"Oh! Good God man, no. We've hardly seen a thing."

"He's coming to see the conservatory, anyway," his wife said.

"Is that so?" he said. "Well, if he's to see everything you'd better get cracking."

He made a jabbing kind of gesture against the air with his glass and he was so close to the window that I thought for a moment he would smash one glass against another. I could not tell if he was nervous or impatient. He covered it up by pouring himself another drink, and his wife said, with acid sweetness:

"There are guests too, my dear."

"No thanks," I said.

"You haven't had anything," the Captain said. "Good God, I feel like beating it up."

"If you still want to see the conservatory I think we'd better go," she said.

I went out of the room with her and we had gone some way to the conservatory, which really turned out to be a hot-house of frilled Victorian pattern beyond the walls on the south side of the house, before I realised that the Captain was not with us.

"Williams," she called several times. "Williams." Big scarlet amaryllis trumpets stared out through the long house of glass. "Ted!"

Presently Williams came out of the potting shed and I thought he seemed startled at the sight of me. He was a man of thirty-five or so with thick lips and carefully combed dark brown hair that he had allowed to grow into a curly pad on his neck There was a kind of stiff correct strength about him as he stared straight back at her.

She introduced me and said: "We'd like to see the conservatory."

"Yes, madam," he said.

It was very beautiful in the conservatory. The pipes were still on and the air was moistly sweet and strangling. The big scarlet and pink and crimson-black amaryllis had a kind of golden frost in their throats. They were very fiery and splendid among banks of maidenhair, and when I admired them Williams said:

"Thank you, sir. They're not bad."

"Don't be so modest," she said. "They're absolutely the best ever."

He smiled.

"What we haven't done to get them up to this," she said.

I walked to the far end by the house to look at a batch of young carnations, and when I turned back the Captain's wife was holding Williams by the coat-sleeve. It was exactly as if she were absent-mindedly picking a piece of dust from it, yet it was also as if she held him locked, in a pair of pincers. I heard her saying something, too, but what it was I never knew, because at that moment the fiery festering figure of the Captain began shouting down the path from the direction of the house. I could not hear what he said, either.

"He's worrying to get you up to the tower," she said. "I'm frightfully sorry you're being dragged about like this."

"Not at all."

Williams opened the door for me. The cuckoo was calling up the hillside, and the Captain, more rosy than ever, was coming up the path.

"Don't want to hurry you, but it takes longer than you think to get up there."

At the door of the conservatory his wife stretched out her hand. "I'll say good-bye," she said, "in case I don't see you again." We shook hands, and her hand, in curious contrast to the moist sweet heat of the house behind her, was dry and cool. Williams did not come to say good-bye. He had hidden himself beyond the central staging of palm and fern.

The Captain and I walked up to the tower. Once again we could see, as from the top of the hill, the whole pattern of the thing: the four avenues of elms flying like long green pennants from the central cross of the house, the quadrangle of stone below, the corn-like bluebells wind-sheaved on the hill. The Captain staggered about, pointing with unsteady fingers at the landscape, and the flag flapped in the wind.

"Curious thing is you can see everything and yet can't see a damned thing," the Captain said. On all sides, across wide elm-patterned fields, there was still no sign of another house. Below us the conservatory glittered in the sun and it was even possible to see, huge and splendidly scarlet under the glass, the amaryllis staring back at us.

The Captain began to cry.

"You get up here and you'd never know any difference," he said. His tears were simply moist negative oozings on the lids of his pink-lidded eyes. They might have been caused by the wind that up there, on the tower, was a little fresher than in the hollow below.

"Never know it was going to pot," he said. "Everything. The whole damn thing."

I felt I had to say something and I remembered the flag.

"Oh! it's simply a thing I found in an attic," he said. "Just looks well. It doesn't mean a thing."

"Nothing heraldic?"

"Oh! Good God, no. Still, got to keep the flag flying." He made an effort at a smile.

I said I had seen somewhere, in the papers, or perhaps it was a book, I could not remember where, that heraldry was simply nothing more than a survival of the fetish and the totem pole, and he said:

"Evil spirits and that sort of thing? Is that so? Damn funny."

Again, not angrily but sadly, biting his nails, with the trembling of his lower lip that was so like the lip of a cow, he stared at the green empty beautiful fields, and once again I felt all the warm sweetness of spring stream past us, stirring the green and scarlet flag, on tender lazy circles of wind.

Below us the Captain's wife and Williams came out of the greenhouse, and I saw them talking inside the winking scarlet roof of glass.

"Well, you've seen everything," the Captain said. "We'll have another snifter before you go."

"No thanks. I really ought—"

"No?" he said. "Then I'll have one for you. Eh? Good enough?"

"Good enough," I said.

We climbed down from the tower and he came to the gate in the fields to say good-bye. Across the fields there were nearly two miles of track, with five gates to open, before you reached the road. The Captain's eyes were full of water and he had begun to bite his nails again and his face was more than ever like a florid fester in the sun.

There was no sign of his wife, and as I put in the gears and let the car move away he looked suddenly very alone and he said something that, above the noise of the car, sounded like:

"Cheers. Thanks frightfully for coming. Jolly glad—"

Half a mile away, as I got out to open the first of the five field gates, I looked back. There was no sign of life at all. The Captain had gone into the house to beat it up. The greenhouse was hidden by the great cross of stone. All that moved was the cuckoo blown once again from the dying elms like a scrap of torn paper, and on the tower, from which the view was so magnificent, the flag curling in the wind.

(1951)

ELAINE

"I suppose the fact is men are more sentimental about them," she said. "Wouldn't you think that was it?"

"No," he said.

Her face, underneath a little hat of striped brown and white fur, was like that of a pretty tigress that did not smile.

"But don't they have them at Oxford?" she said. "Isn't it one of those things there?"

"How can having them at Oxford possibly have anything to do with it?" he said.

"I don't know. I just thought," she said.

As the train rushed forward into spring twilight I could see, everywhere on the rainy green cuttings, pale eyes of primroses winking up from among parallel reflections of carriage lights. Above and beyond the cuttings many apple orchards were in thick wide pink bloom.

"Then what is it you don't like about them?" she said.

"In the first place they're messy. They're not like pansies," he said. "They don't have the flower on a stem. That's what repulses me. They're messy."

"Repulses," she said. "What a word."

His hair, a weak brandy brown, was shredded like tobacco into short separated curls that hung untidily down over the fiery flesh of his neck. His lips were full and pettish. When motionless they were like a thick slit in a red India rubber ball. In the soft fat face the eyes were like blue glass marbles that did not quite fit into their sandy lidded slots and I sometimes got the impression that they would suddenly drop out as he gazed at her.

At this moment she hid behind her newspaper and in the darkening glass of the train windows, across the carriage, we exchanged reflections. I half expected her to smile. Instead I saw the

last of the paling primrose reflections sow themselves lightly across
a pair of dark still eyes that were almost expressionless.

"Another thing is that the smell absolutely nauseates me."

"Why?" she said. "It's so delicious."

"Not to me."

"Oh! that's fantastic," she said. "That heavenly scent. Everybody
thinks so."

"I don't happen to be everybody," he said.

She had lowered her newspaper as she spoke. Now, sharply, she
raised it up again. As she did so she pulled up, very slightly, the skirt
of her dress, so that I could see for a moment or two her small
pretty knees.

"Who was it who made that remark about pansies being one side
of Leicester Square and wallflowers on the other?" she said.

"That was Elaine."

"I knew it was somebody."

"Thank you."

This time I new she would smile at me and I got ready to smile
back at her dark steady reflection in the glass. But to my surprise
she did not smile. She sat transfixed, staring at me as if I were
transparent and she could see through and beyond me into the mass
of fading apple orchards sailing past in the brilliant blue evening
above the cuttings.

"What sort of day did you have?" she said. "What did you do?"

"I had a very bad, tiring day."

"All bad days are tiring," she said. "That's why they're bad."

"Don't be trite."

He began to fuss with a brief-case, taking out first papers, then
books, sorting them over and putting them back again. Between his
knees he held a walking-stick of thick brown cane, the colour
something more than a shade or two paler than the hairs that
crawled down the flanks of his face. In the confusion he let the
walking-stick slip and it fell with a clatter on the carriage floor and
as he leaned forward to pick it up I saw his hands. They were pink
and puffy, as if the flesh had been lightly boiled.

"Why don't you put it on the rack?" she said.

"Because I prefer it here."

"You didn't ask me what I did today," she said.

"If it had been interesting you'd have told me all about it," he said.

After that the girl and I stared at each other for a long time from behind the evening papers, first directly and then, when I could not bear the steady smileless dark eyes looking straight at me any longer, obliquely through the darkening glass. Now and then she moved her body slightly and I could see once again the rounded pretty knees. Then when she saw me looking at the knees she would cover them up again, not quickly, but dreamily, slowly, almost absent-mindedly, fixing me always with the steady eyes from under the tigress hat.

All the time I expected her to smile at me but all this time there was no sign of a smile. I had begun to wonder how long this strange exchange could go on, first the direct stare, then the stare that was like something between two apparitions on two smoky photographic plates, and then the knees uncovering themselves and her hands slowly covering them up again, when she said:

"I think this is frightfully funny. Look at this."

She leaned forward and gave him the evening paper. He took it with puffy casual hands and for the first time I saw her smile. The parting of her lips, revealing her teeth, produced exactly the same effect as the parting of her skirt when it revealed her knees. They were very pretty teeth and he did not notice them either.

"Why funny?" he said.

He gave her back the paper.

"Don't you think it's funny? I do."

"In what way?"

"Well, I don't know—I just think it's funny."

"You mean it's funny because you think it is or you think it's funny because it really is?"

"I just think it's funny—that's all. Don't you?"

"No."

The smile, as it went from her face, reminded me of a flame turned off by a tap. Abruptly she turned it on again; and again the teeth were white and pretty and he did not notice them.

"You can't have looked at the right piece," she said.

She gave him back the paper.

"It made me laugh—"

"It's exactly like the wallflowers," he said. "Just because you think they're sweet it doesn't mean to say they are. That doesn't make it a fact. Don't you see?"

"No."

Furiously he threw the evening paper back in her face. She caught it in silence and held it rigidly in front of her. In this painful moment there was nothing for me to do but to hide behind my own. By this time the evening was fully dark outside and in place of primroses and orchards of apple bloom, candlescent in the twilight, I could see only the rolling phantom lights of little country stations.

For some time I watched these lights. Then there was a long stretch of line with no lights at all and presently from behind my paper I looked at her face again. To my astonishment the smile was still there. It was not only still there but she appeared, it seemed to me, to be nursing it. It was like a light or a piece of fire she did not want to go out.

When she caught me looking at her again she seemed to do the trick of turning the tap again. The pretty teeth were suddenly hidden behind the tight lips. Only the pretty knees remained exposed, delicate and pale and rounded, until with the dreamy absent movement she covered them up again.

Then she began to talk to him from behind her paper.

"Did you have dinner?" she said.

He moved savagely among his books and papers and did not answer.

"With Elaine?"

He did not answer.

"How was Elaine?" she said.

Her voice had raised itself a little. She looked at me hard from behind the paper.

The train screamed through a little station beyond which were woods that were torn with long shrill echoes. I shaded my face with my hand and squinted out and pretended to search among the flashing little old-fashioned station lamps for a name, but darkness rushed in and tall spring woods crowded the sky.

"Dear Elaine," she said.

He suddenly got up and snatched a suitcase from the rack. He banged on its locks as if they were jammed and she said:

"She's a dear. I like her. Did she have her lily-of-the-valley hat on?"

The suitcase yawned open and he began to try to press into it the brief-case with its books and papers. There was not room for it and he banged at it for some time with his podgy fingers like an angry baker pummelling dough.

"Or was it wallflowers? or doesn't she like them?"

He wrestled with the two cases. In a moment or two he gave up the idea of putting one into the other and threw the brief-case on to the seat. Then he shut down the locks of the larger case in two swift metallic snaps and said:

"You take the brief-case. I'll take the two suitcases. We're nearly there."

From behind her newspaper she had nothing to say. Her knees with their delicate rounded prettiness were exposed again, with a naked effect of pure smooth skin but he did not notice them as he leaned forward and said in a voice of slow, cold, enamelled articulation:

"I said would you take the brief-case? Do you mind? I'll take the suitcases. I have only one pair of hands."

"What a funny thing to talk to a woman about," she said. "The scent of wallflowers."

"We shall be there in two minutes," he said.

He reached up for the second suitcase. It was cumbersome, of old shiny worn leather that slipped too easily down through his hands. He prevented its fall with clumsiness and as he did so she stared at me again, full face this time, unsmiling, the dark bright eyes giving that uneasy effect of trying to transfix and penetrate me.

And when she spoke again it was again in a slightly louder voice, gazing straight at me:

"I told you it was because men were more sentimental about them. They always are about flowers."

From the rack he took down a large brown dufflecoat, struggling fatly into it, submerging everything of himself except the untidy mass of brandy brown hair. I could see by this time the lights of the town and I could hear the train brakes grinding on. Sharply he slid back the corridor door but she made no sign of getting up. He did not look at her either. He was unaware of the pretty knees, the

uplifted face, the little tigress hat. He was consumed by the struggle
to get two suitcases through the door at once. Then the train
lurched over points and the sudden motion seemed to throw
himself, the suitcases and the heavy walking-stick in one clattering
mass into the corridor outside.

"Don't forget anything," he said.

A moment later he had disappeared along the corridor. The train
stopped and I heard him banging on an outer door to open it. I saw
him lurch forward under the station lights, grossly out of balance,
head forward, puffing.

She got up and began to gather up her things. I waited behind her
so that she could leave the carriage first and it was only then that I
realised how much he had left for her to carry. She was trying to
gather up an umbrella, a handbag, three parcels, the brief-case and
the evening paper.

"May I help?" I said.

She stared past me coldly.

"No, thank you."

"It's no trouble."

She stared into me this time, rather as she had done so many
times on the journey. For a second or two her eyes were, I thought,
less chilly. I fancied there was perhaps a little relaxing in the lips.
For another second or two I thought of the way she had exposed
her knees and how attractive they were and how pretty. I thought
too of the wallflowers, of Elaine, of the lily-of-the-valley hat and of
how there were pansies on one side of the square and wallflowers on
the other. Most of all I remembered how men were sentimental
about them.

"Are you quite sure?" I said.

"Quite sure."

"It's absolutely no trouble. I have nothing to carry and if—"

"Good night," she said.

Outside, in the station yard, a light rain was falling. As I
stood unlocking the door of my car a sudden wind seemed to
throw her out of the station. She came out without dignity,
as if lost, clutching parcels and brief-case and umbrella and
newspaper, and she could not put up the umbrella against the
rain.

Thirty yards ahead he was striding out, oblivious, still grossly out of balance, brandy-coloured head down against the rain.

When she saw him she gave a little cry and began running. I could see her pretty legs flickering under the lights of the station yard, white against the black spring rain.

"Darling," she called after him. "Darling. Couldn't you wait for me?"

(1955)

COUNTRY SOCIETY

All the vases in Mrs. Clavering's house were filled with sprays of white forced lilac and glossy pittosporum leaves. In January the lilac was almost more expensive than she could afford. But the tall leafless sprays were very distinguished and she hoped they would not fade.

She was going to give everyone white wine to drink at the party. This was partly because she had read somewhere, in a magazine or a newspaper, that that was distinguished too; partly because at the Fanshawes' party she had heard Captain Perigo's wife complaining quite loudly of the stinking drinks you nowadays got out of jugs; and partly because at anther party, the Luffingtons', at the Manor, a Colonel Arber, a newcomer to the district, had started to proclaim his intention of beating things up and had done so, rowdily, on dreadful mixtures of cider and gin. That was exactly what she wanted to avoid. She did not want rowdiness and people complaining, even if they did not mean it, that the drinks you gave them were not strong enough. She thought that nowadays everyone drank too much gin. At one time gin was nothing but a washerwoman's drink but now everyone drank it, everywhere. They tippled it down. White wine sounded so much more reserved and distinguished even if people did not like it so much. She thought too that it was bound to give tone to her attempt to get to know the Paul Vaulkhards. The Paul Vaulkhards, who were new to the county, had taken the house down the hill, and she understood that they were very distinguished too.

All day frost lingered on the trees. It drew a curtain of rimy branches, like chain armour, over the sky, shutting in the large oak-staired house, making it darker than ever, in isolation. It lingered in black ice pools about the road. At three o'clock the caterers' van should have arrived; and nervously, for an hour, Mrs. Clavering

paced about the house, wondering where it had got to; and it was
not until after four o'clock that it arrived, with dented mudguards
and one tray of *vol-au-vent* cakes smashed into crumbs, because of a
skid on the frozen hill.

The three caterers' men grumbled and said the roads were
worse than ever and that everyone ought to have chains. And
then suddenly the western hill of beeches took away the last
strips of frost green daylight too early, as it always did, and the
fields became dark and unkindly, closing in. Mrs. Clavering felt
the awful country isolation extinguish immediately all hope
about the party. She felt that no one would come. She became
doubtful of the coldness of the white wine. There were people
who had to come from considerable distances, such as the Blairs
and Captain Perigo and the principal of the research college and
his wife, very distinguished and important people too, who
would certainly not risk it. She doubted even if the Luffingtons
would risk it from the Manor. With fear and coldness she felt
that the Paul Vaulkhards would not risk it. Nobody of distinction or importance would dare to risk it and she would be left
with people like the dropsical Miss Hemshawe and her mother,
with Miss Ireton and Miss Graves, who lived together and spun
sheep-wool and dyed it into shades of porridge and pale autumnal lichen, and with the Reverend Perks and his elder brother:
with those people whom Mr. Clavering sometimes rudely called
the hen-coop tribe.

"Because they cluck and fuss and scratch and make dirt and pull
each other's feathers out," Mr. Clavering said.

Mrs. Clavering had not succeeded in curing her husband, in
thirty years, of a habit of accurate flippancy, to which he sometimes
added what she felt was deliberate forgetfulness.

Mr. Clavering too, like the caterers, was late coming out from his
office in the town.

"You said you would be here at four!" she called from the first-
floor landing. "Wherever have you been? Did you remember the
pecan nuts? But they were ready! They were telephoned for! All
you had to do was to pick them up from Watsons'—"

"Nobody ate the damn things last time."

"Of course they ate them. They were much appreciated."

In the hall, where Mr. Clavering stood taking off his homberg hat and overcoat, the telephone rang and she called:

"That's the first one. Answer it! I can't bear to—"

Mr. Clavering, answering the telephone, called that it was Mrs. Vaulkhard. "She'd like to speak to you," he said.

"This is it, this is it, this is it," she said. In a constraint of coldness and fear she scurried downstairs and picked up the telephone, trembling, but Mrs. Vaulkhard said:

"I did not want to trouble you. Oh! it was not that. It was simply to ask you—we have my niece here. We thought it would be so nice—No: she is young. Quite young. Seventeen—could we? Would it be any kind of inconvenience?—I did not want you to think—"

With joy Mrs. Clavering forgot the absence of the pecan nuts and a haunting fear that the white wine was, after all, not a suitable drink for so dark and freezing a day.

"Well, *they* will come at any rate. If no one else does—"

"Everybody will come," Mr. Clavering said. "And a few you never thought of."

"I'm sure no one would ever think of doing that sort of thing," she said.

"Everybody will be here," Mr. Clavering said. "The hen-coop tribe. The horse-box tribe. The wool-spinning tribe. The medical tribe. The point-to-pointers. You didn't ask Mrs. Bonnington and Battersby by any chance, did you?"

"Of course I did."

"And Freda O'Connor?"

"Of course."

"Charming, very charming," he said.

"I don't know what you mean. I chose everybody very carefully."

Mrs. Bonnington, who was dark and shapely and in her thirties, kept house for a retired naval commander who amused himself by fishing and sketching in water colour; Mr. Bonnington came down from somewhere at week-ends. The naval commander had a silvery piercing beard, commanding as a stiletto, and ice-blue handsome passionate eyes. Freda O'Connor, a long brown-haired hungry-looking girl with a flaunting bust that was like two full-blown poppy-heads, had left her husband and gone to live, while really preferring horses, with a Major Battersby. In a pleasant way Major

Battersby, brown and shaggy and side-whiskered and untidily muscular, was rather like a large horse himself. Miss O'Connor had succeeded Mrs. Battersby. In the furies of separation Mrs. Battersby, a woman of broad-hipped charm who wore slacks all day, had taken refuge with Mrs. Bonnington. On a horse she looked commanding and taller than she was. It seemed sometimes to Mr. Clavering that Mr. Bonnington arrived at week-ends simply for the purpose of seeing Mrs. Battersby, later departing only to leave Mrs. Bonnington free for the naval commander. He did not know. You could never be quite sure, in the country, about these complicated things and he said:

"You didn't invite Major Battersby too, did you?"

"I invited all the people I thought ought to be invited. After all one has to keep *up*," she said, "one has to keep *in*—"

Mr. Clavering, who would have preferred to live in town, where you could have a leisurely game of snooker or bridge in the evenings at the Invicta Club over a quite glass of whisky, out of reach of women, gave a sigh of pain and said something about not caring whether one was up or in and then added that Mrs. Clavering was wonderful.

Mrs. Clavering replied that she thought Mr. Clavering ought to go and change.

"Change what?" he said.

"That suit of course! You're never coming down in that suit!"

Mr. Clavering, who could see nothing wrong with his suit, began to go upstairs whistling. Mrs. Clavering rushed suddenly past him, remembering she had turned on the bath water. This gave him an opportunity of saying that on second thoughts he would have a quick snifter before the herd arrived, but Mrs. Clavering leaned swiftly over the banisters and called:

"No! Absolutely and utterly not. No snifters. If you want to do something useful see that the lights are switched on in the drive—·"
She was bullying him with affection, and he succumbed.

Some minutes later, as he switched the lights on in the long paved drive that led under canopies of frosted beech boughs up to the front door of the house, he saw that darkness had fallen completely. The lamps set all the low weeping boughs glistening delicately under cold blue air. He stood for a moment watching the sparkling

wintry lace of frosted twigs. He thought how cold and dark and
isolated the garden beyond them seemed, and he thought of the
billiard room of the Invicta Club, where light was coned above
green warm tables in a soft silence broken only by men's voices and
the click of snooker balls. He did not really care much for country
life. The house was really too big and too expensive and too
difficult to keep up; there was always the tiresome problem of
servants who did not want to stay. It was only for his wife's sake
that he kept it up. He was easy-going. She was fond of it all; she
liked country society.

"Isn't there any gin?" he said to the caterers' men in the sitting-
room.

"Only the white wine, Sir," they told him, and he said "Good
God! Wine?" and then recognised that it was another idea of his
wife's designed to make the party different, to elevate and keep up
its tone. He was amused by this and decided to try a glass of the
wine. It was a delicate light green in colour and he thought it
seemed insipid, all taste frozen out of it, and after drinking half a
single frosted glass he went off to grope in the dining-room
cellarette for the gin, but the usual bottle was not there, and with
tolerant amusement he realised his wife had probably hidden it
away.

By soon after six o'clock a dozen people were standing about in
stiff cold groups in the too large hall, grasping chilled glasses of
wine with chilly fingers. The owl-like eyes of the dropsical,
spectacled Miss Hemshawe and her mother prowled to and fro,
searching all newcomers. The Reverend Perks and his elder brother
arrived, looking like two pieces of scraped shin-bone with a little
beef left on, red and fierce at the edges of their ears and noses. Mrs.
Clavering fluttered. Some conversation went on in subdued tones,
and the caterers' men advanced with trays of wine-glasses and
coloured fish-bright snippets of food, eagerly seized upon by the
Reverend Perks and then earnestly recommended by his brother to
Miss Graves and Miss Ireton, who were clad in sheep's wool in the
form of large net-like faded blotting paper.

Soon there was a clucking everywhere, as Mr. Clavering said, of
busy hens. There was even, in the clink of glasses, a sound of
pecking in the air. Presently the hall began to be very full; people

overflowed into the dining-room; and Mr. Clavering found he
could not see everybody, or keep track of everybody, at once. The
wine seemed to him horribly cold and insipid and he hid his glass
behind a vase of lilac without noticing what the sprays of naked
blossom were.

Then his wife came to whisper with despair that it was nearly
seven o'clock and that neither the Paul Vaulkhards nor the Perigos
nor the Blairs had arrived.

"All the best people arrive last," he said, and then looked across
bubbling mole-hills of hats and heads to see Mrs. Battersby
standing on the threshold.

Mrs. Battersby looked outraged and stunned. Her eye sockets
seemed to have lost their pupils and looked like two dark empty
key-holes. Mr. Clavering saw that this sightless stare of dark
outrage was directed at Freda O'Connor. Until that moment he had
not noticed her. Now he saw that her slender skimmed figure,
looking taller than ever, was bound tightly in a long skirt of black
silk, with a brief bodice of white from which her bust protruded
with enforced and enlarged distinction. She was talking to Colonel
Arber, who was not very tall and had the advantage of not needing
to alter the level of his protuberant watery eyes in order to appraise
the parts of her that interested him most. Freda O'Connor looked
casual and hungry and languidly, glamorously indifferent. Her body
lacked the cohesive charm of Mrs. Battersby's, but it seemed
instead to flame. Mrs. Battersby melted away somewhere into
another room. Colonel Arber took another glass of wine, holding it
at the trembling level of Freda O'Connor's bosom, and seemed as if
about to speak with husky passion of something. He guffawed
instead, and the conversation was of horses.

Gradually Mr. Clavering felt that he had seen everybody. The
rooms were impossibly, clamorously full. The Perigos, the Blairs,
the Luffingtons had all arrived. A sound of cracked trumpets came
from the turn of the baronial staircase, echoing into wall displays of
copper cooking-pans, where Dr. Pritchard was telling what Mr.
Clavering thought were probably obstetric stories to Miss Ireton
and Miss Graves, who gazed at him with a kind of rough fondness,
half-masculine. Dr. Pritchard had an inexhaustible fund of stories
drawn from the fountains of illegitimacy and the shallows of

infidelity that he liked to tell for the purpose, most often, of cheering women patients waiting in labour. But maiden ladies liked them too, and sometimes pressed him to tell one rather more *risqué* than they had heard before. In consequence something infectious seemed to float from the foot of the staircase, filling the room with light and progressive laughter.

"I want you, I want you!" Mrs. Clavering whispered. "The Paul Vaulkhards are here!"

He found himself joined to her by the string of a single forefinger that led him through the crowd of guests to where, in a corner, the Paul Vaulkhards and their niece were waiting.

Mr. Vaulkhard was tall and white, and, as Mrs. Clavering had hoped, as distinguished as a statue. Mrs. Clavering fluttered about him, making excited note of his subdued dove-blue waistcoat, so much more élite than red or yellow, and thought that Mr. Clavering must have one too. Mrs. Vaulkhard had the loose baggy charm of a polite pelican covered in an Indian shawl of white and gold.

"Let me introduce my niece," she said. "Miss Dufresne. Olivia."

Charming, distinguished name, Mrs. Clavering thought; and almost before Mr. Clavering had time to shake hands she said:

"Would you look after Miss Dufresne? I'm going to positively drag Mr. and Mrs. Paul Vaulkhard away—that is if they don't mind being dragged. Do you mind being dragged?" She gave a spirited giggle of excuse and excitement and then dragged the Vaulkhards away.

A young dark face looked out from, as it seemed to Mr. Clavering, a crowd of swollen, solid cabbages. It had something of the detachment of a petal that did not belong there. He took from a passing tray a glass of wine and held it out to her, conscious of curious feelings of elevated lightness, of simplification. Out of the constricted clamour of voices he was aware of a core of silence about her that was absorbing and tranquil.

"Are you here for long?" he said. "Do you like the country?"

"No to one," she said. "Yes to the other."

He said something about being glad about one thing and not the other, but a small cloudburst of conversational laughter split the room, drowning what he had to say, and she said:

"I'm terribly sorry, but I couldn't hear what you were saying."

"Let's move a little," he said.

He steered her away through the crowd, watching her light figure. She leaned by the wall at last, sipping her wine and looking at him.

"I don't know that it's any quieter," he said. "Perhaps we should lip-read?"

She laughed, and he said:

"Really instead of standing here I ought to take you round and introduce you. Is there anyone you know?"

"No."

"Is there anyone you'd like to know?"

"What do you think?"

She gave him an engaging delicate smile, brief, almost nervous, and he felt that it was possibly because she was young and not sure of herself. He looked about the room, at the groups of cabbage heads. And suddenly he decided that he did not want to introduce her. He wanted instead to keep her, to isolate her for a little while, letting her remain a stranger.

"Haven't you ever been here before?" he said.

"No."

"And you really like the country?"

"I love it. I think it's beautiful."

Mr. Clavering felt himself appraise the tender, uplifted quality of her voice.

"I think everything's beautiful," the girl said.

"Everything?"

"The lilac," she said, "for instance. That's marvellously beautiful."

"Lilac?"

Absurd of him, he thought, not to have noticed the lilac.

"I noticed it as soon as I came in," she said. "I love white things. Don't you? White flowers. I love snow and frost on the boughs and everything like that."

At this moment Mr. Clavering noticed for the first time that her dress was white too. Frilled about the neck, simply and tastefully, it too had a frosty appearance. It seemed almost to embalm her young body in a cloud of rime.

"What masses of people," she said. "What a marvellous party."

"Are you at school?" he said.

"Me? School?" She gave, he thought, a little petulant toss of the wine glass as she lifted it to her mouth and sipped at it swiftly. "Oh! don't say that. Don't say I still look like a schoolgirl. Do I?"

"No," he said.

Across the room Major Battersby laughed, for the fourth or fifth consecutive time, like a buffalo.

"Who is the man who laughs so much?" she said.

He told her. Battersby was with Freda O'Connor and Mrs. Bonnington and Colonel Arber. The factions had begun to split up. He felt he would not have been surprised to hear from the Battersby group a succession of whinnies instead of laughter. Occasionally Colonel Arber bared his teeth and Freda O'Connor tossed her hair back from her neck and throat like a mane.

"Have you a nice garden?" she said.

Yes, he supposed the garden was nice. He supposed it was pleasant. He thought if anything there were too many trees. It was a bore getting people to work in it nowadays and sometimes he would have preferred a house with a good solid courtyard of concrete all round.

"I love gardens," she said. "Especially gardens like yours with big old trees. I love it at night when you see the car lights on the boughs and then on the very dark trees. It looks so mysterious and wonderfully like old legends and that sort of thing. Don't you think so?"

"Yes," he said. He had never given the slightest thought to the fact that his garden was mysterious with old legends. "I suppose so."

"Oh! It's lovely just to watch people," she said. "Marvellous to wonder who they are—"

Her remark coincided with a thought of his own that his house was full of jibbering monkeys. The rooms were strident with people clamouring with jibberish, sucking at glasses, trying to shout each other down. There was nothing but jibberish everywhere.

"I just love to stand here," she said. "I just love to wonder what's in their minds."

Great God, he thought. Minds? As if hoping for an answer to it all he stared into the glittering, mocking confusion of faces and smoke and glassiness. Minds? He saw that Mrs. Battersby had got together her own faction, joining herself with the Perigos and a woman named Mrs. Peele, who smoked cigarettes from a long ivory holder, and a man named George Carter, who managed kennels for her at which you could buy expensive breeds of dachshunds. There was something of the piquant dachshund broodiness in the face of Mrs. Peele. She was short in the body, with eyes darkly encased in coils of premature wrinkles, and the long cigarette holder gave her a grotesque touch of being top-heavy. There was no doubt that Mrs. Peele and George Carter lived together, just as there was no doubt that the dachshunds were much too expensive for anybody to buy.

"Oh! it's fascinating to watch," the girl said. "Don't you think so?"

A waiter tried to push his way past with a tray of snippets. With guilt Mr. Clavering remembered that he had offered her nothing to eat.

"Please take something," he said.

"Oh! yes, may I? I'm famished. Do you think wine makes you hungry?" She took several fish-filled cases while the waiter stood by, and then a moon-like round of egg. "I adore egg," she said. "Don't you?" and when he did not answer simply because he felt there could be no answer:

"Am I talking too much? I'm not, am I? But the wine gives me a feeling of being gay."

Through smoke-haze he saw his wife, pride-borne and fussy with anxiety, steering the Paul Vaulkhards from, as it were, customer to customer, as if they were sample goods for which you could place an order.

I ought to circulate too, he thought, and then found himself grasping the mild limp dropsical hand of a slightly flushed Miss Hemshawe, who with her mother had come to say good-bye. They must be toddling, Miss Hemshawe said, and under a guise of passiveness gave him a look of unresolved curiosity, because he had been talking for so long a time, alone, to so young a girl.

"Good-bye, Mr. Clavering," they fussed. "Good-bye. Good-bye."

"Sweet," the girl said. She grinned as if the facial distortions of Miss Hemshawe and her mother, toothsome and expansive in farewell, were a secret only she and himself could share.

"Yes," he said, and he knew that now he had only to be seen touching her hand, placing himself an inch or so nearer the frothy delicate rime of her dress, for someone like Miss Hemshawe to begin to build about him too a legend to which he had never given a thought.

Presently he was surrounded by other people coming to say good-bye; every few moments he heard somebody say what a wonderful party it was. His wife, they told him, was so good at these things. He was assailed by shrill voices ejected piercingly from the roar of a dynamo.

The girl pressed herself back against the wall, regarding the scene through eyes limpid with fascination, over the rim of her glass. He was aware of a fear that she would move away and that he did not want her to move away.

"Don't go," he said, and touched her hand.

Before she had time to speak he was involved in the business of saying good-bye to a Mrs. Borden and a Mr. Joyce. He remembered in time that Mrs. Borden was really Mrs. Woodley and that she had changed her name by deed-poll in order to run away with Borden, who had then rejected her in favour of Mrs. Joyce. The complications of this were often beyond him, but now he remembered in time to address her and the consolatory Mr. Joyce correctly.

"Nice party, old boy," Mr. Borden said. "Nice."

He felt that Mrs. Borden had a face like a bruised swedeturnip and that Joyce, red and crusted and staggering, was a little drunk.

"I ought to go too," the girl said. "I think I see them signalling me."

He began to steer her gently through the maze of groups and factions like a man steering a boat through a series of crowded reefs and islands. As he did so he was aware of a minute exultation because, until the last, he had kept her a stranger, apart from the all.

"Oh! Clavering, must say good-bye."

He found himself halted by a clergyman named Chalfont-Beverley, from a parish over the hill. Chalfont-Beverley was tall and young, with a taste for flamboyance that took the form of dressing-up. He was now dressed in a hacking jacket of magnified black-and-white check, with a waistcoat of magenta and a purple tie. His chest had something of the appearance of a decorated altar above which the face was a glow of rose and blue.

"Damn good party, Clavering," he said. His hands were silky. Clavering remembered that he was given to Anglo-Catholicism and occasional appearances at afternoon services dressed in pink-cord riding breeches and spurs below sweeping robes of white and scarlet. "Damn good. Must bear away." There was an odour of talcum powder in the air.

By the time Clavering was free again he saw the girl being taken away, in the hall, by the Paul Vaulkhards. He reached them just in time to be able to hold her coat.

"It isn't far," she said. "I'll just slip it over my shoulders."

She held the collar of the coat close about her neck, so that he felt the young delicacy of her face to be startlingly heightened.

"Good-bye," everyone said. The Paul Vaulkhards said they thought it had been enchanting. Mr. Paul Vaulkhard gave a bow of courteous dignity, holding Mrs. Clavering's hand. Mrs. Paul Vaulkhard said that the Claverings must come to see them too, and not to leave it too long; and he saw his wife exalted.

"Good-bye, Miss Dufresne," he said and again, for the second time, held her hand. "I will see you all out. It's a little tricky. There are steps—"

The Paul Vaulkhards went ahead with Mrs. Clavering, and as he followed through the outer hall he said:

"Did you enjoy it? Would you care to come and see us again before you go away?"

"Oh! it was a marvellous, wonderful exquisite party," she said. "It was beautiful. It was vivid."

The word lit up for him, like an unexpected flash of centralised light, all her eagerness, touching him into his own moment of reserved exultation. He walked with her for a few yards into the frosty drive, where the Paul Vaulkhards were waiting. A chain of light frozen boughs, glistening in the lamplight, seemed to obscure all the upper sky, but she lifted her face in a last gesture of excitement to say:

"Oh! All the stars are out! Look at all the stars!"

"Now remember," he said. "Don't forget to come and see us before you go."

"Oh! I will, I will," she said. She laughed with light confusion. "I mean I will come—I mean I won't forget. I will remember."

He watched her run into the frosty night, down the drive.

Later, in a house deserted except for the caterers' men and shabby everywhere with dirty glasses and still burning cigarettes and a mess of half-gnawed food, his wife said:

"Honestly, *did* you think it went well? *Did* you? You didn't think everybody was awfully stiff and bored?"

"I don't think so," he said.

"Oh! Somehow I thought it never got going. It never jelled. People just stood about in groups and glared and somehow I thought it never worked up. You know how I mean."

"I thought it was nice," he said.

"What about the wine? I knew as soon as we started it was a mistake. People didn't know what to make of it, did they? It was too cold. Didn't you feel they didn't know what to make of it?—it's funny how a little thing like that can go through a party."

Disconsolately, agitatedly picking up glasses and putting them down again, she wandered about the empty rooms. The caterers' men, in their shirt-sleeves, were packing up. In the hall a spray of lilac had become dislodged from its green guard of pittosporum leaves and as Clavering passed through the hall he picked it up and put it back again.

"What do you suppose the Paul Vaulkhards made of it?" his wife called. "Didn't you have an awful feeling they felt they were a bit above it? Not quite their class?"

Opening the front door, he was too far away to answer. He walked for a few paces down the still-lighted drive, looking up at the stars. The night in its rimy frostiness was without wind. With a tenderness he did not want to pursue into anything deeper he remembered how much the girl had liked all things that were white. He remembered how she had thought everything was beautiful.

From the frozen meadows behind the house there was a call of owls and from farther away, from dark coverts, a barkings of foxes.

(1955)

THE EVOLUTION OF SAXBY

I first met him on a black wet night towards the end of the war, in one of those station buffets where the solitary spoon used to be tied to the counter by a piece of string.

He stood patiently waiting for his turn with this spoon, spectacled and undemonstrative and uneager, in a shabby queue, until at last the ration of sugar ran out and nobody had any need for the spoon any longer. As he turned away he caught sight of me stirring my coffee with a key. It seemed to impress him, as if it were a highly original idea he had never thought of, and the thickish spectacles, rather than his own brown kidney-like eyes, gave me an opaque glitter of a smile.

"That's rather natty," he said.

As we talked he clutched firmly to his chest a black leather briefcase on which the monogram of some government department had been embossed in gilt letters that were no longer clear enough to read. He wore a little homberg hat, black, neat, the fraction of a size too small for him, so that it perched high on his head. In peacetime I should have looked for a rose in his buttonhole, and in peacetime, as it afterwards turned out, I often did; and I always found one there.

In the train on which we travelled together he settled himself down in the corner, under the glimmer of those shaded bluish lights we have forgotten now, and opened his brief-case and prepared, as I thought, to read departmental minutes or things of that sort.

Instead he took out his supper. He unfolded with care what seemed to be several crackling layers of disused wallpaper. He was evidently very hungry, because he took out the supper with a slow relish that was also wonderfully eager, revealing the meal as consisting only of sandwiches, rather thickly cut.

He begged me to take one of these, saying: "I hope they're good. I rather think they should be. Anyway they'll make up for what we didn't get at the buffet." His voice, like all his actions, was uneager, mild and very slow.

I remembered the spoon tied to the counter at the buffet and partly because of it and partly because I did not want to offend him I took one of his sandwiches. He took one too. He said something about never getting time to eat at the department and how glad he would be when all this was over, and then he crammed the sandwich eagerly against his mouth.

The shock on his face was a more powerful reflection of my own. His lips suddenly suppurated with revulsion. A mess of saffron yellow, repulsively mixed with bread, hung for a few moments on the lips that had previously been so undemonstrative and uneager. Then he ripped out his handkerchief and spat.

"Don't eat it," he said. "For God's sake don't eat it." He tore the sandwich apart, showing the inside of it as nothing but a vile mess of meatless, butterless mustard spread on dark war-time bread. "Give it to me, for God's sake," he said. "Give it to me. Please don't have that."

As he snatched the sandwich away from me and crumpled it into the paper his hands were quivering masses of tautened sinew. He got up so sharply that I thought he would knock his glasses off. The stiff wallpaper-like package cracked in his hands. His handkerchief had fallen to the seat and he could not find it again and in a spasm of renewed revulsion he spat in air.

The next thing I knew was the window-blind going up like a pistol shot and the window clattering down. The force of the night wind blew his hat off. The keen soapy baldness of his head sprang out with an extraordinary effect of nakedness. He gave the revolting yellow-oozing sandwiches a final infuriated beating with his hands and then hurled them far out of the window into blackness, spitting after them. Then he came groping back for his lost handkerchief and having found it sat down and spat into it over and over again, half-retching, trembling with rage.

He left it to me to deal with the window and the black-out blind. I had some difficulty with the blind, which snapped out of my hands before I could fix it satisfactorily.

When I turned round again I had an impression that the sudden snap of the blind had knocked his spectacles off. He was sitting holding them in his hands. He was breathing very heavily. His distraction was intolerable because without the spectacles he really looked like a person who could not see. He seemed to sit there groping blindly, feeble and myopic after his rush of rage.

His sense of caution, his almost fearsome correctness, returned in an expression of concern about the black-out blind. He got up and went, as it were, head-first into his spectacles, as a man dives into the neck of his shirt. When he emerged with the glasses on he realised, more or less sane now, his vision corrected, that I had put up the blind.

"Oh! You've done it," he said.

A respectable remorse afflicted him.

"Do you think it was seen?" he said. "I hate doing that sort of thing. I've always felt it rather a point to be decent about the regulations."

I said it was probably not serious. It was then nearly March, and I said I thought the war was almost over.

"You really think so?" he said. "What makes you think that? I've got a sort of ghastly feeling it will last for ever. Sort of tunnel we will never get out of."

I said that was a feeling everyone got. His spectacles had grown misty again from the sweat of his eyes. He took them off again and began slowly polishing them and, as if the entire hideous episode of the mustard had never happened, stared down into them and said:

"Where do you live? Have you been able to keep your house on?"

I told him where I lived and he said:

"That isn't awfully far from us. We live at Elham Street, by the station. We have a house that practically looks on the station."

He put on his spectacles and with them all his correctness came back.

"Are you in the country?" he said. "Really in the country?" and when I said yes he said that was really what he himself wanted to do, live in the country. He wanted a small place with a garden—a garden he could see mature.

"You have a garden?" he said.

"Yes."

"Nice one?"

"I hope it will be again when this is over."

"I envy you that," he said.

He picked up his hat and began brushing it thoughtfully with his coat sleeve. I asked him if he had a garden too and he said:

"No. Not yet. The war and everything—you know how it is."

He put on his hat with great care, almost reverently.

"Not only that. We haven't been able to find anywhere that really suits my wife. That's our trouble. She's never well."

"I'm sorry—"

"They can't find out what it is, either," he said. He remembered his handkerchief and as he folded it up and stuck it in his breastpocket the combination of handkerchief and homberg and his own unassertive quietness gave him a look that I thought was unexpressibly lonely and grieved.

"We move about trying to find something," he said, "but—"

He stopped, and I said I hoped she would soon be well again.

"I'm afraid she never will," he said. "It's no use not being frank about it."

His hands, free now of handkerchief and homberg, demonstrated her fragility by making a light cage in the air. His spectacles gave an impervious glint of resignation that I thought was painful.

"It's one of those damnable mysterious conditions of the heart," he said. "She can do things of course. She can get about. But one of these days—"

His hands uplifted themselves and made a light pouf! of gentle extermination.

"That's how it will be," he said.

I was glad at that moment to hear the train slowing down. He heard it too and got up and began to grope about along the hatrack.

"I could have sworn I had my umbrella," he said.

"No," I said.

"That's odd." His face tightened. An effort of memory brought back to it a queer dry little reflection of the anger he had experienced about the sandwiches of mustard. He seemed about to be infuriated by his own absent-mindedness and then he recovered himself and said:

"Oh! no. I remember now."

Two minutes later, as the train slowed into the station, he shook me by the hand, saying how pleasant it had been and how much he had enjoyed it all and how he hoped I might one day, after the war, run over and see him if it were not too far.

"I want to talk to you about gardens," he said.

He stood so smiling and glassy-eyed and uneager again in final good-bye that I began too to feel that his lapse of frenzy about the mustard sandwiches was like one of those episodic sudden bomb-explosions that caught you unawares and five minutes later seemed never to have happened.

"By the way my name is Saxby," he said. "I shall look for you on the train."

Trains are full of men who wear homberg hats and carry brief-cases and forget their umbrellas, and soon, when the war was over, I got tired of looking for Saxby.

Then one day, more than a year later, travelling on a slow train that made halts at every small station on the long high gradient below hills of beech-wood and chalk, I caught sight of a dark pink rose floating serenely across a village platform under a homberg hat.

There was no mistaking Saxby. But for a few seconds, after I had hailed him from the carriage window, it seemed to me that Saxby might have mistaken me. He stared into me with glassy preoccupa-tion. There was a cool and formidable formality about him. For one moment it occurred to me to remind him of the painful episode of the mustard sandwiches, and then a second later he remembered me.

"Of course." His glasses flashed their concealing glitter of a smile as he opened the carriage door. "I always remember you because you listen so well."

This was a virtue of which he took full advantage in the train.

"Yes, we've been here all summer," he said. "You can very nearly see the house from the train." This time he had his umbrella with him and with its crooked malacca handle he pointed south-westward through the open window, along the chalk hillside. "No. The trees are rather too dense. In the early spring you could see it. We had primroses then. You know, it simply magnificent country."

"How is your wife?" I said.

The train, charging noisily into the tunnel, drowned whatever he had to say in answer. He rushed to shut the window against clouds of yellow tunnel fumes and suddenly I was reminded of his noisy and furious charge at the window in the black-out, his nauseated frenzy about the sandwiches. And again it seemed, like an episodic explosion, like the war itself, an unreality that had never happened.

When we emerged from the tunnel black-out into bright summer he said:

"Did you ask me something back there?"

"Your wife," I said. "I wondered how she was."

The railway cutting at that point is a high white declivity softened by many hanging cushions of pink valerian and he stared at it with a sort of composed sadness before he answered me.

"I'm afraid she's rather worse if anything," he said. "You see, it's sort of progressive—an accumulative condition if you understand what I mean. It's rather hard to explain."

He bent his face to the rose in his buttonhole and seemed to draw from it, sadly, a kind of contradictory inspiration about his wife and her painfully irremediable state of health.

It was rather on the lines of what diabetics had, he said. The circle was vicious. You got terribly hungry and terribly thirsty and yet the more you took in the worse it was. With the heart it was rather the same. A certain sort of heart bred excitement and yet was too weak to take it. It was rather like overloading an electric circuit. A fuse had to blow somewhere and sometime.

Perhaps my failure to grasp this was visible in my stare at the railway cutting.

"You see, with electricity it's all right. The fuse blows and you put in another fuse. But with people the heart's the fuse. It blows and—"

Once again he made the light pouf! of extermination with his hands.

I said how sorry I was about all this and how wretched I thought it must be for him.

"I get used to it," he said. "Well, not exactly used to it if you understand what I mean. But I'm prepared. I live in a state of suspended preparation."

That seemed to me so painful a way of life that I did not answer.

"I'm ready for it," he said quietly and without any sort of

detectable desire for sympathy at all. "I know it will just happen at any moment. Any second it will all be over."

There was something very brave about that, I thought.

"Well anyway the war's over," he said cheerfully. "That at least we've got to be thankful for. And we've got this house, which is awfully nice, and we've got the garden, which is nicer still."

"You must be quite high there," I said, "on the hill."

"Nearly five hundred feet," he said. "It's a stiffish climb."

I said I hoped the hills were not too much for his wife and he said:

"Oh! she hardly ever goes out. She's got to that stage."

But the garden, it seemed, was wonderful. He was settling down to the garden. That was his joy. Carnations and phloxes did awfully well there and, surprisingly enough, roses. It was a *Betty Uprichard*, he said, in his buttonhole. That was one of his favourites and so were *Etoile d' Hollande* and *Madame Butterfly*. They were the old ones and on the whole he did not think you could beat the old ones.

"I want gradually to have beds of them," he said. "Large beds of one sort in each. But you need time for that of course. People say you need the right soil for roses—but wasn't there someone who said that to grow roses you first had to have roses in your heart?"

"There was someone who said that," I said.

"It's probably right," he said, "but I think you probably need permanence more. Years and years in one place. Finding out what sorts will do for you. Settling down. Getting the roots anchored— you know?"

The sadness in his face was so peculiar as he said all this that I did not answer.

"Have you been in your house long?" he said.

"Twenty years," I said.

"Really," he said. His eyes groped with diffused wonder at this. "That's marvellous. That's a lifetime."

For the rest of the way we talked—or rather he did, while I did my virtuous act of listening—about the necessity of permanence in living, the wonder of getting anchored down.

"Feeling your own roots are going deeper all the time. Feeding on the soil underneath you," he said. "You know? Nothing like it. No desk stuff can ever give you that."

And then, as the train neared the terminus, he said:

"Look. You must come over. I'd love you to see the place. I'd love to ask you things. I know you're a great gardener. There must be lots you could tell me. Would you come? I'd be awfully grateful if you'd care to come."

I said I should be delighted to come.

"Oh! good, oh! good," he said.

He produced from his vest-pocket the inevitable diary with a silver pencil and began flicking over its leaves.

"Let's fix it now. There's nothing like fixing it now. What about Saturday?"

"All right," I said.

"Good. Saturday's a good day," he said.

He began to pencil in the date and seemed surprised, as he suddenly looked up, that I was not doing the same.

"Won't you forget? Don't you put it down?"

"I shall remember," I said.

"I have to put everything down," he said. "I'm inclined to forget. I get distracted."

So it would be two-thirty or about that on Saturday, he said, and his enthusiasm at the prospect of this was so great that it was, in fact, almost a distraction. He seemed nervously uplifted. He shook hands with energetic delight, repeating several times a number of precise and yet confusing instructions as to how to get to the house, and I was only just in time to save him from a spasm of forgetfulness.

"Don't forget your umbrella," I said.

"Oh! Good God, no," he said. "You can't miss it," he said, meaning the house. "It's got a sort of tower on the end of it. Quite a unique affair. You can't miss it. I shall look out for you."

The house was built of white weatherboard and tile and it hung on the steep chalk-face with the precise and arresting effect of having been carved from the stone. The tower of which Saxby had spoken, and which as he said was impossible to miss, was nothing more than a railed balcony that somebody had built on the roof of a stable, a kind of look-out for a better view. That day it was crutched with scaffolding. In the yard below it there were many piles of builders' rubble and sand and broken timber and beams torn from their sockets. A bloom of cement dust lay thick on old shrubberies of lilac and flowing currant, and in the middle of a small orchard a large pit had been dug. From it too, in the dry heat of summer, a white dust had blown thickly, settling on tall yellow grass and apple leaves and vast umbrellas of seeding rhubarb.

There was nowhere any sign of the garden of which Saxby had spoken so passionately.

It took me some time, as he walked with me to and fro between the derelict boundaries of the place, to grasp that this was so. He was full of explanations: not apologetic, not in the form of excuses but, surprisingly, very pictorial. He drew for me a series of pictures of the ultimate shapes he planned. As we walked armpit deep through grass and thistle—the thistle smoking with dreamy seed in the hot air as we brushed it—he kept saying:

"Ignore this. This is nothing. This will be lawn. We'll get round to this later." Somebody had cut a few desultory swathes through the jungle with a scythe, and a rabbit got up from a seat in a swathe that crackled like tinder as it leapt away. "Ignore this—imagine this isn't here."

Beyond this jungle we emerged to a fence-line on the crest of the hill. The field beyond it lay below us on a shelf and that too, it seemed, belonged to him.

Spreading his hands about, he drew the first of his pictures. There were several others, later, but that was the important one. The farther you got down the slope, it seemed, the better the soil was, and this was his rose garden. These were his beds of *Uprichard* and *Madame Butterfly* and *Sylvia* and all the rest. He planned them in the form of a fan. He had worked it out on an arc of intensifying shades of pink and red. Outer tones of flesh would dissolve with graded delicacy through segments of tenderer, deeper pink until they mounted to an inverted pinnacle of rich sparkling duskiness.

"Rather fine," he said, "don't you think?" and I knew that as far as he was concerned it actually lay there before him, superbly flourishing and unblemished as in a catalogue.

"Very good," I said.

"You really think so?" he said. "I value your opinion terrifically."

"I think it's wonderful," I said.

We had waded some distance back through the jungle of smouldering thistle before I remembered I had not seen his wife; and I
asked him how she was.

"I fancy she's lying down," he said. "She feels the hot weather
quite a bit. I think we shall make quite a place of it, don't you?"

He stopped at the point where the grass had been partially mown
and waved his hand at the wilderness. Below us lay incomparable
country. At that high point of summer it slept for miles in richness.
In the hotter, moister valley masses of meadowsweet spired frothily
above its hedgerows, and in its cleared hayfields new-dipped sheep
grazed in flocks that were a shade mellower and deeper in colour
than the flower.

"It's a marvellous view," I said.

"Now you get what I mean," he said. "The permanence of the
thing. You get a view like that and you can sit and look at it for
ever."

Through a further jungle of grass and thistle, complicated at one
place by an entire armoury of horseradish, we went into the house.

"Sit down," Saxby said. "Make yourself comfortable. My wife
will be here in a moment. There will be some tea."

For the first time since knowing Saxby I became uneasy. It had
been my impression for some time that Saxby was a man who
enjoyed—rather than suffered from—a state of mild hallucination.
Now I felt suddenly that I suffered from it too.

What I first noticed about the room was its windows, shuttered
with narrow Venetian blinds of a beautiful shade of grey-rose. They
only partially concealed long silk curtains pencilled with bands of
fuchsia purple. Most of the furniture was white, but there were a
few exquisite Empire chairs in black and the walls were of the same
grey-rose tint as the blinds. An amazing arrangement of glass
walking-sticks, like rainbows of sweetmeats, was all the decoration
the walls had been allowed to receive with the exception of a
flower-spangled mirror, mostly in tones of rose and magenta, at the
far end. This mirror spread across the entire wall like a lake,
reflecting in great width the cool sparkle of the room in which, on
the edge of an Empire chair, I sat nervously wondering, as I had
done of Saxby's mustard sandwiches, whether what I saw had the
remotest connection with reality.

Into this beautiful show-piece came, presently, Mrs. Saxby.

Mrs. Saxby was an immaculate and disarming woman of fifty with small, magenta-clawed hands. She was dressed coolly in grey silk, almost as if to match the room, and her hair was tinted to the curious shade of blue-grey that you see in fresh carnation leaves. I did not think, that first day, that I had ever met anyone quite so instantly charming, so incessantly alive with compact vibration—or so healthy.

We had hardly shaken hands before she turned to Saxby and said: "They're coming at six o'clock."

Saxby had nothing to say in answer to this. But I thought I saw, behind the flattering glasses, a resentful hardening bulge of the kidney-brown eyes.

Not all beautiful women are charming, and not all charming women are intelligent, but Mrs. Saxby was both intelligent and charming without being beautiful. We talked a great deal during tea—that is, Mrs. Saxby and I talked a great deal, with Saxby putting in the afterthought of a phrase or two here and there.

She mostly ignored this. And of the house, which I admired again and again, she said simply:

"Oh! it's a sort of thing with me. I like playing about with things. Transforming them."

When she said this she smiled. And it was the smile, I decided, that gave me the clue to the fact that she was not beautiful. Her grey eyes were like two hard pearl buttons enclosed by the narrow dark buttonholes of her short lashes. As with the house, there was not a lash out of place. The smile too came from teeth that were as regular, polished and impersonal as piano keys.

It seemed that tea was hardly over before we saw a car draw up among the rubble outside. In the extraordinary transition to the house I had forgotten the rubble. And now as I became aware of it again it was like being reminded of something unpleasantly chaotic. For some uneasy reason I got to thinking that the inside of the house was Mrs. Saxby's palace and that the outside, among the wilderness of plaster and thistle and horse-radish, was Saxby's grave.

The visitors turned out to be a man and wife, both in the sixties, named Bulfield. The woman was composed mainly of a series of

droops. Her brown dress drooped from her large shoulders and
chest and arms like a badly looped curtain. A treble row of pearls
drooped from her neck, from which, in turn, drooped a treble
bagginess of skins. From under her eyes drooped pouches that
seemed once to have been full of something but that were now
merely punctured and drained and flabby. And from her mouth,
most of the time, drooped a cigarette from which she could not
bother to remove the drooping ashes.

Of Bulfield I do not remember much except that he too was large
and was dressed in a tropical suit of white alpaca, with colossal
buckskin brogues.

"Would you like a drink first?" Mrs. Saxby said, "or would you
like to see the house first?"

"I'd like a drink," Mrs. Bulfield said, obviously speaking for both
of them. "If all the house is as terrific as this it will do me. It's
terrific, isn't it, Harry?"

Harry said it was terrific.

Perhaps because of something disturbing about Saxby's silence—
he sat defiantly, mutinously sipping glasses of gin for almost an
hour with scarcely a word—it came to me only very slowly that the
Bulfields had come to buy the place.

It came to me still more slowly—again because I was troubled and
confused about Saxby's part in it all—that the reason the Bulfields
wanted to buy the house was because they were rising in the world.
They sought—in fact desired—to be injected with culture: perhaps
not exactly culture, but the certain flavour that they thought
culture might bring. After the first World War Bulfield would have
been called a profiteer. During the second World War it was, of
course, not possible to profiteer; Bulfield had merely made money.
Mrs. Bulfield must have seen, in magazines and books, perhaps
scores of times, pictures of the kind of house Mrs. Saxby had
created. She must have seen it as a house of taste and culture and
she had come to regard these virtues as she might have regarded
penicillin. Injected with them, she would be immunised from the
danger of contact with lower circumstances. Immunised and elevated, she could at last live in the sort of house she wanted without
being able to create for herself but which Mrs. Saxby—the sick,
slowly expiring Mrs. Saxby—had created for her.

This was as much an hallucination as Saxby's own belief that his rose-garden was already there in the wilderness. But all dreams, like fires, need stoking, and for an hour the Bulfields sat stoking theirs. They drank stodgily, without joy, at a sort of unholy communion of whisky. And by seven o'clock Mrs. Bulfield was loud and stupefied.

Whether it was the moment Mrs. Saxby had been waiting for I don't know, but she suddenly got up from her chair, as full of immaculate and sober charm and vibration as ever, and said:

"Well, would you like to see the rest of the house now?"

"If it's all like this it's as good as done," Mrs. Bulfield said. "It's absolutely terrific. I think it's perfect—where do you keep the coal?"

Bulfield let out thunderclaps of laughter at this, roaring:

"That's it!—we got to see the coal-hole. We must see that. And the whatsit!—we got to see the whatsit too."

"I'm sorry, Mrs. Bulfield," Mrs. Saxby said. "Forgive me— perhaps you'd like to see it in any case?"

"Not me. I'm all right," Mrs. Bulfield said. "I'm like a drain."

"Coal-hole!" Bulfield said. "Come on, Ada. Coal-hole! Got to see the coal-hole!"

"You'll excuse us, won't you?" Mrs. Saxby said to me, and once again the eyes were buttoned-up, grey and charming as the walls of the house, so pale as to be transparent, so that I could look right through them and see nothing at all beyond.

It must have been a quarter of an hour before Saxby spoke again. He drank with a kind of arithmetical regularity: the glass raised, three sips, the glass down. Then a pause. Then the glass up again, three sips, and the glass down. It seemed to me so like a man determined to drink himself silly that I was intensely relieved when he said:

"Let's get a spot of air. Eh? Outside?"

So we wandered out through the back of the house, and his first act there was to point out to me three or four rose trees actually growing on a wall. A bloom of cement dust covered the scarlet and cream and salmon of the flowers. He regarded them for a few moments with uncertainty, appeared about to say something else about them and then walked on.

His evident determination to say nothing more about one hallucination, that of the rose-garden, prepared me for his reluc-

tance to elaborate or surrender another. This was his illusion of the
sick, the expiring Mrs. Saxby.

"She'll kill herself," he said. "She can't stand up to it. She'll just
wear herself down to the bone."

I refrained from saying anything about how healthy I thought
Mrs. Saxby seemed to be.

"You know how many houses she's done this to?" he said. "You
want to know?"

I encouraged him and he said:

"Fifteen. We've lived in fifteen houses in twenty years."

He began to speak of these houses wrathfully, with jealousy and
sadness. He spoke with particular bitterness of a house called *The
Croft*. I gathered it was a big crude mansion of stone in post-
Edwardian style having large bay-windows of indelicate pregnant
massiveness pushing out into shrubberies of laurel and a vast plant
called a gunnera, a kind of giant's castle rhubarb. "Like fat great
paunches they were, the windows," he said, "like great fat commis-
sionaires," and I could see that he hated them as he might have
hated another man.

On one occasion the Saxbys had lived in a windmill. Saxby had
spent a winter carrying buckets of water up and down the stairway,
eating by the light of hurricane lamps, groping across a dark, stark
hillside every morning to catch his train to the office in Whitehall.
Then there had been a coastguard's house by the sea. The shore was
flat and wind-torn and unembellished by a single feather of
tamarisk or sea-holly or rock or weed. Then, because the war came,
there were smaller houses: accessible, easy to run, *chic* and clever,
sops to the new avidity of war, the new, comfortless servantless
heaven for which men were fighting. She roamed restlessly about,
looking for, and at, only those places that to other people seemed
quite impossible: old Victorian junkeries, old stables, old ware-
houses, old cart-sheds, a riverside boat-house, bringing to all of
them the incessant vibration, the intense metamorphosis of her
charm. Her passion for each house was, I gathered, a state of
nervous and tearing exultancy. She poured herself into successive
transformations with an absorption that was violent. She was like a
woman rushing from one amorous orgy to another: hungry and
insatiable and drained away.

She had in fact been unfaithful to him for a series of houses; it amounted to that. She had taken love away from him and had given it with discriminate wantonness to bricks and mortar. I do not say she could help this; but that was how I looked at it. She and Saxby had been married rather late. He was reaching the outer boundaries of middle-aged comfort when he first met her. He had wanted, as men do, a place of his own. He had wanted to come home at night to a decent meal, unassertive kindliness and some sense of permanency. Above all the sense of permanency. He had a touching desire to get his roots down: to plant things, invest in earth, reap the reward of sowing and nurturing things in one place.

He came home instead to that quivering febrile vibration of hers that was so astonishing and charming to other people—people like me—until he could stand it no longer and could only call it a disease. He was really right when he said there was something wrong with her heart. The profundity of its wrongness was perhaps visible only to him. Case-books had no name for her condition or its symptoms or anything else about her—but he had, and he knew it had turned him into a starved wanderer without a home.

That was the second of his pictures: of Mrs. Saxby constantly sick with the pressure of transforming another house, too sick to eat, distraught by builders and decorators and electricians and above all by the ferocious impact of herself. "She's really ill. You don't see it today. She's really ill. She'll kill herself. She lives at that awful pace—"

The third was of himself.

Did I remember the sandwiches, that first night we had met in the train? That was the sort of thing he had to put up with. Could I imagine anything more hideous than that awful bread and mustard? That had been her idea of his supper.

I thought he might well be sick as he spoke of it. And I even thought for a moment I might be sick too. We had again wandered beyond the house into the wilderness of horse-radish and smoking thistle. In the hot late afternoon a plague of big sizzling flies, a fierce blackish emerald turquoise, had settled everywhere on leaves and thistle-heads, in grass mown and unmown. Our steps exploded them. He swung at these repulsive insect-clouds with his hands, trying to beat them off in futile blasphemies that I felt must be

directed, really, in their savagery, against Mrs. Saxby. I could not
help feeling that, in his helpless fury, he wanted to kill her and was
taking it out on the flies.

But he was not taking it out on the flies: not his feelings for Mrs.
Saxby anyway. He took an enormous half-tipsy swipe at a glittering
and bloated mass of flies and spat at them:

"Get out, you sickening creepers, get out! You see," he said to
me, "I wouldn't care so much if it wasn't for the people. She makes
all the houses so lovely—she always does it so beautifully—and then
she sells them to the most ghastly people. Always the most bloody
awful ghastly people. That's what gets me."

From the house, a moment later, came the sound of Mr. Bulfield
triumphantly playing with the appurtenances of the whatsit and of
Mrs. Bulfield, drooping drunkenly from an upstairs window,
trumpeting hoarsely in the direction of the rose-garden that was not
there:

"Now you've started something. Now you've set him off! He'll
spend his life in there."

And I knew, as Saxby did, that another house had gone.

We met only once more: in the late autumn of that year.

On that occasion we travelled down together, into the country, by
the evening train. He seemed preoccupied and did not speak much.
I imagined, perhaps, that another house had been begun, that he
was off again on his homeless, bread-and-mustard wanderings. But
when I spoke of this he simply said:

"The Bulfields haven't even moved in yet. We had some difficulty
about another licence for an extension over the stable."

"How is your wife?" I said.

"She's—"

The word dying was too painful for him to frame. Yet I knew that
it was the word he was trying to say to me; because once again, as
when I had first met him, he lifted his hands in that little pouf! of
sad and light extermination.

"She started another house on the other side of the hill," he said.
"It was too much for her. After all she can't go on like it for ever—"

After he had got out at the little station I could not help feeling
very sorry for him. He had left behind him a queer air of sadness

that haunted me—and also, as if in expression of his great distraction, his umbrella.

And because I did not know when I should see him again I drove over, the following afternoon, to the house on the chalk hillside, taking the umbrella with me.

The house stood enchanting in its wilderness of perishing grass and weeds, yellow with the first burning of frost on them, and a maid in a uniform of pale grey-rose—to match, evidently, the exquisite walls of that room in which Bulfield has roared his joy over the coal-hole and the whatsit—opened the door to me.

"Is Mr. Saxby in?" I said. "I have brought the umbrella he left in the train."

"No, sir," she said. "But Mrs. Saxby is in. Would you care to see Mrs. Saxby?"

"Yes," I said.

I went in and I gave the umbrella to Mrs. Saxby. The day was coolish, with clear fresh sunlight. As I came away she stood for a moment or two at the door, talking to me, the light filling her eyes with delicate illumination, giving her once again that look of being full of charm, of being very alive with an effect of compact vibration—and as healthy as ever.

"I am glad you came over once more," she said. "We are moving out on Saturday."

The dead grasses, scorched by summer and now blanched by frost, waved across the white hillside where the rose-garden should have been.

"I'm afraid it's an awful wilderness," she said. "But we never touch gardens. That's the one thing people prefer to do for themselves."

I drove slowly down the hill in cool sunshine. The country was incomparable. The fires of autumn were burning gold and drowsy in the beeches.

If they seemed sadder than usual it was because I thought of Saxby. I wondered how long he had wanted to be free of her and how long he had wanted her to die. I wondered how many times he had wanted to kill her and if ever he would kill her—or if he would remain, as I fancied he would do, just bound to her for ever.

(1955)

THE MAKER OF COFFINS

Every Sunday evening in summertime she sat at the front window and watched until he came up the hill. Her hands on the horsehair rests of the chair were like pieces of stone-grey paper painted with thin lines of water-colour, palest blue, the skin transparent and the fingers crabbed over the little palms. She always wore a straw hat that had once evidently been purple, the shadows of the trimmings, dark grey, on the mildew grey of the faded, remaining straw.

She sat surrounded by a mass of greenery in brass and china pots, set about on bamboo stands. The curtains in the big bay window were like blankets of red chenille bearing fruitings of soft bobbles down the sides. The old-fashioned gas-brackets over the mantel-shelf bore opaque globes of pink and under them were ornaments of twisted yellow glass from which sprouted dead stalks of feathery brown reed and bunches of paper spills. She made the spills for Luther, with her own hands, every Saturday.

Whenever he came round the corner of the long steep hill she always thought that he looked, in his black suit and carrying the black fiddle case, so much like a doctor. Even from that distance the big rough-angled body dwarfed the fiddle case so that it did not look much larger than a doctor's bag. She had in mind particularly Dr. Farquharson's bag because it was the bag she had known best. It had brought her the twelve children, beginning with Luther.

The illusion of bag and doctor remained with her through his journey up the hill. He walked with a slight groping roll, big feet splayed out as if he wanted to grip the hill with his toes. She knew he did not roll like that because he was drunk but only because his feet were bad. His feet had always been bad. They had been bad ever since the time he was a child and had grown so fast that she could never afford to buy shoes to catch up with him. In those days he had had to suffer a lot of things in that way because he was the first and times were desperate. She felt keenly that she had never been able to do her best for him. The others had been luckier.

When he came into the room at last it was always with a series of bungling noisy clashes as he tried to find a resting-place for the fiddle case somewhere among the many little tables, the piano, the bookcase and the chairs. He could never find room for the damn fiddle, he thought. The bookcase and the piano were both locked up, polished as glass, and she kept the keys on a chain. He groped among the chairs with bull-like stupor but she never at any time took a great deal of notice of it. He had always been clumsy on his feet. He had been a day or two short of nineteen months before he had started walking at all. She always remembered that, of being so afraid that he would never walk: an awful thing, to have a child so fragile that it never walked.

If she was aware of feeling that the enormous body still enshrined the fragile child she did not reveal it. She turned on him with little grunts of peevish affection that had no effect on him at all.

"It'll be dark before you get up here one of these days."

"Had a rush job on. Wonder I got finished at all."

When he had at last disposed of the fiddle he liked to sit by the piano, in the dark patch caused by one end, so that she could not see his face.

"Who was it?" she said. "Thought you said trade was so bad."

"So it is. Man in Canal Street. Burying tomorrow."

"What man?"

"A man named Johnson."

"Who's he? What name?"

"Johnson. Call him Polly Johnson. Kin to Liz Johnson—"

"Nobody I know."

The lines of her face would crease themselves in deeper ruts of disapproval. Her mouth would go on muttering without sound for some moments longer while he settled himself by the piano with hot discomfort and perhaps a belch or two.

"You can take your coat off."

She liked him better with his coat off. It reminded her of the Sundays when all of them were at home, a dinner, all the boys with clean white aprons on, so that the gravy from the Yorkshire pudding did not drop on their chapel suits.

The absence of the coat revealed a man of gross, crusty width, with watery blue eyes starting beerily from a face fired by summer to lines of smouldering bruisy red. His collar-stud pressed brassily on his thick throat and his shirt-sleeves were rolled up above arms massive and blackly haired.

His voice had a yeasty thickness:

"All of 'em gone chapel?"

"Rose and Clarice and Will have gone. Lawrence and Nell went this morning."

Lawrence and Will were good boys: steady boys, fellows with enough ambition to get good jobs and enough sense to hang on to them when they got them. They were solid, pin-stripe men. She had never had any bother with Will and Lawrence; they never troubled her. They did not approve of Luther, but then, they did not understand him.

"Ain't bin out nowhere this week, I reckon? Too hot for you."

"Went up to Rose's Thursday," she said.

"Git the bus?"

"Bus! What d'ya think my legs are for?"

"You wanta git the bus," he said. "One o' these days you'll be doing that traipse up there once too much and you'll be dropping down."

"If I do you'll be there measuring me out 'fore I'm cold," she said swiftly, "I'll warrant that."

"Ah, don't sit there horse-facing so much. You horse-face too much by half."

"Don't you tell me I horse-face," she said.

He did not answer. It pained him when she horse-faced at him. He dreaded the day when he would be measuring her out, he thought. His only compensating thought about that was that he would make her something very nice; something really high-class and lovely; something fitting and worthy of the old lady.

She sat there for some time looking like a bone carving, and at last he broke the silence by saying:

"Anything to eat? I could do with a mite o' something."

"I'll be bound you never got your dinner again, did you?"

"Never had time. Bin at it since daylight."

"Funny how you get so many jobs a-Sundays," she said and her nose rose, pointed as a bird's.

Then because he sat there without moving for a second or two longer she said:

"Well: you know where the pantry is. You don't expect me to put it in your mouth for you, do you?"

Daylight was fading a little when he came lumbering back into the room with hunks of jam tart and cheese and bread and cold new potatoes and a slice of cold Yorkshire pudding on a plate. He sat with the plate on his knees. He knew that he had to be careful of the crumbs; he knew she would horse-face if he dropped the crumbs. But the taste of the new potatoes and the cold Yorkshire pudding were the taste of all the summer Sunday evenings of his boyhood and he crammed them in with blind-eyed pleasure, bolting them down, licking thick red lips and wishing to God she had a pint in the house to wash them down.

She muttered at last:

"Anybody'd think you'd never had a mite in your life. Don't she ever get you nothing a-Sundays?"

"Never care whether I get much a-Sundays," he said.

"It don't look like it," she said.

That was the worst of his mother, he thought. She couldn't hit it off with Edna. He had given up trying to make her now. It was like trying to turn a mule.

"You can get yourself a spill when you want one," she said.

Edna was a bit easy-going, he knew, but on the whole he didn't complain. She had let herself go a bit, perhaps, after the last baby. She was a bit sloppy around the middle. Her face was nothing much to write home about but then he wasn't a picture either. The chief thing was she didn't nag him; he really didn't get drunk very much and if he was late at *The Unicorn* on a Sunday she and the children ate the dinner without him and he pacified her with a pint of Guinness afterwards.

By the time he had finished eating it was almost dark and he got up and did the thing he always did, without fail, every Sunday. He lit one of the gas-lamps above the mantelshelf and then, holding his big red face under the light, adjusted the burner until it gave a pure

white glow. Then he filled his pipe and lit one of her paper spills
from the gas-mantle and put it to his pipe. The flame was sucked
down by his red powerful mouth into the pipe bowl until at last he
blew out strong blue clouds of smoke that almost smothered him.

As she sat in the window she let the smoke come over to her with
her head slightly uplifted, as if it were a cool breeze blowing
through the warm airless room in which no window had been open
all day. There were three moments she really waited for all evening,
and this was the second of them. The first was when she saw him
turn, so like a doctor with the fiddle case, at the bottom of the hill.
The second was the moment of the gas-lamp, the pure white glow
on his face, the great sucked-down flame and the smoke puttering
across the room in blue string clouds. It was the smoke above all
that she associated with that clumsy massiveness of his and after she
smelled it she was aware of the slow dying of cantankerousness
inside herself, a softening of all the edges of the day.

When the pipe was really going she knew what he was going to
do next. She began unconsciously to finger the keys of the piano
and the bookcase that hung on the chain round her neck. That was
the third moment: the moment when he reached for the fiddle case
and undid it and opened it and took out the bow.

He had begun to play the fiddle when he was seven years old.
That had been her ambition for him: a fiddler, a violinist, a great
player of the violin in the household. Mr. Godbold, who had been
a fiddler himself in a great orchestra in Leicester or Birmingham or
some other big city up in that part of the world, gave him lessons in
his front room, twice a week, after school, at two shillings a time.

"He has fine hands," Mr. Godbold said. "He will make a fine
player. He is slow but in the end he will make a fine player."

The walls of Mr. Godbold's front room were hung with many
pictures of Mr. Godbold playing the violin as a soloist or in
orchestras or at social evenings and smoking concerts. She thought
Mr. Godbold, in pieces like *The Spring Song* and excerpts from
Mariana and *Il Trovatore*, played like an angel, and she thought it
would be wonderful if Luther could rise as far as that. The first
winter he persevered through many exercises and the second winter
he came to his first piece, *Robin Adair*. Most children who learned
the piano or the violin went to a Miss Scholes, in the High Street,

where they learned *The Bluebells of Scotland* as their first piece and Miss Scholes gave them sixpence for doing so. Mr. Godbold did not believe in bribing his pupils; they worked hard on exercises that were the real foundation of music and then went straight on to pieces like *Robin Adair*.

Luther stuck at *Robin Adair*. He played it through for a whole winter and then his hands began to grow. By the time he was twelve he was a big awkward gargoyle of a boy in whose hands the violin looked effete and fragile. She thought by that time he could play beautifully: perhaps not quite as beautifully as Mr. Godbold. Perhaps it only seemed to her almost as beautiful because he was so very young.

"You want the key?" she said. She took it off the chain and held it out to him.

The sound of the fifths as he spaced them out on the piano was, she thought, a most wonderful thing. It was different from anything else that was ever heard on the piano: those queer, sharp steps of notes climbing up and starting a trembling on the air. That was the true violin sound: that wonderful prelude of quivering that drew out finally into the glassy, soaring singing of strings.

She had never been very happy about his being a carpenter and at first she opposed it. It was probably that, she thought, that had made his hands so large and clumsy. She was certain the hands of a carpenter could not also be the hands of a violinist; the one could only ruin the other. But his father had said a man had his living to earn and what was wrong with a man being a carpenter? "There was One who was a carpenter and there was no shame in that," he said.

"Play the old un?" Luther said, but she said nothing because she knew he never began with any other.

The time he took to play through *Robin Adair* always seemed to go by, perhaps because she shut her eyes, very quickly. It flew away on the song's own delicacy. He liked to play too with the pipe in his mouth, so that it seemed as if every scrape of the bow gave out its own rank cloud of smoke that finally choked the room with gas-green fog.

After *Robin Adair* he played several other pieces he knew: *The Jolly Miller* and *Oh! Dear What Can the Matter Be?* She thought he played better as he got older; but that, after all, was only natural. That was only as it should be. He was a man of over fifty now. He had been playing the same pieces, on the same violin, for forty years.

"Gittin' dark," Luther would say, after the third piece. "Better be gittin' steady on home."

He sat with the fiddle case on his knee and the pipe and the violin in his right hand, waiting to pack up. There would be just time, he thought, to nip into *The Unicorn* and have a couple of beers, perhaps even three or four beers, before they closed at half-past ten. Old Shady Parker would be there and Bill Flawn and Tom Jaques and Flannel Clarke and they would stand each other a round or two. That would rouse him up nicely and he would go home to Edna happy, belching through the dark summer streets, up and down the hills. Tomorrow he would begin to cut out another coffin. Trade was never what you called good in the summer but someone was always going, unexpected or not, and he mucked along somehow. Damn what the family said. That was good enough for him.

"Better put the key back afore you forget," he would say and she would take the key from him and clip it back on the chain.

The poise of her hands, held for a second or two about her throat, was a signal that she gave him every Sunday.

"Want me to gie y' another?"

"Have you got time? Don't you hang about if you haven't got time."

"Plenty o' time." The big voice was crude and massive as the hands. "You jes' say and I'll play it. Want another? What's it goin' a-be?"

"Play me the old one," she would say.

The old one was *Robin Adair*. As he played it she stared beyond the smoky gaslight into spaces empty of shape. She sat ageless and tranquil as if already embalmed among the greenery of fern-pots, before a shroud of blanketing curtains, under a gas-blue summer sky. The harsh sound of the fiddle strings drew out thinner and thinner across the spaces into which she was staring until her eyes went cloudily after them and she was sightless as she listened.

"Ah! y' can't beat th' old uns," Luther said. "They take a bit o' beatin'."

She did not answer. She felt always that she could hear the sound of the strings long after they were silent. They were like the sound of pigeons' voices echoing each other far away in summer trees, and in the sound of them was all her love.

(1955)

THE COWSLIP FIELD

Pacey sat on the stile, swinging her legs and her cowslip-basket.

Pacey, he thought, was by far the littlest lady he had ever seen. She had very thick dumpy legs and black squashy button boots and a brown felt hat under which bright blue eyes roamed about like jellyfish behind large sun-shot spectacles. On her cheek, just under her right eye, was a big furry brown mole that looked like the top of a bullrush that had been cut off and stuck there.

Pacey was nice, though. He liked Pacey.

"How far is it now to the cowslip field, Pacey?" he said.

"A step or two furder yit," Pacey said.

"It's not *furder*," he said. "It's *further*."

"Oh! is't?" Pacey said. "All right, it's *further*. I never knew such a boy for pickin' me up afore I'm down."

"And it's not *afore*," he said. "It's *before*."

"Oh! is't?" Pacey said. "All right, *before* then. I never knowed sich a boy for whittlin' on me—"

"And it's not *on*," he said. "It's *of*—"

"Here," Pacey said, "for goodness' sake catch holt o' the cowslip-basket and let me git down and let's git on. Else we'll never be there afore bull's-noon."

When Pacey jumped down from the stile her legs sank almost to the top of her button boots in meadow grasses. She was so thick and squatty that she looked like a duck waddling to find the path across the field.

In that field the sun lay hot on sheets of buttercups. Soon when he looked at Pacey's boots they were dusty yellow faces, with rows of funny grinning eyes. At the end of the field rolled long white hedges of hawthorn, thick and foamy as the breakers he had once seen at the seaside, and from a row of sharp green larches, farther on, he heard a cuckoo call.

It was past the time when the larches had little scarlet eyelashes springing from their branches but he still remembered them.

"Pacey," he said, "why do the trees have—"

"Jist hark at that cuckoo," Pacey said. "Afore long it'll charm us all to death."

"Pacey," he said, "why don't cowslips grow in this field?"

"Because it ain't a cowslip field," Pacey said, "don't you know that? Don't you know the difference between a cowslip field and a buttercup field? If you don't it's time you did. Now you jis run on and git to the next stile and sit there quiet and wait fer me."

From the next stile he sat and watched Pacey waddling down the slope of the field, between dazzling sheets of buttercups, under a dazzling high blue sky. In the wide May morning she looked more than ever like a floundering little duck, funnier, tinier than ever.

"Pacey," he said, "will you ever grow any bigger?"

"Not unless me luck changes a lot more'n it's done up to yit."

"Will I grow any bigger?"

" 'Course you will."

"Well then, why won't you?"

"Hark at that cuckoo," Pacey said. "If it's called once this morning, it's called a thousand times."

In the next field brown and white cows were grazing and Pacey took his hand. Some of the cows stood at a pond, over their hocks in water, flicking flies from their white-patched brown rumps in the sun. All across the field there were many ant-hills and Pacey let him run up and down them, as if they were switchbacks, always holding his hand.

Her own hands were rough and clammy and warm and he liked them.

"What do the ants do in their ant-hills all the time, Pacey?" he said.

"They git on with their work," Pacey said, " 'ithout chattering so much."

As they passed the pond he could smell the thick warm odours of may-bloom and fresh dung that the cows had dropped and mud warming in the sun. All the smell of rising summer was in the air. The tips of a few bulrushes, so brown and so like Pacey's mole, were like the last tips of winter, half-strangled by rising reeds.

Then somehow he knew that the next field was the cowslip field and he suddenly broke free of Pacey's hand and ran jumping over the last of the ant-hills until he stood on a small plank bridge that went over a narrow stream where brook-lime grew among bright eyes of wild forget-me-not.

"Pacey, Pacey, Pacey!" he started shouting. "Pacey!"

He knew he had never seen, in all his life, so many cowslips. They covered with their trembling orange heads all the earth between himself and the horizon. When a sudden breeze caught them they ducked and darted very gently away from it and then blew gently back again.

"We'll never gather them all before it's dark, Pacey," he said, "will we?"

"Run and git as many as you can," Pacey said. "It won't be dark yit awhile."

Running, he tripped and fell among cowslips. He did not bother to get to his feet but simply knelt there, in a cowslip forest, picking at the juicy stems. All the fragrance of the field blew down on him along a warm wind that floated past him to shake from larches and oaks and hedges of may-bloom a continuous belling fountain of cuckoo calls.

When he turned to look for Pacey she too was on her knees, dumpier, squattier than ever, filling her hands with golden sheaves of flower.

"Pacey, what will we do with them all?" he said. "What will we do with them all?"

"Mek wine," Pacey said. "And I wouldn't be surprised if it were a drop o' good."

Soon he was running to Pacey with his own sheaves of flower, putting them into the big brown basket. Whenever he ran he buried his face in the heads of flower that were so rich and fragrant and tender. Then as he dropped them into the basket he could not resist dipping his hands into the growing mound of cowslips. They felt like little limp kid gloves. There were so many soft green and yellow fingers.

"The basket'll soon be full, Pacey," he said. "What will we do when the basket's full?"

"Put 'em in we hats," Pacey said. "Hang 'em round we necks or summat."

"Like chains?"

"Chains if you like," Pacey said.

Soon the basket was almost full and Pacey kept saying it was bloomin' hot work and that she could do with a wet and a wind. From a pocket in her skirt she took out a medicine bottle of milk and two cheese cakes and presently he and Pacey were sitting down in the sea of cowslips, resting in the sun.

"The basket's nearly full," he said. "Shall we start making chains?"

"There'll be no peace until you do, I warrant."

"Shall we make one chain or two chains?"

"Two," Pacey said. "I'll mek a big 'un and you mek a little 'un."

As he sat there threading the cowslip stalks one into another, making his chain, he continually looked up at Pacey, peering in her funny way, through her thick jelly spectacles, at her own cowslip chain. He noticed that she held the flowers very close to her eyes, only an inch or two away.

"Pacey," he said, "what makes the sky blue?"

"You git on with your chain," Pacey said.

"Who put the sky there?"

"God did."

"How does it stay up there?"

Pacey made a noise like a cat spitting and put a cowslip stalk into her mouth and sucked it as if it were cotton and she were threading a needle.

"How the 'nation can I thread this 'ere chain," she said, "if you keep a-iffin' and a-whyin' all the time?"

Squinting, she peered even more closely at her cowslips, so that they were now almost at the end of her nose. Then he remembered that that was how she sang from her hymn-book on Sundays, in the front row of the choir. He remembered too how his mother always said that the ladies in the front row of the choir sat there only to show off their hats and so that men could look at them.

"Have you got a young man, Pacey?" he said.

"Oh! dozens," Pacey said. "Scores."

"Which one do you like best?"

"Oh! they're like plums on a tree," Pacey said. "So many I don't know which one on 'em to pick."

"Will you get married, Pacey?"

Pacey sucked a cowslip stalk and threaded it through another.

"Oh! they all want to marry me," Pacey said. "All on 'em."

"When will you?"

"This year, next year," Pacey said. "When I git enough plum-stones."

"Why do you have to have plum-stones?"

"Oh! jist hark at that cuckoo all the time," Pacey said. "Charming us to death a'ready. How's your chain?"

His chain was not so long as Pacey's. She worked neatly and fast, in spite of her thick stumpy fingers. Her chain was as long as a necklace already, with the cowslips ruffled close together, but his own was not much more than a loose golden bracelet.

"Thread twothri more on it," Pacey said, "and then we can git we hats filled and go home to dinner."

When he looked up again from threading his last two cowslip stalks he saw that Pacey had taken off her brown felt hat. Her uncovered hair was very dark and shining in the sun. At the back it was coiled up into a rich, thick roll, like a heavy sausage. There seemed almost too much hair for her stumpy body and he stared at it amazed.

"Is that all your hair, Pacey?" he said.

"Well, it's what they dished out to me. I ain't had another issue yit."

"How long is it?" he said. "It must be very long."

"Prit near down to me waist."

"Oh! Pacey," he said.

As he finished threading his cowslip chain and then joined the ends together he sat staring at Pacey, with her dark hair shining against the blue May sky and her own cowslip chain lying like a gold-green necklace in her lap.

"Does your hair ever come down?" he said, "or does it always stay up like that?"

"Oh! it comes down a time or two now and agin."

"Let it come down now."

"It's time to go home to dinner," Pacey said. "We got to git back—"

"Please, Pacey," he said. "Please."

"You take your hat and git it filled with cowslips and then we can go—"

"Please," he said. "Then I can put my chain on top of your head and it'll look like a crown."

"Oh! you'd wheedle a whelk out of its shell, you would," Pacey said. "You'd wheedle round 'Im up there!"

As she spoke she lifted her face to the blue noon sky so that her spectacles flashed strangely, full of revolving light. A moment later she started to unpin the sausage at the back of her head, putting the black hairpins one by one into her mouth. Then slowly, like an unrolling blind, the massive coil of her hair fell down across her neck and shoulders and back, until it reached her waist.

He had never seen hair so long, or so much of it, and he stared at it with wide eyes as it uncoiled itself, black and shining against the golden cowslip field.

"That's it," Pacey said, "have a good stare."

"Now I've got to put the crown on you," he said.

He knelt by Pacey's lap and reached up, putting his cowslip chain on the top of her head. All the time he did this Pacey sat very still, staring toward the sun.

"Now yours," he said.

He reached up, draping Pacey's own longer necklace across her hair and shoulders. The black hair made the cowslips shine more deeply golden than before and the flowers in turn brought out the lights in the hair.

Pacey sat so still and staring as he did all this that he could not tell what she was thinking and suddenly, without asking, he reached up and took off her spectacles.

A strange transformed woman he did not know, with groping blue eyes, a crown on her head and a necklace locking the dark mass of her hair, stared back at him.

"Well, now I suppose you're satisfied?"

"You look very nice, Pacey," he said. "You look lovely. I like you."

"Well, if you're satisfied let's git ready and start back," Pacey said, "or else I be blamed if we shan't miss we dinners."

Hastily, half-blindly, she started to grope with her hands towards her hair.

"And put my specs back on!" she said. "You took 'em off. Now put 'em back. How the 'nation do you think I can see 'ithout them?"

"It's not *'ithout*," he said. "It's *without*."

"Oh! *without* then! But put 'em back!"

By the time they began to walk back home his hat was full of cowslips. Pacey's brown felt hat was full too and the basket was brimming over with the flowers that were so like tender, kid-gloved fingers.

At the plank across the stream, as Pacey set down the basket and rested for a moment, he turned and looked back. Once again, as before, the cowslips seemed to stretch without break between himself and the bright noon sky.

"There's just as many as when we came," he said. "We didn't make any difference at all, Pacey. You'd think we'd never been, wouldn't you?"

Suddenly, with a cry, Pacey seized him and picked him up, swinging him joyfully round her body and finally holding him upside down.

"Up, round and down!" Pacey said. "Now what can you see?"

"London!"

Pacey laughed loudly, swinging him a second time and then setting him on his feet again.

When he tried to stand still again he found that the world too was swinging. The cowslip field was rolling like a golden sea in the sun and there was a great trembling about Pacey's hair, her necklace and her little crown of gold.

(1959)

DEATH AND THE CHERRY TREE

"You were dead the time before last," he said. "Why don't you stay dead?"

He aimed for the third time down the straight grey barrel of his ash-stick, fixing the black point of a bud like a sight on the face of the girl sitting among pale green masses of curving bracken frond. He had shot her, the first time, between the eyes. He knew that that had killed her. Now she had turned her face away. It was a rather pale delicate face, with short bobbed hair, almost white, airy and separated as thistledown, and he aimed at the shell of her ear.

The sound he made of a bullet going through woodland was something like the high thin note of a tuning fork. He made it with tight-pressed lips, as if he were blowing up a difficult balloon. After it he made noises of grating savagery in his throat. Then he closed one eye, opening it at last to the thinnest crack that revealed slowly the brown bright watchful seed of a pupil squinting down the ash-barrel to the bud, and then beyond the bud to the bullethole.

At this moment the little girl turned and looked him full in the face, slowly too, with eyes so transparent that they were almost colourless.

"Are you ready?" she said.

"You're dead," he said. "You've been dead three times already. You ought to lie down. You can't be dead so many times."

"I don't like being dead. I don't like being killed all the time."

"That's what we're playing," he said. "Being dead."

"You're not," she said.

"I'm playing ambushes," he said. "You're the one that's dead."

He looked at her for some moments longer with puzzled exasperation and then came out, shouldering his ash-stick, from where he had been lying behind a hawthorn bush. A hawthorn bush was the nearest thing he could find to an ambush, which he supposed was also something that grew.

"We can't kill each other now," he said. "We're not playing for a minute. We're having a truce."

He climbed the fence into the orchard. The fence was very rotten and in places no longer a boundary between woodland and the orchard of old, dying cherry trees, moss-grown and tilted, under which bracken was making its invasion in crooked fronds.

"Let's play houses," the girl said.

They had played houses the day before yesterday and she had liked it very much. The house was in the bracken and there was a kitchen where they ate their meals. The saucepans were old tins from the dump in the wood and in one saucepan they had cherries and in another bunches of elder-flower, which were really cauli-flower with cheese on top.

"We'll play wounded," he said. "I'll be wounded and you can bandage me."

"I like houses," the girl said.

"Wounding and killing's more fun," he said. "I'll be wounded."

"How will you be wounded?" she said. "Who's going to wound you? Am I?"

"No," he said. "I get wounded in the jungle, out there." He made brave off-hand gestures in the direction of the woodland. "I'll get wounded and crawl out and you hear me groaning."

He began to retreat in attitudes of stealth through the bracken, crawling under the lowest wire of rotting fence. He was an inch or two taller than the girl and his brown eyes, bright again after the cloud of exasperation, turned from beyond the fence and looked through the middle wires, fixing her with a sort of pained truculence.

"You have to play properly," he said.

She sat gazing at her bare feet with unsure, unwilling eyes. She had taken off her shoes because, in the ambush, she was supposed to be a native and natives, he said, never wore shoes.

"All right," she said.

"When you see me you shriek and start tearing up your petticoat."

"Do I shriek if I'm a nurse?" she said.

"You're not a nurse. There aren't any nurses out here. It's too wild. You're my wife," he said.

When he finally disappeared beyond the fence, into an under-
growth of hazel and elderberry and fern, the girl looked for some
moments in the direction of the sounds he made. The sudden dying
of dry squirrel-like rustlings among fallen leaves left the air filled
with the dead calm of summer, the stillness so deep that when
suddenly the wood was split with the shrieking squawk of a
blackbird she was terribly startled and sprang to her feet and began
screaming too.

"Oh! my dear, my dear, my dear," she said. She ran with her
small hands wringing themselves above the pale thistle-bob of her
hair, her voice wailing in a tiny rabbit-scream.

Almost immediately he emerged from the wood with downcast
arms, plunged into a desperate tiredness.

"They haven't started to shoot me yet," he said. "I haven't had
to fight yet."

"Did I start too soon?"

He fixed his eyes on her with slow, withering adultness.

"You don't see me until I come out of the wood," he said. "Then
you start screaming. Then you run and hold me up and all that."

"I'd rather play houses."

"I'm going home," he said.

He threw down his ash-stick and her eyes became immensely
round and wet, a painful blue under pale, damp, almost invisible
lashes.

"Don't go home yet," she said.

"You never play right," he said. "You always muck the whole
thing up."

"I didn't muck it up when we played houses," she said. "There
was a blackie and I thought it was you. I'll play right this time."

He made a slight upward gesture of his arms, suspending in mid-
expression what seemed to be a great patient and difficult sigh.

"All right, this once," he said. "You wait till I get to the fence,
then scream."

"Can I be in the house getting dinner?"

"All right, you be in the house getting dinner."

"What shall I get?" she said. "Steak and kidney and cauliflower
with cheese on top like we had?"

"No. Lamb!" he said. "Steak and kidney, steak and kidney, steak and kidney—all I get is steak and kidney. How do you expect a man to live and work on that? I want lamb today—lamb with red gravy."

"I'll make mint sauce too, shall I?" she said.

"Good-oh! Plenty of sauce and gravy," he said. "Well, I'll be going now—goodbye!"

"Goodbye, dear," she said.

In the house of bracken she cooked, on two bricks, a length of cherry-bough, making mint sauce of grass. From time to time she straightened the curtains at the windows of bracken and peered happily and delicately out, neat and efficient and no longer dreamy, to the world of woodland and summer and cherry trees.

The meal was almost cooked and she was waiting for the first groans of the wounded when she heard, from across the orchard, the laughing yell of another voice. Slowly she came out of the bracken house and saw, running down between the cherry trees, a girl in a red dress, with two red hair ribbons flying from dark brown plaited hair.

Excitedly the running girl began to wave her hands. The girl beside the small house of bracken did not answer. She watched in silence the running eager figure coming down through the cherry trees and then suddenly the air was nipped with the sound of shot, again like the ting! of a tuning fork. The running girl gave a strange high cry and lifted her hands and then fell, a second later, dead under the cherry tree.

Presently the boy came nonchalantly out of the wood, the ash-gun under his arm, his lips big, spitting at air.

Casually he turned the red dress over and looked briefly down at the stark-eyed face.

"She's dead all right," he said. "I got her."

And then:

"Janey, you're dead."

"How can she speak if she's dead?" the fair-haired child said. "The lamb and mint sauce is ready."

He ignored lamb and mint sauce and put the toe of one shoe under the waist of the girl in the red dress, gently kicking her.

"She can if I say so. Janey! you're dead. You can get up now."

When Janey got up, smiling, her brown hair, with its dark firm plaits, gave her an air of confidence and certainty. It did not seem possible, as with the fairer, smaller child, to see her suddenly and lightly blown away.

"That was the most wonderful fall down dead I ever saw," the boy said.

"Shall we have dinner now?" the fair child said. "Let's have dinner."

"Did I do it right?"

"It was marvellously marvellously marvellous," he said.

"What are we playing?"

"We're going to have lamb and mint sauce and red gravy," the small child began to say, but the boy said:

"Ambushes. That's the ambush over there."

"Can I play? Can I be ambushed?"

"I think the meal will get cold if we don't have it," the small child said. "You know how lamb gets cold."

"I'm in the ambush and you come along the road here. You can fire back if you like. I fire first because I'm behind the ambush. Then you fire back and we have a battle."

"Do I get killed?"

"You get killed in the end," he said, "and I get wounded."

"I'm going to tear up my petticoat," the small child said.

But the boy was already running for the wood, making renewed and now more ferocious noises of savagery in his throat and turning at the fence to say:

"It's a Sten-gun now. Not an ordinary gun. It fires all the time."

"I'm going to tear up my petticoat," the small girl said.

The dark girl gave a quick scarlet swing of her plaits. "They don't tear up petticoats now. It's old-fashioned. Sometimes they tear up sheets but not petticoats."

"Tom said petticoats."

"They don't tear up petticoats, do they, Tom?"

"No," he said. "That's daft."

"I'll be in the house," the small girl said. "I'll be keeping the lamb warm."

As she crouched down, hiding herself with quietness in the house of bracken, the red flash of dress and hair-bows ran up the slope of the orchard with a whine of jeep-sounds.

For a few moments afterwards the air was silent, only the breath

of summer making a slow stir in high boughs of oak and cherry.
The sky seemed to be filled with pale blue milk and among the
rising bracken the thistle-head of the girl, not ruffled, was shining
and white as silk in the sun.

Suddenly the jeep came down the slope and a second or two later
the Sten-gun was firing with bright stutters from behind the
hawthorn. The scarlet dress rolled in the road, over and over, and
then straightened on its face, muttering strenuous resistance, firing
back. Sometimes the girl yelled in her excitement and once the boy
shouted back:

"I give you one more chance. I'm giving you one more
chance and then I use tear-gas," and for a second she lifted her
head and before she could lower it again the Sten-gun beat her
to pieces.

She was still dead in the road, eyes flat to the sky, when the boy
came over and said:

"That was a trap, Janey. That's how I got you. When I said about
the tear-gas it was a trap."

"I know," she said.

"I'll see if I can trap you again," he said. "Some other way."

"What about dinner?" the small child said. "Let's have dinner."

"We don't want dinner," the dark girl said. "You're always
talking about dinner. Why don't you shut up about dinner? If you
don't want to play go home."

"I was here first," the small one said. "I was here before you."

"What difference does that make?" she said. "It doesn't make
any difference, does it, Tom?"

"No," he said.

"There you are—Tom says so."

"You don't even know how to fall down dead," Tom said.

This time, as the battle began, she did not go into the house of
bracken, with its cooling lamb and mint sauce of grass and the
cauliflower with cheese sauce on top that now looked, in its rusty
tin, like nothing so much as squashed sprays of elder-flower.

She did not look much at the battle either. She knew it was a very
good battle because the shots from the wood never stopped and
once there was a bang, preceded by a long whistle, that was a bomb.
At the end of it the girl with the scarlet dress was dead again and

she and Tom were lying together in the grass, rolling about, laughing excitedly.

"Come on. Again," Tom said. "I blew the jeep to bits. This time you're a convoy."

"No," she said. "This time I'll ambush you."

"No. I'm the ambush. I'm the man. I have to be the ambush."

"No," she said. "I want to be the ambush this time."

The boy seemed to hesitate. He seemed very slightly bewildered by the slow warm character of her smile.

"I'll let you kill me just the same," she said.

Her brown eyes held him for a moment fully and now the expression on her lips was only a half-smile.

"Good-oh!" he said. "Come on."

"Aren't we going to play houses? With dinner?" the fair child said.

"No. Not now. We don't want to," he said. "You go home."

She did not speak. Presently she walked away up the slope of orchard, under the cherry trees, in a series of stops and starts, like a piece of slow-blown thistle-down now and then gently stopped in its progress by blades of grass. At the top of the slope she paused to look back. Under the cherry tree, where the house was, the sound of battle was dying away and she saw the girl climbing out of the ambush through the wires of the fence to the road where the boy was standing with his arms held over his head, in surrender.

She stood staring at all this for some time longer. She had forgotten her shoes and now she dared not go back for them. Her eyes were big and colourless. One of her small stony lips was held tight above the other and it might have been that she wished, after all, that she too was dead.

(1959)

THE BUTTERFLY

Mr. Pascoe, laughing, made himself another piece of toast. It popped from the automatic toaster like a wingless dying bird shot by an invisible gun, laying itself on the appliqué tablecloth with the neatness of a brown plucked offering. Mr. Pascoe spread butter on it with pleasant smoothing strokes and said:

"Is there anything you want? Something you feel you'd like to have?"

Outside, in the garden, heat was already beginning to quiver beyond a low line of rambler roses, burning in tremulous waves that reminded the boy of the air that danced above the hot bellies of steam rollers on tarry streets in summertime. To his father the toaster was a plaything he used every breakfast time.

"No. I don't think so," he said.

"Now is the time to say if there is."

"I don't think so."

"What about a bow and arrow? You were keen on that last time."

"I don't think so." The boy saw the summer heat above the rambler roses crinkle as if from a fire. "I think it's going to be too hot—"

"Hot?" his father said. "I don't think you have the slightest idea what hot is."

Another piece of toast leapt like a dying bird from the toaster. Mr. Pascoe made an attempt to catch it, one-handed, with what was to have been amusing brilliance, but failed. He laughed, revealing brown crumbs of toast on his bluish lips. The toaster was very funny; he did not know quite why the toaster always made him laugh so much and yet failed to amuse the boy.

"We have a hundred and thirty degrees sometimes," he said. "You feel your eye-balls frizzle."

"You said you would bring me a butterfly," the boy said. "One of the big blue ones."

"I did?" Mr. Pascoe found it hard to remember when he had made promises about a butterfly. "I can't remember that."

"It was when you and Mother went to Kwala Pilah with Mr. Kitson—"

"Oh! that fellow."

He destroyed the second piece of toast with a snap of his fingers, breaking it into singed fragments which he began to pick up with the buttery end of his knife.

"Well, is there anything you want? Have you thought of anything?"

"Only the butterfly."

"No: I mean here. Before I go. There's only this morning. You could go into town with Miss Jackson. Or both of you could come with me."

As the boy stared at the hot rambler roses, thinking first of Miss Jackson, who had wet slobbery teeth like a dog, and then of his father and mother going with Mr. Kitson for the drive on which they had seen the butterflies, he could not understand why his father did not remember that trip. His mother remembered it perfectly.

"So large—as large as my hands." He recalled with acute vividness the fanning spread of his mother's delicate fingers as she vivaciously described for him the great width of the butterflies. "It was at the top of that hill. They came out of the tree ferns—because don't you remember John Kitson said he thought for a moment they were blue hibiscus?"

His mother's fingers were a lovely pale yellow, with grey-pink nails, but when he remembered her it was easy to think of them as a brilliant scorching blue, dancing and unfolding like wings.

That was two years ago, but he remembered it perfectly. "We should bring Peter one next time we come home," his mother said, and his father said: "Oh! you know how it is. Things get smashed up. You want the thing properly mounted—"

"Well, all right. We can get it properly mounted. There's no need to snap about it—"

"Oh! all right, we'll get it mounted then. There's a fellow in the Palmerston Road."

"You will love it," his mother said. "I shall never forget seeing them on that hill. Marvellous. Crowds of them flying off like petals. As blue as cornflowers."

"Switch off the toaster," his father said. "We don't want it any more."

He had an idea his father had bought the toaster to amuse him because his mother had not come back. He supposed that was why he laughed so much every time the toast jumped out. "We had one exactly like it in Singapore. They're American. I didn't think you could get them here."

Miss Jackson had a habit of snapping her wet teeth down over her bottom lip whenever he spoke of his mother. Miss Jackson didn't know why his mother hadn't come back; she had a good reason no doubt, a perfectly good reason; it was no use asking her. His father said: "You've got to remember the trip is very expensive for two people. We had an idea I could come this year and then your mother could come next. That will save you that big gap."

In winter, on the coldest, darkest days, he was obsessed with a feeling that summer would never come. His father and mother always came home in the summer so as to escape the worst of the equatorial weather. He had to wait a long time for the summer. His mother was beautifully thin and nervous and excitable and in summer she wore white silk dresses made by a Chinese dressmaker and the silk made her look more sheer, more exquisite and more lively than ever.

His mother liked joking too; but not in the way his father liked joking. He could not always laugh at the things his father thought were funny, but his mother was mischievous and her sort of laughter was catching.

He remembered running with her in the garden, in full summer, when the currant-trees were thick. His father began calling her and she said: "Hide, lie down. Let's hide so he can't find us any more," and he remembered how they lay behind the currant-trees, on hot earth, in secret, laughing all the time his father called. "He can't find us!—he'll never find us again!" she said and he hid his face in her cool silky dress and smelled her body and the scent of silk and strong currant leaves and hot earth. That was the funniest thing they had ever done together.

His father did not think it was funny. The boy remembered a

darkness in his face. "Oh! of course if you think it funny that's perfectly all right. That's all there is to it of course."

It was not exactly anger his father felt. The hairs of his face seemed to bristle pompously. That was funny too and after he had stalked into the house the boy and his mother began laughing again, pressing their faces into their hands. He thought his mother would never stop laughing, but at last she said:

"Now we've really got to stop. We must. Peter, we mustn't laugh at people." Bubbles of laughter kept bursting through her handkerchief as she dried her eyes. Tears of laughter made her eyes more lively and more beautiful. "Now we've really got to stop—Peter, we really must—Oh! good Lord, I'm going to start again—!"

He knew that day that he belonged to his mother. All his feelings for her were enshrined in the laughter, the smell of hot currant leaves and hot earth, the secretive feeling of the white silk dress.

When she went away again Miss Jackson took charge of him. He could not see that there was really any reason for the existence of Miss Jackson, but his father explained that:

"We must keep the house on. You must have somewhere you can think of as home."

In winter the currant-trees were bare, with big fat buds on them. Snow came and the feeling of summer became for ever destroyed. Miss Jackson hung pieces of bread and bacon-rind in apple-boughs above the lawn in frosty weather and blue-tits swung on the brown bristly skin and punctured the fat until it was knobbly like the paper he found in chocolate boxes. He watched the blue-tits and wondered if they were as blue as the butterflies of which his mother talked. He thought the butterflies must be even bigger, bluer and more wonderful. With her vivacious spreading hands his mother had made them seem like that.

"I am going to get a hair-cut," his father said. "You could come down in the car with me and then if there was anything you wanted—"

"Would you see if you can think of the butterfly next time?" the boy said. He knew that his mother would not fail to remember it and he said:

"Tie a piece of cotton round your finger. That's what Miss

Jackson does. Then you'll remember it was the time you and Mummy went on the drive with Mr. Kitson—"

"What makes you keep talking about Kitson?" his father said. "Who spoke to you about Kitson?"

"Mother did. She used to talk about him—"

"What sort of talk? In what way?"

"I can't remember," he said. "It was just—"

"Did she talk often? Can't you remember if she talked often?"

"No. Just sometimes. Only just laughing and talking sometimes."

His father's face was cloudy and stodgy. He searched it vainly for a break of light, a touch of the vivacity he found in his mother's, even a remnant of the breakfast humour about the toaster. All of his father seemed instead to recede, to stiffen and dry up. He got up from the table and said:

"Perhaps after all it would be better if you stayed in the garden. You could help Miss Jackson shell peas or something."

The boy stared from the window at the hot quivering rambler roses. His father seemed as if he suddenly saw in his face a reflection of his own stodgy gravity and he said:

"Now you're not going to mope, are you? Just because I spoke. You said you wouldn't do that."

"No." He knew his father was angry because he had spoken of Mr. Kitson.

"You're getting too big for that. You're nearly seven. And I've got something to tell you—" He paused and then manufactured, with a quick spurt of the lips, a sudden smile. "I've been saving this up for you."

"Yes?"

"On your birthday," Mr. Pascoe said, "I'm going to ring you up. I'm going to telephone all the way from the Straits and say Hullo and wish you many happy returns."

"I see."

"I had the idea on the plane. I thought how wonderful it would be."

"Shall I be able to talk to both of you?"

"It's nearly ten thousand miles," Mr. Pascoe said. "But if we're lucky you'll be able to hear me just as clear as now. Only when I'm speaking it won't be exactly the same time as it is with you."

"Why won't it?"

"It never is. It's to do with the earth going round."

"Shall I be able to talk to both of you?"

"You can talk as long as you like," Mr. Pascoe said. "Six minutes if you like. It's expensive but it doesn't matter."

"What about Mother? Will she be there—?"

"Yes, yes. I said so, didn't I? We'll arrange all that."

He tried to imagine the voice of his mother and father talking to him across the world. It seemed strange; it did not excite him very much; and he felt he would rather have had the butterfly. Since his mother had not come back there were times when his head seemed to grow large and hollow and droning with the sound of his own blood wandering through it; and soon it was his whole self, wandering about the world. His head and the world: droning and empty and hollow and echoing, and himself striding with rubbery steps across it, all alone, bouncing. It was the lightheadedness, Miss Jackson said. A powder would put that right. It was the dreams again, after too much supper. It was head under the clothes again. That was no good, this hot weather, that was a habit he must get out of.

"Well, I'll go now and have my wool shorn," his father said. "Are you sure there's nothing you want?"

"No, thank you."

"Now's the time to say. It'll be too late tomorrow."

"No, thank you."

After his father had gone he went into the garden and stood there alone, watching the quiver of heat above the rambler roses. The leaves on the apple trees were very thick, hiding the dirty pieces of string on which Miss Jackson hung ham-rind in the winter. He thought of the day when he and his mother had hidden behind the currant-trees and she had said "Let's hide so that he can't find us any more." His birthday was a long way away, in December. He tried to imagine what it would be like in winter, with the birds pecking at ham-rind on frosty boughs, with dark afternoons and windy rain and the voice of his mother coming to meet him across the world.

When his father came back from having the hair-cut he must remember to tell him about the string on his finger, so that he in turn would remember to tell his mother about the butterfly and the wonderful day with Mr. Kitson in the hills.

He remembered his mother's hands, fanning and excitable and wing-like, so that she too was like a butterfly. With the string on his finger his father would surely remember them too?

(1959)

WHERE THE CLOUD BREAKS

Colonel Gracie, who had decided to boil himself two new-laid eggs for lunch, came into the kitchen from the garden and laid his panama hat on top of the stove, put the eggs into it and then, after some moments of blissful concentration, looked inside to see if they were cooking.

Presently he sensed that something was vaguely wrong about all this and began to search for a saucepan. Having found it, a small blue enamel one much blackened by fire, he gazed at it with intent inquiry for some moments, half made a gesture as if to put it on his head and then decided to drop the eggs into it, without benefit of water. In the course of doing this he twice dipped the sleeve of his white duck jacket into a dish of raspberry jam, originally put out on the kitchen table for breakfast. The jam dish was in fact a candlestick, in pewter, the candle part of which had broken away.

Soon the Colonel, in the process of making himself some toast, found himself wondering what day it was. He couldn't be sure. He had recently given up taking *The Times* and it was this that made things difficult. He knew the month was July, although the calendar hanging by the side of the stove actually said it was September, but that of course didn't help much about the day. He guessed it might be Tuesday; but you never really knew when you lived alone. Still, it helped sometimes to know whether it was Tuesday or Sunday, just in case he ran short of tobacco and walked all the way to the village shop only to find it closed.

Was it Tuesday? The days were normally fixed quite clearly in his mind by a system of colouration. Tuesday was a most distinct shade of raspberry rose. Thursday was brown and Sunday a pleasant yellow, that particularly bright gold you got in sunflowers. Today seemed, he thought, rather a dark green, much more like a Wednesday. It was most important to differentiate, because if it

were really Wednesday it would be not the slightest use his walking
down to the shop to get stamps after lunch, since Wednesday was
early closing day.

There was nothing for it, he told himself, but to semaphore his
friend Miss Wilkinson. With a piece of toast in his hand he set
about finding his signalling flags, which he always kept in a
cupboard under the stairs. As he stooped to unlatch the cupboard
door a skein of onions left over from the previous winter dropped
from a fragile string on the wall and fell on his neck without
alarming him visibly.

One of the flags was bright yellow, the other an agreeable shade of
chicory blue. Experience had shown that these two colours showed
up far better than all others against the surrounding landscape of
lush chestnut copse and woodland. They were clearly visible for a
good half mile.

In the army, from which he was now long retired, signalling had
been the Colonel's special pigeon. He had helped to train a
considerable number of men with extreme proficiency. Miss
Wilkinson, who was sixty, wasn't of course quite so apt a pupil as a
soldier in his prime, but she had nevertheless been overjoyed to
learn what was not altogether a difficult art. It had been the greatest
fun for them both; it had whiled away an enormous number of
lonely hours.

For the past five weeks Miss Wilkinson had been away, staying on
the south coast with a sister, and the Colonel had missed her
greatly. Not only had there been no one to whom he could signal
his questions, doubts and thoughts; he had never really been quite
sure, all that time, what day it was.

After now having had the remarkable presence of mind to put an
inch or two of water into the egg saucepan the Colonel set out with
the flags to walk to the bottom of the garden, which sloped fairly
steeply to its southern boundary, a three foot hedge of hawthorn.
Along the hedge thirty or forty gigantic heads of sunflower were in
full flower, the huge faces staring like yellow guardians across the
three sloping open meadows that lay between the Colonel and Miss
Wilkinson, who lived in a small white weatherboard house down
on the edge of a narrow stream. Sometimes after torrential winter
rains the little stream rose with devastating rapidity, flooding Miss

Wilkinson, so that the Colonel had to be there at the double, to bale her out.

In the centre of the hedge was a stile and the Colonel, who in his crumpled suit of white duck looked something like a cadaverous baker out of work, now stood up on it and blew three sharp blasts on a whistle. This was the signal to fetch Miss Wilkinson from the kitchen, the greenhouse, the potting shed, or wherever she happened to be. The system of whistle and flag suited both the Colonel and Miss Wilkinson admirably, the Colonel because he hated the telephone so much and Miss Wilkinson because she couldn't afford to have the instrument installed. For the same reasons neither of them owned either television or radio, the Colonel having laid it down in expressly severe terms, almost as if in holy writ, that he would not only never have such antisocial devices in the house but that they were also, in a sense, degenerate: if not immoral.

Miss Wilkinson having appeared in her garden in a large pink sun hat and a loose summery blue dress with flowers all over it, the Colonel addressed her by smartly raising his yellow flag. Miss Wilkinson replied by promptly raising her blue one. This meant that they were receiving each other loud and clear.

The day in fact was so beautifully clear that the Colonel could actually not only see Miss Wilkinson in detail as she stood on the small wooden bridge that spanned the stream but he could also pick out slender spires of purple loosestrife among the many tall reeds that lined the banks like dark green swords. Both he and Miss Wilkinson, among their many other things in common, were crazy about flowers.

Having given himself another moment to get into correct position, the Colonel presently signalled to Miss Wilkinson that he was frightfully sorry to trouble her but would she very much mind telling him what day it was?

To his infinite astonishment Miss Wilkinson signalled back that it was Thursday and, as if determined to leave no doubt about it, added that it was also August the second.

August? the Colonel replied. He was much surprised. He thought it was July.

No, no, it was August, Miss Wilkinson told him. Thursday the second—the day he was coming to tea.

The Colonel had spent the morning since ten o'clock in a rush of perspiring industry, cleaning out the hens. The fact that he was going to tea with Miss Wilkinson had, like the precise date and month, somehow slipped his mind.

"You hadn't forgotten, had you?"

"Oh! no, no, I hadn't forgotten. Had an awfully long morning, that's all. Would you mind telling me what time it is now?"

In the clear summer air the Colonel could distinctly see the movement of Miss Wilkinson's arm as she raised it to look at her watch. He himself never wore a watch. Though altogether less pernicious than telephone, television and radio, a watch nevertheless belonged, in his estimation, to that category of inventions that one could well do without.

"Ten to four."

Good God, the Colonel thought, now struck by the sudden realisation that he hadn't had lunch yet.

"I was expecting you in about ten minutes. It's so lovely I thought we'd have tea outside. Under the willow tree."

Admirable idea, the Colonel thought, without signalling it. What, by the way, had he done with the eggs? Were they on the boil or not? He couldn't for the life of him remember.

"Do you wish any eggs?" he asked. "I have heaps."

"No, thank you all the same. I have some." It might have been a laugh or merely a bird-cry that the Colonel heard coming across the meadows. "Don't be too long. I have a surprise for you."

As he hurried back to the house the Colonel wondered, in a dreamy sort of way, what kind of surprise Miss Wilkinson could possibly have for him and as he wondered he felt a sort of whisper travel across his heart. It was the sort of tremor he often experienced when he was on the way to see her or when he looked at the nape of her neck or when she spoke to him in some specially direct or unexpected sort of way. He would like to have put this feeling into words of some kind—signalling was child's play by comparison—but he was both too inarticulate and too shy to do so.

Half an hour later, after walking down through the meadows, he fully expected to see Miss Wilkinson waiting for him on the bank of the stream under the willow-tree, where the tea-table, cool with lace cloth, was already laid. But there was no sign of her there or in the greenhouse, where cucumbers were growing on humid vines, or in the kitchen.

Then, to his great surprise, he heard her voice calling him from some distance off and a moment later he saw her twenty yards or so away, paddling in the stream.

"Just remembered I'd seen a bed of watercress yesterday and I thought how nice it would be. Beautifully cool, the water."

As he watched her approaching, legs bare and white above emerald skim of water-weed, the Colonel again experienced the tremor that circumvented his heart like a whisper. This time it was actually touched with pain and there was nothing he could say.

"Last year there was a bed much farther upstream. But I suppose the seeds get carried down."

Miss Wilkinson was fair and pink, almost cherubic, her voice jolly. A dew-lap rather like those seen in ageing dogs hung floppily down on the collar of her cream shantung dress, giving her a look of obese friendliness and charm.

"The kettle's on already," she said. "Sit yourself down while I go in and get my feet dried."

The Colonel, watching her white feet half-running, half-trotting across the lawn, thought again of the surprise she had in store for him and wondered if paddling in the stream was it. No other, he thought, could have had a sharper effect on him.

When she came back, carrying a silver hot water jug and tea-pot, she laughed quite gaily in reply to his query about the surprise. No: it wasn't paddling in the stream. And she was afraid he would have to wait until after tea before she could tell him, anyway.

"Oh! how stupid of me," she said, abruptly pausing in the act of pouring tea, "I've gone and forgotten the watercress."

"I'll get it, I'll get it," the Colonel said, at once leaping up to go into the house.

"Oh! no, you don't," she said. "Not on your life. My surprise is in there."

Later, drinking tea and munching brown bread and butter and cool sprigs of watercress dipped in salt, the Colonel found it impossible to dwell ˙on the question of the surprise without uneasiness. In an effort to take his mind off the subject he remarked

on how good the sunflowers were this year and what a fine crop of
seeds there would be. He fed them to the hens.

"I think it's the sunflowers that give the eggs that deep brown
colour," he said.

"You do?" she said. "By the way did you like the pie I made for
you?"

"Pie?"

With silent distress the Colonel recalled a pie of morello cherries,
baked and bestowed on him the day before yesterday. He had put it
into the larder and had forgotten that too.

"It was delicious. I'm saving half of it for supper."

Miss Wilkinson, looking at him rather as dogs sometimes look,
head sideways, with a meditative glint in her eye, asked suddenly
what he had had for lunch? Not eggs again?

"Eggs are so easy."

"I've told you before. You can't live on eggs all the time," she
said. "I've been making pork brawn this morning. Would you care
for some of that?"

"Yes, I would. Thank you. I would indeed."

From these trivial discussions on food it seemed to the Colonel
that a curious and elusive sense of intimacy sprang up. It was
difficult to define but it was almost as if either he or Miss
Wilkinson had proposed to each other and had been, in spirit at
least, accepted.

This made him so uneasy again that he suddenly said:

"By the way, I don't think I told you. I've given up *The Times*."

"Oh! really. Isn't that rather rash?"

"I don't think so. I'd been considering it for some time actually.
You see, one is so busy with the hens and the garden and all that
sort of thing that quite often one gets no time to read until ten
o'clock. Which is absurd. I thought that from time to time I might
perhaps borrow yours?"

"Of course."

The Colonel, thinking that perhaps he was talking too much, sat
silent. How pretty the stream looked, he thought. The purple
loosestrife had such dignity by the waterside. He must go fishing
again one day. The stream held a few trout and in the deeper pools
there were chub.

"Are you quite sure you won't feel lost without a paper? I think I should."

"No, no. I don't think so. One gets surfeited anyway with these wretched conferences and ministerial comings and goings and world tension and so on. One wants to be away from it all."

"One mustn't run away from life, nevertheless."

Life was what you made it, the Colonel pointed out. He preferred it as much as possible untrammelled.

Accepting Miss Wilkinson's offer of a third cup of tea and another plate of the delicious watercress he suddenly realised that he was ravenously hungry. There was a round plum cake on the table and his eye kept wandering back to it with the poignant voracity of a boy after a game of football. After a time Miss Wilkinson noticed this and started to cut the cake in readiness.

"I'm thinking of going fishing again very soon," the Colonel said. "If I bag a trout or two perhaps you might care to join me for supper?"

"I should absolutely love to."

It was remarks of such direct intimacy, delivered in a moist, jolly voice, that had the Colonel's heart in its curious whispering state again. In silence he comtemplated the almost too pleasant prospect of having Miss Wilkinson to supper. He would try his best to cook the trout nicely, in butter, and not burn them. Perhaps he would also be able to manage a glass of wine.

"I have a beautiful white delphinium in bloom," Miss Wilkinson said. "I want to show it you after tea."

"That isn't the surprise?"

Miss Wilkinson laughed with almost incautious jollity.

"You must forget all about the surprise. You're like a small boy who can't wait for Christmas."

The Colonel apologised for what seemed to be impatience and then followed this with a second apology, saying he was sorry he'd forgotten to ask Miss Wilkinson if she had enjoyed the long visit to her sister.

"Oh! splendidly. It really did me the world of good. One gets sort of ham-strung by one's habits, don't you think? It's good to get away."

To the Colonel her long absence had seemed exactly the opposite.

He would like to have told her how much he had missed her. Instead something made him say:

"I picked up a dead gold-finch in the garden this morning. It had fallen among the sea kale. Its yellow wing was open on one of the grey leaves and I thought it was a flower."

"The cat, I suppose?"

"No, no. There was no sign of violence at all."

Away downstream a dove cooed, breaking and yet deepening all the drowsiness of the summer afternoon. What did one want with world affairs, presidential speeches, threats of war and all those things? the Colonel wondered. What had newspapers ever given to the world that could be compared with that one sound, the solo voice of the dove by the waterside?

"No, no. No more tea, thank you. Perhaps another piece of cake, yes. That's excellent, thank you."

The last crumb of cake having been consumed, the Colonel followed Miss Wilkinson into the flower garden to look at the white delphinium. It's snowy grace filled him with an almost ethereal sense of calm. He couldn't have been, he thought, more happy.

"Very beautiful. Most beautiful."

"I'm going to divide it in the spring," Miss Wilkinson said, "and give you a piece."

After a single murmur of acceptance for this blessing the Colonel remained for some moments speechless, another tremor travelling round his heart, this time like the quivering of a tightened wire.

"Well now," Miss Wilkinson said, "I think I might let you see the surprise if you're ready."

He was not only ready but even eager, the Colonel thought.

"I'll lead the way," Miss Wilkinson said.

She led the way into the sitting room, which was beautifully cool and full of the scent of small red carnations. The Colonel, who was not even conscious of being a hopelessly untidy person himself, nevertheless was always struck by the pervading neatness, the laundered freshness, of all parts of Miss Wilkinson's house. It was like a little chintz holy-of-holies, always embalmed, always the same.

"Well, what do you say? There it is."

The Colonel, with customary blissful absent-mindedness, stared about the room without being able to note that anything had changed since his last visit there.

"I must say I don't really see anything in the nature of a surprise."

"Oh! you do. Don't be silly."

No, the Colonel had to confess, there was nothing he could see. It was all exactly as he had seen it the last time.

"Over there. In the corner. Of course it's rather a small one. Not as big as my sister's."

It slowly began to reach the blissfully preoccupied cloisters of the Colonel's mind that he was gazing at a television set. A cramping chill went round his heart. For a few unblissful moments he stared hard in front of him, tormented by a sense of being unfairly trapped, with nothing to say.

"My sister gave it to me. She's just bought herself a new one. You see you get so little allowed for an old one in part exchange that it's hardly worth—"

"You mean you've actually got it permanently?"

"Why, yes. Of course."

The Colonel found himself speaking with a voice so constricted that it seemed almost to be disembodied.

"But I always thought you hated those things."

"Well, I suppose there comes a day. I must say it was a bit of a revelation at my sister's. Some of the things one saw were absorbing. For instance there was a program about a remote Indian tribe in the forests of South America that I found quite marvellous." The Colonel was stiff, remote-eyed, as if not listening. "This tribe was in complete decay. It was actually dying out, corrupted—"

"Corrupted by what? By civilisation my guess would be."

"As a matter of fact they were. For one thing they die like flies from measles."

"Naturally. That," the Colonel said, "is what I am always trying to say."

"Yes, but there are other viewpoints. One comes to realise that."

"The parallel seems to me to be an exact one," the Colonel said.

"I'm afraid I can't agree."

There was now a certain chill, almost an iciness, in the air. The

ethereal calm of the afternoon, its emblem the white delphinium,
seemed splintered and blackened. The Colonel, though feeling that
Miss Wilkinson had acted in some way like a traitor, at the same
time had no way of saying so. It was all so callous, he thought, so
shockingly out of character. He managed to blurt out:

"I really didn't think you'd come down to this."

"I didn't come down to it, as you so candidly put it. It was simply
a gift from my sister. You talk about it as if I'd started taking some
sort of horrible drug."

"In a sense you have."

"I'm afraid I disagree again."

"All these things are drugs. Cinemas, radio, television, telephone,
even newspapers. That's really why I've given up *The Times*. I
thought we always agreed on that?"

"We may have done. At one time. Now we'll have to agree to
differ."

"Very well."

A hard lump rose in the Colonel's throat and stuck there. A
miserable sense of impotence seized him and kept him stiff, with
nothing more to say.

"I might have shown you a few minutes of it and converted you,"
Miss Wilkinson said. "But the aerial isn't up yet. It's coming this
evening."

"I don't think I want to be converted, thank you."

"I hoped you'd like it and perhaps come down in the evenings
sometimes and watch."

"Thank you, I shall be perfectly happy in my own way."

"Very well. I'm sorry you're so stubborn about it."

The Colonel was about to say with acidity that he was not
stubborn and then changed his mind and said curtly that he must
go. After a painful silence Miss Wilkinson said:

"Well, if you must I'll get the pork brawn."

"I don't think I care for the pork brawn, thank you."

"Just as you like."

At the door of the sitting room the Colonel paused, if anything
stiffer than ever, and remarked that if there was something he
particularly wanted he would signal her.

"I shan't be answering any signals," Miss Wilkinson said.

"You won't be answering any signals?"

An agony of disbelief went twisting through the Colonel, imposing on him a momentary paralysis. He could only stare.

"No: I shan't be answering any signals."

"Does that mean you won't be speaking to me again?"

"I didn't say that."

"I think it rather sounds like that."

"Then you must go on thinking it sounds like that, that's all."

It was exactly as if Miss Wilkinson had slapped him harshly in the face; it was precisely as if he had proposed and been rudely rejected.

"Good-bye," he said in a cold and impotent voice.

"Good-bye," she said. "I'll see you out."

"There's no need to see me out, thank you. I'll find my way alone."

Back in his own kitchen the Colonel discovered that the eggs had boiled black in the saucepan. He had forgotten to close the door of the stove. Brown smoke was hanging everywhere. Trying absentmindedly to clear up the mess he twice put his sleeve in the jam dish without noticing it and then wiped his sleeve across the tablecloth, uncleared since breakfast-time.

In the garden the dead gold-finch still lay on the silvery leaf of sea kale and he stood staring at it for a long time, stiff-eyed and impotent, unable to think one coherent simple thought.

Finally he went back to the house, took out the signalling flags and went over to the stile. Standing on it, he gave three difficult blasts on the whistle but nothing happened in answer except that one of two men standing on the roof of Miss Wilkinson's house, erecting the television aerial, casually turned his head.

Then he decided to send a signal. The three words he wanted so much to send were "Please forgive me" but after some moments of contemplation he found that he had neither the heart nor the will to raise a flag.

Instead he simply stood immovable by the stile, staring across the meadows in the evening sun. His eyes were blank. They seemed to be groping in immeasurable appeal for something and

as if in answer to it the long row of great yellow sunflower
faces, the seeds of which were so excellent for the hens, stared
back at him, in that wide, laughing, almost mocking way that
sunflowers have.

(1961)

MRS. EGLANTINE

Every morning Mrs. Eglantine sat at the round bamboo bar of the New Pacific Hotel and drank her breakfast. This consisted of two quick large brandies, followed by several slower ones. By noon breakfast had become lunch and by two o'clock the pouches under and above Mrs. Eglantine's bleared blue eyes began to look like large puffed pink prawns.

"I suppose you know you've got her name wrong?" my friend the doctor said to me. "It's really Eglinton. What makes you call her Eglantine?"

"She must have been rather sweet at some time."

"You think so?" he said. "What has Eglantine got to do with that?"

"The Sweet-briar," I said, "or the Vine, or the twisted Eglantine."

For a woman of nearly fifty Mrs. Eglantine wore her blue lined shorts very neatly. Her legs were brown, well-shaped and spare. Her arms were slim and hairless and her nails well-manicured. She had pretty delicate ears and very soft pale blue eyes. Her hair, though several shades too yellow, was smooth and always well-brushed, with a slight upward curl where it fell on her tanned slender shoulders.

Her only habit of untidiness was that sometimes, as she sat at the bar, she let one or both of her yellow sandals fall off. After that she often staggered about the verandah with one shoe on, and one in her hand; or with both shoes off, carrying them and saying:

"Whose bloody shoes are these? Anybody know whose bloody shoes these are?"

Soon, when she got to know me a little better, she would slap one of her sandals on the seat of the bar-stool next to her and say:

"Here, England, come and sit here." She always called me England. "Come and sit down and talk to me. I'm British too.

Come and sit down. Nice to meet someone from the old country in this lousy frog-crowd. What do you make of Tahiti?''

I had never time to tell her what I thought of Tahiti before, licking brandy from her lips, she would say something like:

"Swindle. The big myth. The great South-sea bubble. The great South-sea paradise. Not a decent hotel in the place. All the shops owned by Chinks. Everybody bone-lazy. Takes you all day to cash a cheque at the bank. Hot and dirty. Still, what else do you expect with the Froggies running the show?''

Presently, after another brandy or two, she would begin to call me dear.

"You've seen the travel posters, haven't you, dear? Those nice white sands and the Polynesian girls with naked bosoms climbing the palms? All a myth, dear. All a bloody swindle. All taken in the Cook Islands, hundreds of miles away.''

Talking of the swindle of white sands and Polynesian girls she would point with her well-kept hands to the shore:

"Look at the beach, dear. Just look at it. I ask you. Black sand, millions of sea-eggs, thousands of those liverish-looking sea-snakes. Coral island, my foot. I can bear most things, England, but not black sand. Not a beach that looks like a foundry yard.''

It was true that the beaches of Tahiti were black, that the sea, where shallow, was thick with sea-eggs and at low tide with creatures looking like inert lumps of yellow intestine. But there were also shoals of blue and yellow fish, like delicate underwater sails, with sometimes a flying fish or a crowd of exquisite blue torpedoes flashing in bluest water.

It occurred to me that something, perhaps, had made her ignore these things.

"How long have you been here now?'' I said.

"Ever been to Australia?'' she said. "That's the place for beaches. Miles of them. Endless. You've seen the Cook Islands? White as that. Me? Six months, dear. Nearly seven months now.''

"Why don't you take the sea-plane and get out,'' I said, "if you hate it so much?''

"Long story, England,'' she said. "Bloody complicated.''

Every afternoon she staggered away, slept in her room and re-appeared about six, in time for sunset. By that time she had changed her shorts for a dress, generally something very simple in cotton or silk that, from a distance or behind, with her brief lean figure, made her look attractive, fresh and quite young.

I noticed that, in the evening, she did not go at once to the bar. For perhaps ten minutes or a quarter of an hour she would stand in silence at the rail of the verandah, gazing at the sunset.

The sunsets across the lagoon at Tahiti, looking towards the great chimneys of Moorea, are the most beautiful in the world. As the sun dips across the Pacific the entire sky behind the mountains opens up like a blast furnace, flaming pure and violent fire. Over the upper sky roll clouds of scarlet petal, then orange, then yellow, then pink, and then swan-white as they sail away, high, and slowly, over the ocean to the north. In the last minutes before darkness there is left only a thunderous purple map of smouldering ash across the sky.

"It's so beautiful, England dear," she said to me. "God, it's so beautiful it takes your breath away. I always want to cry."

Once or twice she actually did cry but soon, when sunset was over and the enormous soft southern stars were breaking the deep black sky, she would be back to brandy and the bar. Once again her eyes would take on the appearance of swollen prawns. One by one her shoes would fall off, leaving her to grope barefooted, carrying her shoes about the verandah, not knowing whose they were.

"Sweet people," she said once. "Very sweet people, you and Mrs. England. Good old England. That's a sweet dress she has on. What would you say, Mrs. England, if you wanted to marry someone here and they wouldn't let you?"

She laughed. From much brandy her skin was hot and baggy. Her eyes, looking as if they were still in tears from the sunset, could no longer focus themselves.

"A Froggy too," she said, "which I call damn funny. Rather a nice Froggy too."

Her voice was thick and bitter.

Rather funny? she said. "I come all this way from Australia to meet him here and then find they've sent him to New Caledonia. Administrative post. Administrative trick, dear, see?"

I said something about how simple it was, nowadays, to fly from one side of the Pacific to the other, and she said:

"Can't get permission, dear. Got to get permission from the Froggies to go to Froggy territory," she went on. "Of course he'll come back here in time."

I said something about how simple it was to wait here, in Tahiti, where she was, and she said:

"Can't get permission, dear. Got to get permission from the Froggies to stay in Froggy territory. Froggy red tape, dear. Can't stay here, can't go there. Next week my permit expires."

I made some expression of sympathy about all this and she said:

"All a trick, dear. Complete wangle. His father's a friend of the governor. Father doesn't like me. Governor doesn't like me. Undesirable type, dear. Divorced and drink too much. Bad combination. British too. They don't want the British here. Leaves more Tahitian girls for the Froggies to set up fancy house with."

There were, as my friend the doctor said, only two general types in Tahiti: those who took one look at the island, wanted to depart next day and never set eyes on it again; and those who, from the first moment, wanted to stay there for ever. Now I had met a third.

"Going to make my last appeal for an extension of my permit tomorrow," Mrs. Eglantine said. "Suppose you wouldn't like to write it for me, would you, England dear? It'll need to be bloody well put, that's sure."

"Where will you go?" I said. "If you have to go?"

"Nearest British possession, dear. Cook Islands. Wait there."

The Cook Islands are very beautiful. Across a long, shallow, sharkless lagoon flying-boats glide down between soft fringes of palm and purest hot white coral sand. At the little rest-house, by the anchorage, the prettiest and friendliest of Polynesian girls serve tea and cakes, giggling constantly, shaking back their long loose black hair.

"Yes, it's very lovely," I said. "You couldn't have a better place to go than that. That's a paradise."

"And a dry one," she said, "in case you didn't know it. Worse than prohibition. They allow you a bottle of something stronger than lime-juice once a month, dear, and you even need a permit for that."

We left her under the moth-charged lights of the verandah groping for her shoes.

"*Dormez bien*, dears," she said. "Which is more than I shall do."

"She must have been very pretty once," my wife said.

"She's pretty now," I said, "sweet and rather pretty."

Five days later she flew out with us on the morning plane. Half way to the Cook Islands I brought her breakfast and she said, as she knocked it back, "Bless you, England dear."

In the lagoon, by the anchorage, a little crowd of Polynesians, mostly women and girls, sat under the shade of palm-trees, out of the pure blistering heat of white coral sand, singing songs of farewell to a young man leaving by the plane.

The songs of Polynesia have a great sadness in them that is very haunting. A few of the women were weeping. Then at the last moment a girl rushed on bare feet along the jetty towards the waiting launch, wringing her hands in sorrow, her long hair flying, bitterly weeping final words of good-bye.

On the scalding white coral beach, under the palms, Mrs. Eglantine was nowhere to be seen. And presently, as the launch moved away, I could no longer hear the songs of sad farewell or the haunting voice of the girl who was weeping. But only, running through my head, haunting too:

"The Sweet-briar, or the Vine, or the twisted Eglantine."

(1961)

THE CHORDS OF YOUTH

"I would absolutely stake my life," my Aunt Leonora said "that it's Otto. The same, same old Otto. Even after thirty years I'd know that marvellous forehead anywhere. That fine brow."

With a rising shrillness in her voice, never in any case an instrument much subdued, she brandished a copy of the *Flimshurst Courier & Gazette* in front of my face with all the excited ardour of a messenger arriving with news of some positive and splendid victory.

"Look at that face. Look at it. Wouldn't you know it anywhere?"

With what I hoped was pointed if casual gentleness I reminded my Aunt Leonora that I had never met Otto. I had never, until that moment, even heard of Otto. Otto, for all I knew or could guess, might never have existed. He was yet another of those figures out of the vast social mythology that, over the years, Aunt Leonora conjured up so smoothly and sweetly to amuse herself and deceive and infuriate the rest of us. Otto, without a doubt, belonged to those picnics she thought had been arranged but hadn't, those couples she thought were in love but weren't, to all those various misguided and tangled lives she thought ought to be re-moulded nearer to her particular heart's desire simply in order to give her the serene satisfaction of feeling that their new-shaped destinies were her own.

"We met," she suddenly said with that inconsequent entanglement of near-truth and near-falsehood, not quite downright lying, that formed the greater part of her charm, "in Switzerland. We climbed the Zugspitze together."

"The Zugspitze happens," I said, "to be in Germany."

"Well, wherever it was. I know it was somewhere near the frontier."

"The nearest frontier to the Zugspitze," I pointed out, "is Austria."

"Very well, Austria then. I know it was somewhere there. Why on earth do you always have to split hairs?"

I was about to point out, with all the blandness in the world, that there were times when some degree of accuracy helped, one way or another, when she smartly brandished the copy of *The Courier & Gazette* at me a second time. Didn't I agree that it was Otto? That it couldn't possibly be anyone else but Otto?

"You see," she said, now baring her long teeth in one of those maddeningly disarming smiles of hers, "it's so typical. I mean this twinning of towns idea. Adopting one another, one English and one German. He was all for that sort of thing, fraternity and so on. Aren't you? You've heard of it, haven't you?"

One moment she was flashing her golden spectacles at me in insistent demand for an answer; the next she was wheeling round with affectionate vehemence on my Uncle Freddie, who was sitting with sublime comfort in his easy chair, sopping a slice of buttered toast in his tea.

"I—" Freddie said, "What?—"

"That was Otto all over," she said. "That's how we all were at the Hirschen. The Gasthof. At six o'clock in the evening none of us knew each other—German, Swiss, English, Austrian, total strangers, the lot—by midnight we were all in love. Next day we were all haring up the Zugspitze."

A gift for exaggeration is not the least of my Aunt Leonora's charms. A sudden monstrous turn of phrase will serve to extinguish, as if by magic, all her tiresome, fibbing garrulity. In consequence, I loved the sentence "haring up the Zugspitze." It endeared her so much to you that you forgave her all tedium, all chatter. It even made me smile.

"I can't think what there is to smile at," she said, "and keep those eyes of yours to yourself. They're always wandering." She gave me one of those dark accusatory glares of hers, at the same time half-hinting that I was somehow corrupting Freddie. "It's no use looking at Freddie, either. He's all for it, too."

All for what I didn't know and had no time to ask before she went on, with an almost blithe shrillness of joy:

"That's the thing that makes me so sure it is Otto. It's so exactly like him. He'd have everybody blood-brothers in no time. I mean anybody, no matter. For instance this exchange of towns idea. The mayor of this in Germany and the mayor of that in England. Just like him. I think we really ought to try to love the Germans, don't you?"

"No."

"What do you mean?—no?"

"No."

In a withering second she turned cold on me; her spectacles were icy.

"No? I'm shocked. I thought you were so frightfully keen on that sort of thing?"

"What sort of thing?"

"International good-will and all that. International understanding. You're always on about it, anyway. It's one of your hobby-horses."

It was a typical, blatant, outrageous lie. I will admit, it is true, to a few hobby-horses, but international good-will is not one of them. I am, on the whole, less interested in that subject than in the love-making of snails. It was now my turn to be icy.

"And that, I suppose, is a picture of the great Otto you've got there?"

She snapped *The Courier & Gazette* at me with all the crackling vehemence of a pistol trigger being cocked.

"I don't know what's behind that word great," she said, "but there isn't a doubt that's him, being greeted by the Mayor of Flimshurst at the quayside."

"Not the mayor. The Chairman of the Urban District Council."

"Well, whatever he is. Anyway, I think he ought to be Mayor. It sounds so much more equal."

Eagerly but coldly watched by Aunt Leonora, I turned to the picture, on the front page of *The Courier & Gazette*, of Anglo-German friendship. The Chairman of the Urban District Council looked, except for a thick ecclesiastical bunch of white hair curling in his neck, remarkably like a well-gnawed bone. He also looked to me like the kind of man who smiles too easily. A glittering chain of office was looped about his neck.

In his left hand he was holding aloft the German flag; with his right he was shaking hands in smiling effusion with a bald-headed man whose face looked like a pot of lard that has boiled over and eventually congealed in white, flabby, unhealthy drifts and folds. He was waving the Union Jack. Enthusiastic and even strenuous though this gesture was, he somehow hardly looked to me like a man who had ever, even in youth, scaled high mountains. Nor could I detect in the heavy Teutonic furrows of his face any sign of that marvellous forehead, that fine brow.

"And what," I said, "did you say that Otto's other name was?"

"Oh! Heimberger. Hunnegar. Honnegger. Heimburg. Something like that."

"According to the paper here this is a Herr Otto Untermeyer."

"Oh! is it? Oh! yes, I suppose it could be. After all these years. Untermeyer—well, yes, it isn't all that—anyway, it does say Otto?"

"It does say Otto."

"Good, then it must be. It positively couldn't be anyone else."

Here I thought it pertinent to ask:

"Yes, but does it look anything like the man? Would you recognise him again, for instance?"

"I shall invite him to tea. No, lunch. That would give us more time." She actually laughed as she suddenly stopped talking of lunch and scaled the inconsequent steps of memory. "The thing I remember most is the wild flowers. Gentians and soldonellas and anemones—those lovely big greyish-yellow ones. And the butter-flies. And the vast amounts of sausage. *Wurst—Lieberwurst, Brat-wurst*—Oh! it became quite a joke, the *wurst*. Especially with Otto. Follow me, all, he would say—*Achtung!* all will now follow—*Achtung!*—I will go *wurst! Wurst*, you see?—first!"

I said I saw; Uncle Freddie, at the same moment, rather dismally started to sop the last piece of buttered toast in his tea.

Abruptly and unexpectedly, as she often did, Aunt Leonora became pensive. Behind the dancing golden spectacles, so icy a few minutes before, her eyes became dreamy, wide and globular. She might for a second or two have been living again some long-uncaptured moment of Teutonic romance, gentian-starred, listening to a thousand-belled peal of soldonellas between summer meadows and summer snow—or that, at least, is what I thought until with equal abruptness all her dreaminess evaporated and she said with that simplicity that both endeared and disarmed:

"I should like to show him something really English. A real English memory. Like the *wurst* is for me. As German as that is, only English. You know?"

I was about to say I didn't know and then to make some innocent suggestion about fish-and-chips when she suddenly gave a series of chirps, either of delight or revelation or both, and danced across the room to pick up the telephone directory.

"Oh! what is his name, that man, that Chairman of the Council fellow? I know it as well as my own. Doesn't he keep a shop or something?"

"Several. Among other things."

"Other things? What other things?"

"Anything that will earn a dishonest penny."

She glowered at me with extreme accusation.

"I always thought you judged people too hastily," she said. "There's good in everybody."

I said I didn't doubt it; you had to be good to go as far as her George Wilbram, Chairman of the Urban Council, had done.

"What was that? What did you say? Don't mumble so. I'm always telling you."

"You'll find him under Wilbram," I said. "Or Augustine Developments or Abbey Enterprises."

"What charming names. I think I'll try Augustine. Will you come to lunch too? I think you'd adore Otto. Something tells me you'd have a great deal in common."

While waiting for Mr. Wilbram's number to come through she several times urged me to put my thinking-cap on in the matter of German wines. We had to do our utmost to do Otto well on that score; we had to match the vintage to the guest.

"Rather *soignée*," she said. "You know what I mean? I don't know the German word. There must be one, mustn't there?"

I started to say that undoubtedly there must and turned in readiness to wink at Uncle Freddie, only to find that he had dropped off, head on chest, the last piece of buttered toast precariously poised in his fingers, like some half-smoked cigar.

"Oh! Mr. Wilbram? You won't know me, but—I saw all about that marvellous Anglo-German unity thing of yours. Yes. In the paper. Oh! yes, I'm a great friend of Otto. We once climbed together."

Ten minutes later, after a conversation as one-sided as the progress of a snow-fed torrent careering down one of the many valleys at the foot of the Zugspitze, Aunt Leonora at last drew breath, went in brief silence to the window and looked across, eastward and southward, to the modest summer hills that grace the skyline like folds of gentlest green cloth between her house and the sea.

In the sigh that she finally and suddenly gave there was, I thought, a depth not unmystical. It revealed too, like her words, how tender and endearing at heart she really was.

"If we can't show him gentians and anemones and soldonellas and all that we can at least show him the orchids. All those rare native ones of ours that grow up there—the Spider, the Butterfly, the Bee, the Soldier—you know—they're so English, aren't they? And to think that the Romans must have seen them too— marvellous thought!"

She actually gave a short, ecstatic clap of her hands. Much startled, Uncle Freddie woke with a jump. The remaining piece of buttered toast dropped into his tea-cup. With feverish haste he scrambled to his feet, knocking cup into saucer, looking rather like a pink, fat baby roused cruelly from milky slumber, and said:

"What was that? I thought you called me."

"The most marvellous thing has happened," she said. "A sort of Prodigal Son thing—in a way, sort of." She suddenly turned to me those inquisitive innocent spectacles of hers, as if seeking some confirmation of this preposterous parallel of hers. "Don't you think so? It *is* rather like that, don't you feel?—Otto coming back. Quite a miracle in a way. Don't you think so?"

"No."

"Oh?" For a single second she looked wildly hurt. Then she looked utterly stern. "And if it isn't a miracle what in your precious book is it then?"

Something prompted me to say "the trump of doom," but I remembered myself in time and said:

"Never mind about the miracles. What are you going to give them to eat? I'd like the wine and the food to marry as well as they can."

"Steak and kidney pudding," she said with such promptitude that

Uncle Freddie actually emerged into full consciousness, like a schoolboy bidden to a sudden banquet. "And Christmas pudding for afters. I always keep one or two back—one for Easter and one for emergencies."

Uncle Freddie actually gave something like a cheer. "The old Kate and Sidney!" he started to say when she abruptly interrupted him with renewed sternness, as if rebuking the man for interrupting holy ritual.

"That will do," she said and suddenly rose inconsequently away from both of us and such worldly matters as steak and kidney pudding by saying very softly, in a sentence now more mysterious than mystical: "I'd have you know the chords of youth are sometimes very slender," leaving us both abruptly chastened and without an answer.

It was only some long time later that it occurred to me that the word might well have been "tender."

*   *   *

For lunch on the following Friday I selected a white wine, a *Deidesheimer Hofstück '59*. That this was unlikely to marry very well with the steak and kidney pudding, or for that matter with the Christmas pudding either, was something that hardly seemed to matter. Nothing else would marry anyway. The choice was merely a gesture in the cause of Anglo-German unity. With the *Deidesheimer Hofstück '59* we made our bow, so to speak, to the Reich. With the two puddings we raised the English standard high.

For some time before lunch I had an uneasy feeling that Aunt Leonora might take the cause of friendship even further. For some reason or other I was over-possessed by the notion that the chords of youth might well prompt her to go, ridiculous though it may sound, all Bavarian, peasant costume and all. I need hardly have worried. She finally appeared in a mustard-and-pepper tweed costume, a shirt blouse and brown brogue shoes.

These, she said, were just the stuff for walking.

"Oh! Herr Untermeyer. Otto. It was weather just like this, wasn't it? You remember? A little mist first thing and then— *achtung*! the sun. *Wurst*!"

Herr Untermeyer looked much more than startled. I could have sworn that his transparent pork-like eyes, too small for the immense inflated paper-bag of his face, turned pink. He looked, gross and flabby in a grey summer suit cut to disguise the vast lines of his figure and now much-creased with travelling, very like a prisoner rudely captured on a foreign field, nervously wondering if his captors were about to treat him well or not.

"Wasn't this a piece of luck, Mr. Wilbram? It was just by chance that I saw it in the paper. What's the name of the town you're twinning with, or adopting, or whatever it is?"

"Traben. It's—"

"Oh! would that be near the Zugspitze? Have you been to that part, Mr. Wilbram? There's a marvellous blue lake there. All blue."

"No, I haven't," Mr. Wilbram said. "It's farther north—Traben, I mean."

"You've talked to Otto about how we met and climbed the Zugspitze and all that, I suppose? It's all of thirty years."

"Herr Untermeyer doesn't speak English very easily," Mr. Wilbram said. "He's all right if he takes it slowly."

"Really? It used to be so beautiful."

"Yes? I suppose you tend to forget it over the years."

Mr. Wilbram might, I thought, have been a medieval prelate. His lean countenance—face is too simple a word—exuded goodness as a ripe plum exudes juice, except that there was neither juice nor ripeness in Mr. Wilbram. The goodness of his eye was cold. His hair, white and slightly curled as fresh lamb's wool, as I had noted in the picture in the newspaper, had been allowed to grow rather long in his neck, where you felt it had been carefully tended with a comb of piety.

"Now what about a drink? You," she said to me, "organise the drinks with Freddie. A pink gin for me. And you, Mr. Wilbram, what for you?"

"For me, nothing. I rarely—"

"No? Not even for an occasion—a day like this?"

"For an occasion, sometimes. But midday, never."

"But Otto will. Herr Untermeyer? You'll have a little—*schniff*, you know? You remember *schniff*? You remember how we all used to have *schniffs*? I said in English we called it snifter and you said in

German it was *schnapps* and so in the end it got to *schniffs*. Eh? You
remember? That was a good example of Anglo-German unity all
right, Mr. Wilbram, wasn't it? *Schniffs?*"

"I suppose it was," Mr. Wilbram said.

"And that," she said, "in the early days of the Nasties too. I
always called them the Nasties. So much nearer the truth. Still,
we'll forget all that. Enough of that. This is *our* day, isn't it, Otto?
What about a *schniff* now?"

Herr Untermeyer, it seemed to me, didn't seem to think it was
their day. Nor, I thought, was he much inclined to *schniffs*.
Prisoner-like still, he stood painfully erect, as if under orders of
silence, awaiting the terms of his sentence.

"I know! I'll give him red-currant wine," she said. "After all it
was Germany I first drank it. And you, Mr. Wilbram, too? Yes? It's
my own—from a German recipe. *Guht*, yes? Red-current, Otto, you
understand? That will do you?"

"So," Herr Untermeyer said.

"Your pink gin," I said, "or would you rather have red-currant
now?"

"Oh! red-currant, I think, now, don't you? I think so. It's all the
better for the unity."

So we drank red-current for unity. Even Mr. Wilbram drank a
modest half-glass, sipping it with something between a touch of
disapprobation and an air of penance, rather as if it were communion wine. By contrast Herr Untermeyer seemed to approve
greatly. Uncle Freddie had somehow drawn him aside, towards the
window, through which and over ruby glasses they were contemplating the hills.

"Orchids," I heard Uncle Freddie say. "Very rare." Uncle Freddie
raised his glass, in what might have been a gesture of salutation.
"You know them? Orchids? They are disappearing fast."

"*So?* Disappearing?"

"My wife," Uncle Freddie said, making another gesture with his
glass towards the hills, "will show them to you. After lunch. Up
there. You like the wine?"

"Was good."

"I'm rather for it myself," Uncle Freddie said and reached out to
a side-table for the bottle. In re-filling Herr Untermeyer's glass and

his own he referred once or twice more to the orchids. It was a great shame. They were disappearing fast. A tragedy. Being stolen, he explained. It was the same in Germany, he supposed? Picnickers and motorists and all that?—"

"The rape of the countryside," Aunt Leonora said. "Oh! I'm sure it goes on everywhere. That at least we have in common."

"In common? Rape?" Herr Untermeyer stared at Aunt Leonora greatly mystified, eyes rapidly growing pinker. "So? This word I am not knowing. And orchids? *Was* is orchids?"

"They are referring," Mr. Wilbram said, "to a certain kind of flower. *Blümen*."

"Ah! *blümen. So?*"

"Some," Aunt Leonora said, "are shaped like soldiers. And some like spiders. And some like men."

"Soldiers?" Herr Untermeyer said. "*Blümen?* This I am not—"

"Soldiers," Aunt Leonora said. "What is the German for soldiers? *Wehrmacht?*"

"No, no, *Soldaten*," Mr. Wilbram said. "*Soldaten*."

"We have them shaped like butterflies too," Uncle Freddie said. "And bees. And there is one, the *Military*—"

"*Soldaten?* Ah! you are in military service?"

"Do I smell something boiling over?" I said.

Aunt Leonora promptly rushed to the kitchen, calling as she went, "Don't rush, don't rush. We'll be ten minutes yet. Give everybody another *schniff*, dear boy, will you? Don't let Otto get dry."

I immediately armed myself with a fresh bottle of red-currant.

"Another *schniff*, Herr Untermeyer?"

"*Danke. Schniff?* What is this word *schniff?*"

I was about to say that it was a word born out of international fraternity or something of that sort when Mr. Wilbram said:

"From here, Herr Untermeyer, we are actually looking straight across to where the Romans camped. Straight up there."

Herr Untermeyer, glass replenished, eyes pinker than ever, slowly followed the direction of Mr. Wilbram's pointing finger to the line of hills a mile or two away.

"Takes you back a bit, doesn't it?" Uncle Freddie said. "Always gives me a sense of history. To think the Romans—"

"Romans?" Herr Untermeyer said. His eyes were fixed on the hills in a kind of jellified mystification. "Romans?"

"Caesar's soldiers," Mr. Wilbram said. "*Soldaten—Romanisch—*"

"*Ja, ja!*" Herr Untermeyer said. "*So!* I understood." All mystification gone, all military secrets unravelled, Herr Untermeyer actually laughed, bellying guffaws, begging us please to excuse the badness of his understanding about the *blümen*. He had foolishly confused them with the military. *Blümen* were for gardens, *ja*?

"You do much climbing now?" Uncle Freddie said.

What answer Herr Untermeyer was about to give to this discomforting question I never knew. In that same moment Aunt Leonora came back from the kitchen, instantly seized Herr Untermeyer affectionately by the arm and led him to the window. For an awful moment or two I saw us being launched yet again on the tortuous seas of flora and fauna, of orchids and Romans, *blümen* and the military, when to my infinite surprise she looked Otto straight in the face and said:

"Let's have a good look at you. No. You really haven't changed. Not all that much. I'd have known you again—even without the photograph." In a gesture of affection quite touching in its disarming simplicity she held up her pink gin. "*Schniff*, eh, Otto? Cheers! *Wurst*! It's such a pleasure to have you here."

"Also for me it is a great pleasure. Also to be in England."

"Herr Untermeyer loves England," Mr. Wilbram said. "Except for the sausages, eh, Herr Untermeyer!" Mr. Wilbram gave a brief, harsh crackle of a laugh. "Not the sausages."

"Not the sausages?" Aunt Leonora said. "No? Not the *wurst*?"

"He thinks they are very bad," Mr. Wilbram said. "Very bad."

"Bad. Bad. Very bad," Otto said. "Most bad. Most."

"Good God, what's wrong with them?" Uncle Freddie said. "I get raring hungry at the thought of them. When can we eat, dear?"

"Bad, the sausage, very bad. The *wurst*, in England, very bad. They are not ripe."

"Ah, ah! We have had this before," Mr. Wilbram said. "By ripe— I should explain—he means they have no flavour."

"They have not the strong!" Herr Untermeyer said, suddenly making gestures of powerful vehemence with his clenched massive lardy fists, so that for a moment or two Aunt Leonora recoiled, positively alarmed. "They have not the force! You understood?"

"The melons," my Aunt Leonora suddenly said, in one of those typically inconsequent moments of hers that both charm and dismay, "weren't quite as ripe as I should have liked them—they're a little bit tricky as late as this in August. So we have to begin without them, I'm afraid." With those long, disengaging teeth of hers she flashed at each of us in turn, a separate disarming smile. "Aren't I lucky? Four men. Shall we go in before everything gets cold?"

"Praise the Lord and pass the ammunition!" Uncle Freddie said. "The good old Kate and Sidney."

There were always moments when Uncle Freddie, fired by an extra glass or two of something, particularly red-currant wine, was liable to become harmlessly jocular, but now I thought I detected in the cold goodness of Mr. Wilbram's eye an answering glint of disquiet, as if Freddie had been guilty of a spasm of blasphemy.

Undeterred, ripe-faced and famished, Freddie stood at the head of the lunch table, brandishing a knife and fork over the steak and kidney pudding like a priest preparing a sacrifice.

"Nothing like the good old Kate and Sidney!"

"Kate and Sidney?" Mr. Wilbram said, his cold good eyes fixed on the puffed white crust of the pudding, large as a football, his voice again frosty, as if once more a slight blasphemy had been committed.

"*Gate und—*"

Herr Untermeyer too looked confused, pink, questioning eyes on the pudding, from the crust of which Uncle Freddie now proceeded to cut a generous slice, so that steam rose forth.

"I never heard it called this before," Mr. Wilbram said, rather as if he had just heard that some alien clause had been introduced into the *Sermon on the Mount.* " 'Kate and Sidney'—?"

"It's a kind of joke," I said.

"Rhyming slang," Uncle Freddie said. "By God, the crust's beautiful. Apples and pears. Trouble and strife. Tit for tat. Plates, please, plates. Where are the plates?"

"Right in front of your eyes, dear."

"We have this special kind of slang," I started to explain to Herr Untermeyer, who looked increasingly bewildered, "Tit for tat: hat.

So you get titfer. It's a joke—a *scherz*," I said, this being the only German word I could think of that meant light. "A joke-*scherz*," I repeated several times. "You see?"

Herr Untermeyer, who had been standing at attention all this time, said he did not understood.

"Oh! do please sit down, everybody," Aunt Leonora said. "And stop prattling,"—this to me, quite sharply, as if I had been guilty of more or less continued flippancy. "The wine is far more important. Show Otto the wine."

"*Wasser, bitte*," Herr Untermeyer started to say and for one uneasy moment I thought that the carefully chosen *Deidesheimer Hofstück '59* might after all go unappreciated. "Pliss may I—"

"Oh! yes, I'm sorry," Mr. Wilbram said. "It's my fault. Herr Untermeyer has to have a glass of water. He has tablets to take."

"For the hard." Herr Untermeyer tapped his chest several times. "Also when the bad wind is blowing. From the East—"

"I'll go, I'll go," Aunt Leonora said and then as suddenly gave the water-fetching task to me. "You go. I must hand the vegetables. We have no help, Otto, you see."

When I got back to the lunch table again, a glass of water in one hand and a bottle of the *Deidesheimer Hofstück '59* in the other, Herr Untermeyer had a private array of bottles set out in front of him, one containing green pills, one pink and two white.

I set the glass of water in front of him and at the same time prepared to show him the *Deidesheimer Hofstück '59*. A rich and seductive odour of meat pudding filled the air. Assailed by this, by the sight of the wine-bottle and by the enforced necessity of pill-taking, Herr Untermeyer sat in further confusion, painfully beset by the opposing forces of denial and indulgence, his large frame breathing heavily.

"I hope you will like the wine, Herr Untermeyer," I said and to my relief he turned on the bottle with a gesture of hardly concealed joy, actually caressing it with his fat fingers. "Ah! is *gubt*. Is very nice. From my part of Germany. You understood?"

In the same moment Aunt Leonora set in front of him a plate generously heaped with pudding, mashed potatoes flecked with parsley butter, French beans and cauliflower, the whole caressed by the rich dark gravy of the Kate and Sidney.

As Herr Untermeyer gazed down on this with an almost tortured expression of pleasure and anticipation I heard Mr. Wilbram plead with Aunt Leonora in a whisper almost deathly:

"A mere half of that for me, Mrs. Elphinstone. A mere half. Less if possible. Even less. I am not a very great eater."

As Mr. Wilbram's frame bore a sharp resemblance to one of those pallid marble effigies, horizontally embalmed for ever in stony piety, that one sees in churches, it was impossible to imagine that he ever ate much at all, except perhaps toast and dry cornflakes.

"Would you please try the wine, Herr Untermeyer?" I said.

"You know you're not really supposed to, Otto," Mr. Wilbram said.

"Ah? You say?"

"*Verboten*, Otto," Mr. Wilbram said. "*Verboten*."

"*Mit* the pills, yes, yes. I can do. Is all right."

"No, no. *Verboten*. Remember now. You told me yourself. One glass and then *verboten*."

"No, no! *Mit* the pills," Herr Untermeyer said, "is *gubt*. Is all right."

Mr. Wilbram shook his head with a gesture of sad goodness, gloomily exhorting Herr Untermeyer to remember that after all it was he, not Mr. Wilbram, who would suffer.

In answer Herr Untermeyer suddenly tasted the wine with a positive gasp of pleasure.

"*Wunderbar!*"

"Well, well, have it your way," Mr. Wilbram said. The tone of his voice was that of one icily delivering judgment.

"Don't say I didn't warn you. You remember the attack in Traben last year?"

"That," Herr Untermeyer said, "was not the same. Was different on that occasion. Was then the *lieber*. Now, *mit* the pills, the *lieber* is *gubt*. The *wein* I can in little bits take now."

"All right, all right. It's on your head," Mr. Wilbram said. "It's on your head."

"Oh! come, a little wine after all," Aunt Leonora said, "for thy stomach's sake. It maketh glad the heart of man, surely. And anyway this is something of an occasion. Nothing like wine for warming up the international fellowship, is there? We saw that at the Hirschen, didn't we, Otto?''

"I'll bet it wasn't backward in flowing forward at Traben last year either," Uncle Freddie said. "By God, the Kate and Sidney's good. Sorry if I've started."

"Oh! yes, do start, Otto," Aunt Leonora said. "Please don't let it get cold."

Herr Untermeyer at once struck into the steak and kidney pudding with the enthusiasm of a man long deprived of nourishment. The pills stood before him forgotten. The gross nature of his pleasure was now and then reflected in monosyllables richly content and sometimes, unlike the English sausage, ripe. "*Schön!*" was one of these and "*Budding*" another.

"How you call this *budding* again? A *joke*?" Herr Untermeyer turned on from the depths of his stomach a positive diapason of voluptuous approval and pleasure. "This is not *joke*. This is *himmel*! *Was* is this flesh?" he said, holding up a succulent square of steak speared at the end of his fork. "How is this called?"

"Not flesh," Mr. Wilbram said. "Meat. Steak."

"To rhyme with Kate," Uncle Freddie said.

"How is this. Ah! this you call it? Kate? How you say like that? Kate?"

"No, steak," Mr. Wilbram said. "Steak. Kate is a figure of speech. So to speak."

"So? *Kate budding*, so? This I love. This is *himmel*, Frau Elphinstein, *himmel*. My bestest congratulations on your kitchen. *Danke*. I give you *Schniff*!"

"*Schniff*!" Aunt Leonora said. "*Schniff*! Oh! how that word takes me back."

"The chords of youth," I said and raised my glass of *Deidesheimer Hofstück '59*.

"What was that?" she said sharply. "I've told you before. Don't mumble so."

"I was simply praising the pudding."

"Oh! were you? All I can say is it sounded a funny sort of praise."

In my own praise was odd and whispered, that of Herr Untermeyer continued to be splendidly articulate. Between gargantuan mouthfuls of meat and vegetable and crust he hardly paused for breath. Nor, for a man who wasn't a very great eater, did Mr. Wilbram, I thought, appear to be doing badly either. Spots of gravy actually dribbled down the front of his shirt as he pushed his loaded fork into his mouth. Only now and then, as if some force in him slightly disapproved of the enjoyments of the flesh, did he suddenly desist, glance genially at Aunt Leonora as if in fear that his plate might be empty before that of Otto, and then forge on again.

He need have had no qualms about the plates; Otto's was white and clean while Mr. Wilbram was still mopping up the last forkfuls of kidney and potato.

"Now, now, come along, everybody. I want none of it left. More for you, Otto? Yes!"

"*Schön! Schön! Schön* beyond speak. No? That is not right? What is right then? Unspeak?—unspeakable?"

Uncle Freddie and I laughed aloud and Aunt Leonora, beaming with those long, impossible white teeth of hers, said:

"Oh! you're quite a dear, Otto. You're really a great dear. You don't change a scrap. Give Otto more wine. And I won't say 'No' either."

"Better open another bottle, dear boy," Uncle Freddie said. "That's if there *is* a second?"

"And a third," I said.

"Good show. There's a certain something about this German wine."

"Oh! we drank oceans of it at the Hirschen, didn't we, Otto? Positive oceans."

"*Wein* we may have in Germany. *Guht wein*. Much *wein*. But not this *budding*. No."

Soon, I noticed, even Mr. Wilbram was enjoying that certain something in the German wine. Its influence rose about the lunch table like a breath of flowers. We *schniffed* exhaustively. Aunt Leonora *schniffed* to the *Zugspitze* and Herr Untermeyer, actually standing up, glass upraised, *schniffed* to England, and to my great surprise, "the gliffs of Dover." This gliffs of Dover had, it seemed, moved him immeasurably.

"From the sea, from the ship, I am seeing this gliffs. So white. They are so *schön* and white and I am weeping."

"May I in return," Mr. Wilbram said, "pledge our faith in Germany? Perhaps I ought to say the new Germany?"

"I think you'd better," Aunt Leonora said, in one of those charmingly swift diplomatic thrusts of hers that are always over before you can do anything about them. "To hell with the old. I mean the Nasties. You know what I mean."

"That," Mr. Wilbram said, "is what we are all trying to forget."

"You may be," she said, "but not me."

On this very slightly discordant note she got up from the table and started to clear the dishes, urging us all at the same time to stay where we were, and then presently went off to the kitchen, whispering as she passed me:

"Brandy or rum, do you think?"

"Rum," I said. "It burns better."

As we waited for her return I drained the second bottle of *Deidesheimer Hofstück '59*. This led Uncle Freddie to praise it, not for the first time, as a wine that one could drink a good deal of and not feel the difference.

Herr Untermeyer strongly agreed. "That is so. You are not feeling it. Not in the head. Not in the legs. Only in the hard. How do you say this?—this *wein* is like—how are you saying?—a *lieder?*—"

"A song."

"A song, *jawohl*. That is so. A song. A song for the hard."

"Brings back the good old days, I'll bet," Uncle Freddie said. "Slopes of the Zugspitze and all that. I often wonder what you got up to on that mountain."

"International fellowship," I said.

Any glint of remonstrance in Mr. Wilbram's eye was promptly extinguished by the entrance of Aunt Leonora, bringing the Christmas pudding, bearing it aloft like some blue-famed dark head on a charger.

"My God, she's well alight," Uncle Freddie said.

"It's the rum," I said. "Far better than brandy."

"Let's have a drop more on, dear boy," Freddie said. "Don't let her die down. Splendid show."

As Aunt Leonora finally bore the flaming pudding to the table Uncle Freddie and I raised an appropriate cheer. Herr Untermeyer, pink eyes transfixed by this newly offered sacrifice, actually clapped his fat hands, delighted as a child at the rum-fed flames.

"Looks marvellous," Uncle Freddie said.

"I only hope it will be good," Aunt Leonora said. "I always think they taste better for keeping. Don't you think so, Mr. Wilbram? Does your wife keep yours?"

Mr. Wilbram said he rather thought not. They were rarely at home for Christmas. He suddenly ran his finger round his shirt collar, looking flushed and discomforted. Wasn't it rather warm, didn't we think? Would anyone mind if we opened a window?

It was rather warm, Aunt Leonora suddenly confessed, and while Uncle Freddie was feeding the expiring flames on the pudding with more rum I went to the window and opened it, surprised to see how the day had flowered from an early morning fogginess, clothed in softest white cloud, to a blazing afternoon. The hills shone golden with a purity of light that only the marriage of sea and late summer could give.

"Perfect afternoon," I said. "Splendid for walking."

Uncle Freddie gave me a sharpish sort of look, which I ignored, and Aunt Leonora said while I was up would I hand her the cream? As I picked up the cream-boat from the sideboard I heard Mr. Wilbram say:

"I don't want to put a damper on things, Mrs. Elphinstone, but I feel I ought to say that Herr Untermeyer has an engagement at five. He's christening a bus."

"Good God, man," she said, "since when have buses had to be christened?"

"It's a joint Anglo-German effort," Mr. Wilbram said. "The two towns have shared the cost, Traben and ours. It's for the old people. Excursions and so on. It's going to be called *The Lorelei*. It's Herr Untermeyer's idea."

"The chords of youth again," I said.

"What did you say?" Mr. Wilbram said, "I didn't quite catch that."

"Oh! take no notice," Aunt Leonora said. "In any case there's plenty of time for the bus. It isn't two o'clock yet. You'll want to walk your lunch down, won't you?"

Mr. Wilbram, I thought, didn't look at all as if he wanted to walk his lunch down.

"Ah! the fire is now out," Herr Untermeyer said, rubbing his hands.

"Drop more rum do you think?" Uncle Freddie said and was about to feed the dying flames a second time when Aunt Leonora waved him aside and started to cut generous wedges of Christmas pudding, at the same time saying to Herr Untermeyer:

"Now, Otto, you'll taste this? Something very specially English. They don't even have it in Scotland." What this had to do with it I simply couldn't think. "I'm sorry there aren't any good-luck charms. But then we're grown-up, aren't we?"

"This also is a *budding*?"

"Yes, but for Christmas."

"Ah! so? But Christmas it is not now. It is now summer."

"Yes, but we saved it from last year."

The expression on Herr Untermeyer's face clouded from mere bewilderment to fogged mystification. The Christmas pudding steamed with richness. Aunt Leonora drowned a mountainous wedge of it in cream, Uncle Freddie topped up the wine glasses and Mr. Wilbram further complicated things by saying:

"I suppose it's something left over from pre-Christian times. I mean the dried fruit and all that. The feast of the Winter Solstice and so on. Very little for me, Mrs. Elphinstone, please, very little. I've really had an excellent sufficiency."

"I admit it does blow you up a bit," Uncle Freddie said.

"Winter?" Herr Untermeyer said. "Winter? Why you now say winter?"

"Oh! you'll soon walk that off," Aunt Leonora said and carved Mr. Wilbram a slice of pudding, darkly rich and steaming, as generous as Otto's, topping it with cream. "Anyway you can always run down the hills. If not up them."

With dismay Mr. Wilbram picked up his fork and started to toy with the pudding. His normally pallid effigy of a face had already turned a rich, sweaty rose. At the same time it was restless, I thought, even melancholy.

By contrast Herr Untermeyer sucked at his lumps of pudding as eagerly as a baby sucks at a dummy-teat. Cream ran down his chin. Currants slipped from his spoon. His tongue, like that of an eager dog, leapt out and licked up morsels and dribbles with the deftness of a conjuror, with no pause for either word or breath.

Once Aunt Leonora remarked that it was a treat to see people eat.

The pudding, I had to admit, was a poem, if rather a stolid one, and presently I began to feel my own face expanding, over-fed with rum, fruit, and cream, into a flushed, almost feverish bag, my eyes moist and somnolent.

With much scraping and sucking, Herr Untermeyer left his platter clean-licked would almost have been the appropriate word—and then, glass suddenly high, *schniffed* the *budding*, red lips spluttering a sentence half-English, half-German, in which I several times caught, I thought, the word "engels."

Aunt Leonora instantly demanded to know what all this meant and I, not really having more than the faintest idea myself, as instantly translated it as:

"Otto says the pudding could only have been made by the hands of angels."

It might have been a trick I'd learned from her. It might have been one of her own inspired half-truths. At any rate with a cry of joy she jumped up from the table, waltzed round it to Otto and excitedly kissed him, continental fashion, on both cheeks. Then, before he had time to recover from this affectionate onslaught, she kissed him with what I thought was astonishingly vigorous ardour on the lips, saying:

"And that one's for the Zugspitze. For luck. For old times. Who says there's any lack of Anglo-German unity?"

My swift examination of Mr. Wilbram's face found it far gone beyond melancholy. It was sunk in reproving gloom. At the same time his eye was arid. There were clearly excessive heights of passion towards which even Christmas pudding could not be permitted to reach. There were limits even to Anglo-German fellowship.

It wasn't surprising that, after all this, Otto took a second helping of pudding or that Aunt Leonora cut it even larger than the first. While he attacked it with that unremitting vigour Aunt Leonora found such a delight Uncle Freddie topped up the wine glasses, Otto at once seizing his and holding it aloft to *schniff* us all in general and the pudding again in particular, saying that he could only wish it was always Christmas in summer-time.

"In Germany we have never this. Never this festival in *sommer*."

"Oh! who says anything about angels?" Aunt Leonora said.

"You're the angel if ever there was one. Oh! Otto, you haven't changed a bit. *Spoem*, remember?"

This new and sweeping word, this new marriage of German and English, suddenly fell on us, I thought, like an entrancing rocket.

"You remember *spoem*, surely, Otto?"

"*Bitte?*"

"It was the second night at the Hirschen. We'd all been drinking that wild raspberry drink. Not *framboise*, that's French. *Himbeer* or something like that, isn't it? We'd been drinking it for hours. Perhaps I was a little far gone, I don't know, but suddenly I turned to you and said 'S'lovely, isn't it? S'poem, isn't it?' *Spoem*—it became one of those words—*spoem*, like *schniff*, you know? *Spoem*—you surely remember?"

"*Bitte? Ah, so, so.*"

"Anyway," she said, with one of those entrancing and wholly unexpected turns of mind that sometimes makes her, in fact, a sort of *spoem* herself, "who's for cheese?"

Uncle Freddie, Mr. Wilbram and I were, reluctantly, not for cheese, but Otto was.

"Ah! the Stilton," Aunt Leonora said. "At the last moment I remembered it. There must be one more very, very English thing, I thought, and Stilton was it."

While Aunt Leonora danced to the kitchen to fetch the Stilton Uncle Freddie went to the sideboard and came back with a decanter.

"Well, if Stilton must be eaten," he said, "then port must be drunk. Agree, dear boy?"

I said I very much agreed and in the same moment saw Mr. Wilbram take a quick, cold look at his watch. Then as Freddie started to find glasses for the port Mr. Wilbram whispered something into Herr Untermeyer's ear and Herr Untermeyer looked at his watch too.

"*Ah! so.* Fine, fine. Is plenty."

"Ah! port!" Aunt Leonora came back into the room bearing dishes of butter and biscuits and a half Stilton. "Splendid idea. Have we time?" She looked at her watch too. "Oh! oceans, oceans. That little orchid trip won't take us the whisk of a donkey's tail."

Here I thought it prudent to remind her that the orchids were not only rare but widely scattered, that their habitat was as jealously guarded as a state secret and that, in any case, the flowering season of many of them was already over; to which she replied, characteristically:

"Well, we don't expect to see all Rome in a day, do we? Of course we shan't see them all. That isn't the point. It's the feeling that they *might* be there."

Herr Untermeyer attacked the Stilton. With an ardour undiminished he married it with the port. It was all, like the Kate and Sidney, the Christmas pudding and the *Deidesheimer Hofstück '59, schön*, the work of angels. Every moment he looked more richly, expansively content.

"A little more Stilton, Otto? Another drop of port? A *soupçon— kleine?*—"

Mr. Wilbram, by this time, had grown visibly impatient. He didn't want to interrupt things, he said, coldly, but he felt he had to remind Mrs. Elphinstone about the bus. The bus had to be christened. At five o'clock prompt. And afterwards representatives of the two towns had to take a ride in it and this too couldn't be delayed. Was this—this other—so important?

"Of course, it's important." She gave him one of those characteristically dark, accusatory glares of hers that had him silenced completely. "It's important to show him our heritage and all that, isn't it? That's what he's here for, isn't he?"

It is always hard to reply to these caustic darts of Aunt Leonora's; they disarm the best of men; and Mr. Wilbram remained miserably, but I thought wisely, silent.

"After all it is the little things that count. It's neglecting them that leads to wars." After this astonishing statement of untruth she declared, rather sharply, that she would get the coffee. "It's only a matter of a mile, anyway. Goodness gracious, it isn't a route march, is it? The walk will do us all the world of good."

Our hills are not high; their grassy slopes, rich with cowslips in spring and light drifts of harebells in summer, have nothing in common with the slopes of the Zugspitze; but they rise with sudden abruptness, hard, dry bosoms of grass that present, to those who have just lunched well on two sorts of pudding, two of wine, Stilton cheese and coffee, obstacles as formidable as those in a steeplechase.

"We might possibly see the Spider," Aunt Leonora said. We were all struggling up the steep rough hillside, she and Otto ahead together, I next, Mr. Wilbram last, in single file, in the heat of afternoon. "And the Bee. But not of course anything so rare as the Military. That's only known to a dozen or more choice spirits."

I always admired certain phrases of Aunt Leonora's and "choice spirits," I thought, was good.

"We are not seeing this military?" Herr Untermeyer stopped suddenly to say. "This camp?"

"No, no, Otto. You don't quite understand. The Military is not a camp. It's a flower."

"Not a camp? But this Romans?—"

"That," she said, "is quite a different matter."

"So?"

"Left fork here!"

At the command Herr Untermeyer turned, stomping behind Aunt Leonora up an even steeper path. Before I joined them something made me stop and look back. Twenty yards behind me, bent at the knees, head well down, Mr. Wilbram had stopped for breath.

"Everything all right?" I called. "Shall I wait for you?"

There was no sound in answer; Mr. Wilbram merely waved one hand, flat, like a man counting a boxer out.

A minute or two later, as I climbed the path, I saw that Aunt Leonora and Herr Untermeyer had also paused. They seemed, I thought, to be having something of an argument. It became evident, presently, that Herr Untermeyer wasn't happy about the military. I heard him declare, rather aggressively, that he was confused, that he did not understood.

It was very hot and a slight breeze blowing from the sea only seemed to make the air more burning. But with a coolness I thought remarkable Aunt Leonora started to explain, clearly not for the first time, that the military on the one hand wasn't quite the same as the military on the other. To make it worse she explained that in any case we wouldn't see either.

"So? But Herr Wilbram is spoking of a camp."

"I know Mr. Wilbram spoke of a camp. But there is nothing to be seen. It has all disappeared. You can only stand on the spot and say 'It was here.' Or rather probably."

"Ah! it is here?"

"No, no, it isn't here. It was probably a mile or two over there. There were probably two camps anyway."

"Ah! two camps? This is why you are spoking of the military twice?"

In answer Aunt Leonora developed a sudden sharp concern for Mr. Wilbram. Where was the man? She turned and looked back to where Mr. Wilbram, practically on all fours now, seemed to be fumbling for the right fork in the path. Good God, she said, speaking as if the man were slacking, did he expect them to stand around and wait? They hadn't got all day.

Here I suggested that Mr. Wilbram might perhaps be feeling the effects of lunch, particularly the puddings. Herr Untermeyer at once struck his chest a resounding blow.

"No, no, that can't be so. You are not feeling this *buddings*. Not here." He struck his chest again. "With the bestest cooking you are not feeling it. In one half hour it is not felt."

With these praises falling enthusiastically on her ears Aunt Leonora positively purred.

"Shall we press on to the top then? Best foot forward. *Achtung!*"

Promptly Herr Untermeyer stomped ahead, now as it were in command, the *fuehrer* leading us. I felt warm sweat dribble down my hair into my neck and I turned to take yet another look at Mr. Wilbram. His position on all fours seemed, I thought, to have become infinitely more acute, as if he had in fact resigned himself to the idea of crawling the rest of the way to the top.

"I think perhaps I ought to wait for Mr. Wilbram," I called.

"Oh! do no such thing. He'll catch up. He isn't tied to his mother's apron strings, is he? Press on!"

"Right," I said. I started to press on. "Excelsior!"

Herr Untermeyer, in spite of years, fat, puddings and port, pressed on too, climbing at a punishing pace. Even Aunt Leonora, inspired no doubt by memories of other, more youthful ascents, could hardly keep up. Nor in fact could I.

Far down the hillside Mr. Wilbram crawled like a tortoise in pain.

I paused once, looking back, to offer succour, but Mr. Wilbram seemed merely to be sunk in an attitude of prayer.

By the time I reached the crest of the hillside Herr Untermeyer and Aunt Leonora were surveying the wide pastoral scene below them, its uttermost fringes pencilled with the faint line of the sea, with an air of triumphant satisfaction, almost if not quite smug.

"I said it was only a jaunt. I can't think why that man Wilbram makes so much fuss of it."

"Herr Wilbram is tired? He does not seem to have the strong."

Clearly Mr. Wilbram had not the strong. A little concerned now, I made the suggestion that I should go back and help him to the top, an idea Aunt Leonora greeted with withering scorn.

"Good God, man, let him fend for himself. He'll be needing a rope next."

Flabby-kneed, panting wretchedly, Mr. Wilbram took nearly another five minutes to drag himself to the top, only to be greeted by Aunt Leonora, never the most tactful of women, saying:

"Well, you made it. Next time we'll bring an ice-axe."

Herr Untermeyer laughed stentoriously. It was a laugh, fruity and slightly coarse, in which you could fairly hear the heavy power of puddings and it fell on Mr. Wilbram, still periodically gasping for breath, like a mocking blow.

"I don't see that there's anything particularly funny about it."

"No?" Herr Untermeyer merely let out another laugh, fruitier and coarser than the first.

"Oh! very well, if that's how you feel about it."

Unexpectedly Herr Untermeyer now revealed a sense of humour hitherto entirely unexpected; or perhaps it was merely the good humour of the *Deidesheimer Hofstück '59*, the port and the flaming rum that was speaking.

"We should perhaps have brought a *dachshund*, eh, *mit* brandy?"

"I don't quite follow that remark," Mr. Wilbram said.

"*So?*" Herr Untermeyer laughed yet again, this time I thought a little loftily, with a touch of the master-race. "On the great mountain you have the great *hund*. *St. Bernard*. On the small mountain you have the small. You follow?"

Mr. Wilbram did not follow; he turned, instead, very icy.

"Was that illustration meant as a personal affront," he said, "or what?"

"Oh! it was a bit of light-heartedness," Aunt Leonora said.

"It was not exactly," Mr. Wilbram said, "my idea of light-heartedness. But of course there's a difference between English and German humour."

"Oh! is there? I never noticed it."

"We are dragged up here on some—some pretext," Mr. Wilbram said, "and I find myself laughed at. I say 'we.' All except Mr. Elphinstone, of course. I noticed he didn't come."

Hitherto no one had remarked on the absence of Uncle Freddie who, as was customary, had conveniently stayed behind to have a zizz.

"My husband has nothing to do with it. He always retires after lunch."

"So do I."

"Then," she said with one of those wide, enchanting, large-toothed smiles of hers, "you should have said so."

Mr. Wilbram gasped impotently. Herr Untermeyer stood erect, very stiff. A train, crossing the valley far below, gave a sudden shrilling whistle, the sound ripping the warm still air.

"Men make such a song and dance about little things," Aunt Leonora went on. "You could have had a zizz too if you'd wanted to. You only had to say."

"A what?"

"A zizz. A nap. Good gracious me, you might have thought we'd asked you to climb the Matterhorn."

"Of course some of us," Mr. Wilbram said, "have the advantage of being mountain climbers."

"We were all so jolly and friendly," she said, "and then suddenly you went all spokey."

"Spokey? I must say you use the oddest words sometimes. What exactly does that mean?"

"It means," I said, "bloody-minded."

"Oh! it does? Do you mind cutting out the bad language? I don't think that helps."

I didn't say anything; I didn't think, at that moment, that anything would help. There was a feeling in the air, it seemed to me, of undeclared conflict. The forces of Anglo-German unity had drifted rather far apart.

"Well," Aunt Leonora said, with remarkable poise and cordiality, "shall we sort of drift back?"

I loved the expression "sort of drift back"; but if it was intended as balm on the troubled air it failed completely.

"Oh! do exactly as you like," Mr. Wilbram said. "Take no notice of me. I don't want to break up the afternoon."

"Would you like to go back, Otto?" Aunt Leonora said. "There'd be just time for a cup of tea."

"I am thinking yet," Herr Untermeyer said, "of the military. This perhaps we have time to see?"

"No, no, Otto. I've already explained. There isn't any military. Except for the orchid. And that's quite different."

"Exactly. Why don't you tell him," Mr. Wilbram said, "that there aren't any orchids either? I don't want to press the point, but could we get back? We've got a bus to christen."

Without waiting for an answer, Mr. Wilbram started back down the hill. Aunt Leonora, under her breath, said she wished people wouldn't get so huffy and spokey and then, in a voice deliberately loud, said:

"Otto. Straight across there—right across—so far as you can see—is Hastings. Where the great battle was fought."

"Oh! who cares about the Battle of Hastings?" Mr. Wilbram said. "We're late now."

"I do for one," she said. "I care about it awfully. We wouldn't be the same without it, would we? It's part of our heritage, isn't it?" And then, in one of those delightfully diplomatic thrusts of hers: "It might do a bit more good if you showed the flag."

"Flag?" Mr. Wilbram said. "What flag?"

"Our flag. You were fast enough showing that German one."

Oh! indeed and where was that? Mr. Wilbram wanted to know.

"In that wretched paper. You were waving the German one and Otto had the Union Jack."

"That," Mr. Wilbram said, "is what it is all about. In case you've missed the point."

"Oh! is it? Then I can only say it would have made more sense if you'd have waved ours instead of theirs. What next? I expect we'll all soon be waving the hammer-and-sickle."

"Oh! my dear woman—"

For the second time Mr. Wilbram started down the hill-side. I thought it prudent to follow and then heard Otto say:

"This battle. This is the affair military we are coming to see?"

"No, no, Otto. We should go. You have your bus to christen."

"You are speaking also of flags."

"Well, yes, just in passing. Shall I lead the way?"

"Herr Wilbram is angry? Yes, I think. Why is Herr Wilbram angry?"

"I told him he was waving the wrong flag."

"So? Which is the wrong flag?"

"The German flag."

"So? You are not liking the German flag?"

There are moments when my Aunt Leonora, divine crackpot that she is, is capable of the most deliberate, endearing honesty.

"No," she said. "It does something to me. It curls me up inside."

We descended the hillside in absolute silence. The heat of the sun, coming more from the westward now, seemed more burning than ever. A chalky dust rose from our footsteps. I now felt powerfully thirsty and, unlike Herr Untermeyer, could feel the two puddings engaged in heavy, sometimes windy, conflict inside me.

By the time we reached the foot of the hill some hidden force had conquered Mr. Wilbram's lethargy. Armed with second wind, he was striding out strongly, fifty yards ahead. Long before we reached Aunt Leonora's house he had doubled the distance and by the time we reached it too he was already sitting, pale and impatient, at the wheel of his car.

"Wouldn't you all care for a cup of tea?"

"I'm afraid we haven't the time."

"It won't take a minute. I'll have the kettle on in a jiff."

"English tea?" Otto suddenly said. "This I am liking very much. *Mit* toast, eh? This is something splendid."

"Good. Then we'll all go in, shall we? Freddie'll be awake now."

Perhaps the very thought of Freddie having been asleep all afternoon, deeply lapped in a zizz, roused some demon in Mr.

Wilbram. At any rate he suddenly thrust his head out of the window of his car and positively barked:

"Otto! *There is no time*!"

"You mean for tea?" Aunt Leonora spoke with the utmost sweetness, itself as maddening as anything could be, smiling blandly with those long teeth of hers. "Of course there's time. There's oceans of time."

"Otto, we must go. There simply isn't the time."

"Oh! don't be such a fidget. Of course there's time."

"I am not a fidget!"

"Then don't be so spokey. If Otto wants a cup of tea then he can have a cup of tea, can't he? Don't make such an issue of it."

"I am not making an issue of it. But Herr Untermeyer has a program to keep."

"Then he must do a Francis Drake, mustn't he? Have a cup of tea with plenty of time to beat the Spaniards afterwards—"

"Otto! We haven't the time. *We must get going*. Spaniards!—"

Otto was already half-way up the garden path, with Aunt Leonora not far behind. As if this were not irritation enough in itself the front door of the house suddenly opened and Uncle Freddie appeared, fresh and vibrant from sleep, eager with smiling welcome.

"Ah! there you all are. Tongues hanging out, I expect. I've got the kettle on."

I suppose it was "tongues hanging out" that provided the last extreme force that unloosed the puritanical demon in Mr. Wilbram. Suddenly he yapped like an infuriated dog:

"Once and for all, Otto, we have to go." He was actually out of the car now. Paler than ever, he strode as far as the garden gate. "For heaven's sake, don't you realize it's nearly five o'clock? Why on earth must you have tea?"

"Because I am thirsty."

"Then get Mrs. Elphinstone to give you a glass of water and let's get going. Quickly."

"Glass of water, my foot," Aunt Leonora said. "The man's entitled to tea if he wants to have tea, isn't he? Without being bossed around."

"The tea I am taking only in small portion. Most quickly. In one moment."

Mr. Wilbram banged with his fists on top of the garden gate, shouting:

"Otto, if you don't come now, I wash my hands of the whole affair. I disclaim responsibility. We shall only be just in time as it is. It's on your head. I warn you, it's on your head."

Herr Untermeyer too strode to the garden gate.

"You are spoking very loud at me?"

"I am and I will."

"Ah! *so*? You wish conflict?"

"I am not talking of conflict. I am talking of time. Getting to places on time. People are waiting. Don't you understand?"

"I do not understand when you are making loud words!"

"Now, now," Aunt Leonora said. "You two. You mustn't get at loggerheads."

"Loggerheads?" Otto said. "Loggerheads? What is this word? Explain to me, please."

"Oh! damn the explaining! I don't often use strong language, but really, really! Damn the word! Damn the man!—"

"This word I am knowing. This damn. This is not polite."

"Oh! it's an everyday word nowadays," Aunt Leonora said. "Nobody takes any notice. Like bloody. Anyway, you shouldn't swear at your visitor, Mr. Wilbram, should you?"

"I am not swearing at him!" Mr. Wilbram actually shook his fist in the air. "I am simply saying that if he doesn't come now, this minute, I'll wash my hands of the whole affair."

"Oh! why don't you all come in?" Uncle Freddie called from the doorway. "The tea's already made."

"I come!" Otto said. "The tea I will take at once! Like *blitzen*—quick take!"

"You will do no such thing. We've had to deal with this German obstinacy before," Mr. Wilbram explained. "This wretched Teutonic—whatever it is—"

"Bloody-mindedness," I said.

"Well, whatever it is! The only way is to treat with obstinacy in return. I say we go now! I say no tea! You understand?"

"I understood. You wish conflict again, ah? This is catastroff!"

Herr Untermeyer actually raised his fist and shook it so aggressively that I thought he would, for one moment, poke Mr. Wilbram in the eye. The two men faced each other, one red with passion, one pale with ashen indignation, both speechless, at a point of thunderflash, until suddenly my Aunt Leonora said with disarming sweetness:

"Into the car, the pair of you. The tea-party can wait until some other time. We don't want another Boston on top of us, do we?"

Like two scowling dogs, anger unappeased, Mr. Wilbram and Herr Untermeyer got into the car.

"Good-bye, Otto," Aunt Leonora said, almost as if nothing had happened. "*Auf Wiedersehen*. You won't be late. It's been like old times. Come again."

"It is catastroff!" I heard Herr Untermeyer say. "Castastroff!"

The car drove away. The pair of hands that waved the briefest of farewells, one German, one English, were scarcely flags of cordiality.

Slowly I walked back to the house with Aunt Leonora. Above us the hills were bathed in serenity. The golden summer air was utterly silent. Nothing could have been more peaceful. Only she herself seemed, for once, I thought, more than a little perturbed.

"I wouldn't have expected that from Otto," she said at last and her voice was hurt. "Why did he have to behave like that? It wasn't like him at all. It wasn't a bit like he used to be. I do wish people wouldn't change so. It would make it so much easier if they always remained the same, don't you think?"

As I looked back at the tranquil hills, in the golden August sun, it was suddenly on the tip of my tongue to say that the chords of youth were very tender; but I kept quiet instead, content to know that I had no answer.

(1968)

THE SONG OF THE WREN

Miss Shuttleworth, moving with an air of delicate vacancy that also had something quite seriously studious about it, walked up and down the banks of the little stream running through the bottom of her garden, carefully distributing various sandwiches from a big blue plate.

Those of cucumber she placed on a large stone urn filled with budding violet petunias. Half a dozen of tomato she arranged about a clump of wild yellow irises growing at the water's edge. An assortment of anchovy paste, cream cheese, blackberry jam and Gentleman's Relish she set out at carefully measured intervals on the lawn that bordered the stream. When all had been distributed she stood back in a silence of contemplation that was almost reverent, surveying the result as if it were some fastidiously moulded work of art.

Finally she sat down on the lawn, legs carefully folded and tucked under her, and stared dreamily first at the sandwiches and then at the water sparkling in the warm June sunshine. Since she was wearing a floppy pink cotton dress and an even floppier pink straw hat from which straggling grey curls fell untidily to her shoulders, she looked not unlike a big, resting pink moth. Her intense blue eyes, large in concentration, gave her the impression of not belonging, quite, to this world.

Presently the eyes gave a sudden flutter of expectancy and then of positive, almost child-like delight.

"We're not alone, we're not alone," she suddenly said in a sort of expanding whisper, "we're not alone, we're not alone."

Two pairs of birds, a male and female blue tit, then a male and female chaffinch, flew with a delicate flicker over the stream, the blue tits going straight for the cream cheese, the chaffinches for the Gentleman's Relish.

"Good, good, good," Miss Shuttleworth said, again in a carefully expanded whisper, "splendid, splendid. Clever creatures."

Amazing how they knew, Miss Shuttleworth told herself. How did they know? Why was it the chaffinches always went, without fail, for the Gentleman's Relish and the blue tits for the cream cheese? Was it by some divine intuition or something of that sort? or perhaps a question of taste? However it was it struck her, always, as being little short of miraculous.

Half a minute later her wonder at these things was being enlarged to include a cock robin flying perkily over the clump of yellow irises.

"Don't fail me, don't fail me," Miss Shuttleworth whispered, "don't fail me."

Before she had finished speaking the robin had settled among the tomato sandwiches. Now why always the tomato? Frequently Miss Shuttleworth was disposed to tell herself that it had something to do with coloration, the red of the tomato having some mysterious affinity with the red of the robin's breast. Could that be it? The fact that there was no answer merely served to increase her wonder.

It was still further increased when a bevy of sparrows descended in chattering disharmony on the anchovy paste, quarrelling greedily. She watched it all with excitement, well knowing that when the anchovy paste had all gone there would be a shrill rush for the blackberry jam. It was just like a properly organized meal, with the fish being followed by a sweet course. Naturally it didn't always work out quite like that, sparrows being what they were. Often they flouted the rules and raided the robin's tomato. Not that you could play fast and loose with cock robins for long. They were sharp enough to have their own back in no time.

Over on the far side of the stream a wren was singing his heart out in a willow tree, the notes pure silver. The wren too was a source of wonder. Why did the wren never, ever come to the sandwiches? Pure shyness? Indifference? She had asked herself these and a dozen other questions time and time again and had never come up, yet, with an answer.

For fully another three or four minutes she sat utterly absorbed in the brilliance of the wren's song, embalmed in a trance of fascination.

"Excuse me, madam."

It was less the voice of a man speaking from somewhere behind

her than the surprised fluttering of disturbed tits, sparrows, chaffinches and the cock robin that suddenly woke her out of her song-
imprisoned trance.

"Oh! you startled me. Why—"

"I must apologize for the intrusion, madam. But I'm engaged in
making a social survey and I wondered if you would mind
answering a few questions."

"A survey? About what? Why me? Is it something personal?"

"It's a general survey on a great variety of subjects."

"What is the point of it?"

"Eventually all the answers will go into a computer and the
results will, I hope, become a book."

Miss Shuttleworth could think of nothing to say. She thought the
man was perhaps thirty-five. His large, black-rimmed glasses did
not conceal the deadly seriousness of his eyes.

He now proceeded to sit down on the grass, at the same time
producing from an attaché case a thick blue notebook, several
sheets of foolscap paper and a ballpoint pen. A consultation of the
sheets of foolscap kept him utterly quiet for fully a minute, during
which the tits and sparrows began to fly back.

"What an extraordinary, amazing, astonishing thing. The tits
have gone for the Gentleman's Relish. They've never, ever done
that before."

"I'm sorry, madam. What did you say?"

"I said the tits have gone for the Gentleman's Relish. Why, I
wonder? I suppose they could have sensed the presence of a
stranger."

"I'm sorry, madam. I don't think I quite understand what you're
talking about."

"My birds. I allot them certain sandwiches every day. They
always go for the same ones. They sort of do it according to the
Laws of the Medes and Persians."

"Oh! they do, do they?"

The man stared hard, eyes big and serious with disbelief, into the
sun. This caused him suddenly to sneeze loudly and violently and
Miss Shuttleworth said:

"Blessings upon you. Blessings upon you."

"And what exactly does that mean?"

"Oh! one always says that, doesn't one? I even say it to the birds. Starlings give a sort of sneeze sometimes. Of course they're great imitators, starlings. I suppose they might well pick it up from us humans. The sneezing, I mean."

In silent disbelief the man stared at his notebook, momentarily lost in a trance of his own. Coming out of it at last he said:

"Oh! by the way, my name's Adamson. Would you mind if I asked you a few questions now?"

"Oh! ask away. For the life of me I can't think what I can do to help, I mean, why me?"

"It isn't merely a question of one person. It's a complex cross-section and sub-sections of views on an infinity of subjects. From them the computer will build up a picture. For instance what do you think about the Common Market?"

"What market?"

"The Common Market. What are your views on that?"

Miss Shuttleworth, eyes slowly revolving in order to catch a possible glimpse of birds coming back, was obliged to confess she had never heard of the Common Market.

"Oh! but you must have. After all it's been top news in all the papers for weeks."

Miss Shuttleworth was also obliged to confess that she never read newspapers.

"But you must have heard it mentioned on radio and television. Or both."

Miss Shuttleworth was now obliged to confess that she had neither radio nor television, a confession that caused Mr. Adamson to make a protracted entry in his notebook.

"Well, what about space? What are your views on that? You see any purpose, for instance, in further exploration?"

"I often wonder what birds think about when they're flying about in space. Do you suppose birds think?"

"No. Not in the sense that we do."

"But I do, you see, I do. I mean the sandwiches, for instance. They must think about those, you see. It must be conscious thought that makes them do what they do."

"Oh? Well, we'll leave space for the moment. What about the permissive society?"

"The what society?"

"The permissive society."

"Is it for the prevention of something? I never heard of it. Can one join?"

"Not exactly. It's a sort of breaking down of rigid rules and pre-accepted social behaviour and moral attitudes and so on. I mean should the young indulge in pre-marital intercourse for instance?"

"Well, they always have, haven't they?"

"What I mean is that there seems to be an entirely new manifestation of it. Do you approve of that or not?"

"Birds don't get married, do they? Why should humans simply in order to propagate the species?"

"I'm sorry, but I don't think you quite get my point."

"Well, what is the point?"

"A whole new pattern of social behaviour is emerging and sex would seem to be the mainspring of it. Have you any views on that?"

"Oh! just hark at that wren. If that isn't sheer divinity I'd like to know what is. Exquisite, so exquisite. Ethereal, in fact, ethereal."

"All right, divinity. What are your views on religion?"

"Which one?"

"Accepted religion. Organized. The church."

"Would you be surprised if I told you I worshipped birds?"

"I'm very fond of birds myself. But they've nothing to do with religion."

"But they have, they have. They *are* religion. That wren is just as surely an apostle as any who fished the Sea of Galilee."

"Well, we'll leave religion. What about life after death?"

"Now I've a question for you. I was asked it by a small boy the other day. He comes into the garden sometimes with his fishing rod and a bent pin and a worm and tries to catch fish in the stream. And the other day as he was putting a worm on his hook he asked me if I thought a worm had a heart? Now there's a question for your computer."

"Possibly. But hardly one of much social significance."

"I disagree. I disagree. Are not two sparrows sold for a farthing?"

"I'm sorry, but I think we're straying from the main purpose."

"Surely not. The question of whether a worm has a heart or

whether two sparrows are sold for a farthing is just as significant as your permissive market."

"Society."

"But society is a market. In which, if I'm not much mistaken, sex is sold."

"Yes, yes. Do you mind if I make a note?" With serious concentration Mr. Adamson made a note in his big blue book. After doing so he took off his spectacles, breathed on them and then polished the lenses with his handkerchief. As he did this his eyes looked remarkably, even innocently, naked.

He then turned to his sheets of foolscap. On them were a number of questions for which he still sought answers: abortion, the multiracial society, immigration, the pill and whether sex should be taught in schools, but suddenly, before he could ask Miss Shuttleworth for her views on such matters, she leapt to her feet as if startled.

"Good gracious, I hear the church clock striking twelve! I must go and feed the hens. They'll never forgive me if I forget them. I have one that talks, you know."

"Indeed."

"In her own language of course, though I understand it perfectly—as in fact I should by now. I've had her donkey's years. Of course people are inclined to laugh when I say I hold conversations with a hen, but after all people talk to their dogs, don't they? And anyway I'd rather talk to my Biddy than to a lot of people I could name. You will forgive me if I go?"

"Of course. Thank you for giving me so much of your time."

"Why don't you come too?" Miss Shuttleworth actually laughed, her voice pitched excitedly high. "You could ask Biddy a question for your computer. For instance what it feels like to go cluck."

"Cluck?"

"Broody. Cluck is the local word. Sometimes I feel like going cluck myself. Do you ever?"

Mr. Adamson refrained from saying whether he himself ever felt like going cluck and proceeded to pack his notebook and papers into his attaché case.

"I must fly!" Miss Shuttleworth said. "Fly. Do excuse me. Goodbye."

Miss Shuttleworth seemed positively to take to the air as she swept across the lawn, looking more than ever like a huge floppy pink moth.

For a few seconds Mr. Adamson stared after her. "Mad. Quite, quite mad," he told himself. "Has a worm got a heart? Do birds think? Are not two sparrows sold for a farthing? Really, sometimes one really doesn't know. One really wonders."

Across the stream the wren again poured out its ethereal cadence of song, all sweetness on the warm June air, but Mr. Adamson, pausing to extract his notebook from the attaché case and record in it a quick, earnest note, appeared not to be listening.

There were clearly things of greater importance on his mind.

(1972)

ABOUT H. E. BATES

H. E. Bates was born in 1905 at Rushden in Northamptonshire and was educated at Kettering Grammar School. He worked as a journalist and clerk on a local newspaper before publishing his first book, *The Two Sisters*, when he was twenty. In the next fifteen years he acquired a distinguished reputation for his stories about English country life. During the Second World War, he was a Squadron Leader in the R.A.F. and some of his stories of service life, *The Greatest People in the World* (1942), *How Sleep the Brave* (1943) and *The Face of England* (1953) were written under the pseudonym of 'Flying Officer X'. His subsequent novels of Burma, *The Purple Plain* and *The Jacaranda Tree*, and of India, *The Scarlet Sword*, stemmed directly or indirectly from his war experience in the Eastern theatre of war.

In 1958 his writing took a new direction with the appearance of *The Darling Buds of May*, the first of the popular Larkin family novels, which was followed by *A Breath of French Air, When the Green Woods Laugh, Oh! To Be in England* (1963) and *A Little of What You Fancy*. His autobiography appeared in three volumes, *The Vanished World* (1969), *The Blossoming World* (1971) and *The World in Ripeness* (1972). His last works included the novel, *The Triple Echo* (1971) and a collection of short stories, *The Song of the Wren* (1972). Perhaps one of the most famous works of fiction is the best-selling novel *Fair Stood the Wind for France* (1944). H. E. Bates also wrote miscellaneous works on country life, several plays including *The Day of Glory* (1945), *The Modern Short Story* (1941) and a story for children, *The White Admiral* (1968). His works have been translated into sixteen languages and a posthumous collection of his stories, *The Yellow Meads of Asphodel*, appeared in 1976.

H. E. Bates was awarded the C.B.E. in 1973 and died in January 1974. He was married in 1931 and had four children.

THE REVIVED MODERN CLASSICS

Sherwood Anderson, *Poor White* • H.E. Bates, *A Month by the Lake & Other Stories. A Party for the Girls. Elephant's Nest in a Rhubarb Tree* • Kay Boyle, *Death of a Man. Fifty Stories. Life Being the Best & Other Stories. Three Short Novels* • Mikhail Bulgakov, *The Life of Monsieur de Molière* • Joyce Cary, The Second Trilogy: *Prisoner of Grace, Except the Lord, Not Honour More. A House of Children. Mister Johnson* • Maurice Collis, *The Land of the Great Image. She Was a Queen* • Shusaku Endo, *The Sea & Poison. Stained Glass Elegies* • Ronald Firbank, *Three More Novels* • Romain Gary, *The Life Before Us. Promise at Dawn* • William Gerhardie, *Futility* • Dezsö Kosztolányi, *Anna Édes* • Miroslav Krleza, *On the Edge of Reason* • Madame de Lafayette, *The Princess of Cleves* • Siegfried Lenz, *The German Lesson* • Henri Michaux, *A Barbarian in Asia* • Henry Miller, *Aller Retour New York* • Vladimir Nabokov, *Laughter in the Dark* • Eça de Queiròs, *The Illustrious House of Ramires* • Raymond Queneau, *The Blue Flowers* • Kenneth Rexroth, *An Autobiographical Novel. Classics Revisited. More Classics Revisited* • William Saroyan, *The Man with the Heart in the Highlands & Other Early Stories* • Muriel Spark, *The Public Image. The Comforters* • Stevie Smith, *Novel on Yellow Paper* • Stendhal, *Three Italian Chronicles* • Niccolò Tucci, *The Rain Came Last & Other Stories* • Robert Penn Warren, *At Heaven's Gate.*

PLEASE WRITE FOR A FREE COMPLETE CATALOG FROM
NEW DIRECTIONS, 80 EIGHTH AVENUE, NEW YORK, 10011.